SOLVING FOR EX

BY LEIGH ANN KOPANS

ISBN-10: 1492819689

ISBN-13: 978-1492819684

PRAISE FOR SOLVING FOR EX:

"Amazing! If you like Sarah Dessen you will LOVE this."

~ Emma Pass, author of *Acid*
and *The Fearless* (Random House)

"Putting a modern spin on a Jane Austen classic, *Solving for Ex* proves that brains can be sexier than brawn. In this complicated equation of high school drama, mean girls, mathletics, and romance, Leigh Ann delivers yet another beautifully written young adult novel that authentically captures teenage emotions while also capturing the reader's heart."

~ Nikki Godwin, author of *Chasing Forever Down*,
American Girl on Saturn, and the upcoming
Falling from the Sky

"Ashley is the kind of girl you want to root for, smart and capable and self-assured, despite of, or maybe because of, her vulnerabilities. And in Brenden, LeighAnn has crafted a boy worth of such a girl. Through all the heartbreak and angst of high school, their connection is undeniable and pressing. It's elementary, dear readers—*Solving for Ex* is one must-read romance."

~ Jenny Kaczorowski, author of
The Art of Falling (Bloomsbury 2013)

If you only read one book in 2014, make sure it's *Solving For Ex*! I sincerely doubt that you'd regret reading it; it's intelligent, hilarious, intense and touching...Honestly one of the most amazing books I have ever read.

For my daughters, who I hope, like Ashley, always make their best judgment their first consideration.

We have all a better guide in ourselves,
if we would attend to it,
than any other person can be.

~Jane Austen, *Mansfield Park*

CHAPTER ONE

the means of settling well

If every problem had as clear and quick an answer as those on the Mathletes exam, I would have been winning at life. Too bad things didn't work like that, and Brendan, the guy I was hopelessly in love with, reminded me of the fact every day.

I could almost hear the smirk on his face from behind me on the rickety metal grated walkway at the top of Squirrel Hill's water tower. "If a is less than b, and three squared plus four squared plus five squared plus twelve squared equals a squared plus b squared is satisfied by only one pair of positive integers, what is the value of a plus b?"

I yawned. "Eighteen."

"Damn, Ashley. You didn't even write that down."

"I did in my head." I grinned, lining up my shot.

"Doesn't count. You've been practicing, haven't you? We swore we wouldn't practice. Now you'll be faster than me!"

"Not possible. And I haven't been practicing. Not that much." Only a couple of hours a day.

"I knew you were awesome, but man. That's fast."

My heart seriously skipped a beat.

1

I was in love with Brendan because he was Brendan, and I was me, and we were perfect for each other.

We weren't together because I didn't have the balls to tell him.

"So. You're psyched to be back, right?"

"Was there ever a question?" The truth was, wild horses couldn't drag me back to my old school.

It was the last Saturday morning before classes started for the year at Mansfield Prep, and in Squirrel Hill, Pennsylvania, summer had overstayed its welcome. If I hadn't known better, I would have sworn the fog was steam. It draped itself over the sleepy Pittsburgh district like a blanket, conforming to the curves and angles of every street lamp, late-summer rose, and porch swing. And whoever sat on them. Including me.

Even though I knew sitting up here would make the top layer of my freshly straightened hair frizz, I loved the feel of the warm wet air on my face. I loved the mountains pushing up all around the moat of rivers that cradled the city of Pittsburgh. I loved how the fog diffused even the harshest summer-morning sunshine and cast the glittering skyscraper windows in a magical mist.

It was a welcome change from the farming town of Williamson, where my parents lived. Where I'd lived, until eight months ago.

Brendan nudged his shoulder against mine. "So you finally learned to use that thing?"

"Yeah, I actually really like it. I'm glad your parents got you such an expensive and completely inappropriate gift for no particular reason."

He laughed. "What's new, right? And couldn't we have looked at foggy trees a little closer to the house? Or a little later in the morning?"

I shook my head and jutted my chin out toward the landscape. "Carpe diem, and all that. Don't tell me you don't think this is gorgeous." Brendan yawned loudly. "Okay, point taken," I said. "I owe you, okay? What are you so exhausted for, anyway?"

"Late night. Mom was out with friends and I wanted to wait up for her."

"Your dad out of town again?"

He shrugged, confirming it, but telling me it was no big deal. "I was messing with you. I know how important the sunrise is."

"I've missed this view," I said. I've missed you.

He smiled that soft smile of his, the one that made the corners of his eyes crinkle in that way that melted my insides. That was the biggest hazard of hanging out with Brendan every Saturday morning. As if subjecting myself to pining for him every weekday at school wasn't enough, I had to do this to myself on the weekend, too.

He slung his arm around my shoulders, catching my neck in the crook of his elbow, and pulled me to him. I was thankful that he was so tall, because my face tucked neatly into his shoulder and he couldn't see the way my eyes fluttered shut as I breathed him in—shampoo and grapefruit and a little bit of aftershave. Summer or winter, indoors or out—my Brendan.

"I can't believe you're the first person to ever convince me to climb up here."

I stared at him. "Don't tell me you've never climbed the water tower."

He gave a short laugh. "Don't tell me I remind you of those delinquents who have nothing better to do on a Friday night."

"Oh, please. It's hardly breaking and entering. I just want to get some good shots. The sun'll be up soon, and then I'll have missed the foggy sunrise." I shifted my weight to the side to wedge my foot beneath me for a steadier angled shot. The whole rickety walkway trembled, and Brendan grabbed my forearm, digging his fingers in. I was already sweating in the summer morning's wet heat, but as soon as his skin touched mine, a whole new kind of heat ran through me.

"Trying to cuddle with me?" I attempted a laugh, but my voice just shook.

"Shut up. You know it's the height."

Brendan was deathly afraid of heights, which is why it was that much crazier that he was even up here with me. "Well, if you made it up here, I'd say you're doing pretty well. A few more times and it'll be a piece of cake."

He stared out at the horizon while he caught his breath. "It's your fault I'm even up here, anyway. Your aunt would kill me if I let anything happen to you."

"True." I metered, fired another test shot, and winced at the result.

"You've been making faces at that thing for five minutes now. Why don't you put it on auto, get the shot, and we can get out of here? I'll even buy you breakfast."

"Hush," I said, pressing my eye to the viewfinder again. "You'll buy me breakfast anyway." I fired another shot. Dammit. Still dark. I clicked into the data readout to check the settings there.

Something bony dug into my collarbone. I turned my head and almost ran my nose straight into Brendan's—he'd rested his chin on my shoulder and was staring at the LCD. My heart stopped. His lips were so close to mine that one quick move would have them pressed together. And of course, I suddenly couldn't move a muscle.

"How do you even read that?" he asked, jabbing his finger at the histogram, before he sat up and leaned back on his palms. I started to stammer a response, but he'd already stood up on shaky legs and reached a hand down to me. "C'mon, Ash. Let's get out of here. I'm starving."

I grabbed his hand and smiled back, telling myself it didn't really matter what we talked about after a long summer apart. Hell, I was happy just to be hearing his voice. I'd been in touch with him a lot over the summer, but it was mostly through email. The camp where I worked for nine weeks every summer didn't get cell phone service and I could only really email him a couple of times a week without looking like a stalker. Then, for the few weeks I was bored out of my mind back home, he was on some crazy European cruise with his family.

It sucked not being able to talk to him, especially since we'd seen each other every day since I'd first arrived in Squirrel Hill. I'd been sitting inside the house sniffling and sobbing for the past twenty-four hours, and it was clear that Aunt Kristin and Uncle Bruce didn't really know what to do with me anymore. That January morning, I'd been sitting in the front yard, frigid though it was, and had kept right up with my crying. The tears rolled down my face like my eyes were fountains—they flowed out like they were a natural and permanent part of who I was. I wasn't even really aware of them anymore.—Depression'll do that to you. Everything was black and cold and stupid and hopeless and it was hard to tell how much of that was real or only inside my head.

Brendan had been walking his Great Dane and had come

and sat next to me, made the dog sit next to him, and handed me a tissue. We'd sat there together, watching cars go by, for a couple minutes. And then, still looking out across the street, he'd said, "Why did the cookie cry?"

"Excuse me?"

"Why did the cookie cry?"

"Um..."

"Because his best friend was away for so long." He snorted.

"I'm sorry, I don't..."

"Get it? A wafer so long?"

I turned to look at him then, and he was already looking at me, with a goofy grin on his face, flashing impossibly white teeth. He had a square face, floppy hair, a solid jaw, and the biggest, most unreal deep blue-green eyes I'd ever seen. As upset as I'd been a few minutes earlier—pretty damn upset—I started giggling, then full-on laughing. He'd laughed too, and then I found I couldn't stop until I started crying again.

"Hey, hey. Don't do that. This is Pittsburgh. Your tears'll freeze on your face. Do you think breakfast would help?"

"Actually...maybe." I don't know what made me think that having breakfast with a total stranger was okay, but I was pretty sure it had something to do with the fact that he was the only person who'd been able to make me laugh in the last four months.

That first Saturday morning breakfast with Brendan, I'd

finally started to pull myself out of the black hole of depression that had been my life, and it was his hand that dangled over the edge, waiting for me to grab onto it.

The diner hadn't changed a bit since that freezing January morning, but I had. I could laugh and smile again, and I mostly owed it to him. As I settled into my seat in our usual booth and let my mug of hot coffee warm my hands, I knew I was exactly where I belonged. Brendan doused his pancakes with half the pitcher of syrup and spoke through a half-full mouth. "So, are you ready for your second first day at Mansfield?"

"Way more ready than I was last year. Yeah. And you can swallow before you speak, you know. That's gross." Even with his stunning lack of table manners, I couldn't keep the smile off my face.

He rolled his eyes and gulped down the pancakes, never missing a beat. "To be fair, you weren't ready for anything last winter."

He was right. Last Christmas, I was nothing but pissed about moving in with Aunt Kristin and Uncle Bruce. But there was no way I would have been able to go out for breakfast back home. In such a small town, when a girl is the cause of such a big high school scandal—sleeping with the lacrosse captain when he was going out with the captain of the cheer squad—that girl can barely show her face outside of her car to pump gas. I would have owned up to it, taken the social knocks for breaking up the prom king and queen like a champ. If I had actually slept with Carson Barret. But I hadn't. What I had done was refuse to do his math homework for his girlfriend's best friend. She'd done the initial rumor-spreading herself, and the cheer squad had gleefully taken care of the rest.

In the space of a week, I couldn't set foot inside the school without getting something messy and rotting thrown at me, or having my stuff vandalized. It was when my tires got slashed and my car got spray-painted with the "Ashley is a Whore"in angry red letters that my parents finally let me stay home for the rest of the year. My grades were good enough that I could quietly finish the rest of my homework and exams after Thanksgiving break in the safety of my own bedroom.

I snorted. "Yeah, that's true. I wasn't even ready to talk to anyone, let alone make friends. But," I said, raising my eyes, "I'm glad you came over and said hi. Really glad. No matter how hideous the angsty sobbing made me."My heart tripped and stuttered as I waited for his response.

"Me too. Besides, it's not like I minded having an excuse to have breakfast here every week. You're just party to my Pamela's pancake addiction."He grinned at me, and my heart completely stopped for exactly two point one five seconds. "And you could never look hideous, Ash."

I took a deep breath, smiled, and struggled to compose

myself.

If he had an idea how much those breakfast dates helped me, he never showed it. A week and a half before Christmas, Kristin and Bruce had invited me to live with them in Squirrel Hill, a sweet suburb on the outskirts of Pittsburgh. But they had been the only people I knew here. Breakfast dates with Brendan were literally the only reason I ever left the house for non-school reasons, especially considering that it had taken a Spartan regimen of Xanax and Lexapro to get me to agree to getting out of bed every morning.

If he had any idea how much not being able to tell him how I felt killed me, he never showed that, either. But Brendan was the only reason being the new kid at snobby Mansfield Prep in the middle of sophomore year hadn't dragged me even further into the horrible cycle of depression. Even though I would have much preferred holding hands as we walked down the hallway instead of bumping shoulders, and sharing kisses during movies instead of just popcorn, I was happier being his best friend than I'd been in years. Given that, the status quo of our relationship was just fine with me.

Until it suddenly, horribly, wasn't anymore.

CHAPTER TWO

motives of vanity

It was our first day back at Mansfield Prep, and I hadn't seen Brendan at all since we'd gone our separate ways at the front door. Still, everything was going as well as could be expected for a first day—classes interesting enough for the most part, and at least the ones that weren't had teachers that would leave me alone. I was headed to Brendan's locker before lunch when everything turned upside down.

The freaking goddess Aphrodite walked down the hallway, right toward me.

There were plenty of pretty girls in our school. It was easy enough when everyone was rich, and when almost every girl had a ton of cash to get a professional makeup consult, wardrobe designer, even a diet plan or nose job, to fit into this school's image of "pretty." Big, bouncy hair, petite nose, big eyes and lips. Exactly the right shoes, bag, and watch to go along with the school uniform. So, yeah, I saw pretty all around me every day.

But this girl? Was beautiful. She had bouncing waves of chestnut-brown hair, sky-blue eyes, and a dimple that could kill anyone on sight. Flawless skin, and toned legs that stretched to eternity. When she walked down the hallway, you could see the guys stop, gawk, and drool in a wave of patheticness.

When she passed me, I discovered the worst part of her—the way she smelled. God, she smelled amazing. Like she rolled in a field of flowers every morning and stuffed her bra with them in the process, so that the perfume followed her everywhere. I bet she even smelled good when she jogged. Because she definitely jogged. No way she didn't with a body like that.

A guy about four inches taller than she was walked next to her. I almost gasped when he turned back and looked at me. With his high cheekbones and solid, chiseled jaw, pouty lips and rich deep brown eyes all topped off with a mop of golden-brown curls, he was literally stunning.

Thankfully, Brendan's sister Julia, who was also one of my only other friends at Mansfield, didn't notice my own patheticness when I stopped for a second, just to take a longer look. When I turned to her, I realized it was because she was staring, too. "Hey," I tugged on Julia's sleeve, "Do you know who the new kids are? Did she bring her own boyfriend?"

"Nope! That's her brother. Twins." She stopped in her tracks, too, but she stared at the guy instead of the girl. "Isn't he incredible?"

"I wouldn't know. I've never met him."

Julia rolled her eyes, still smiling that same stupid smile.

"You know what I mean. Gorgeous. Absolutely..."

"Oh my God, is that all you ever think about? You're a freshman, it's your first day, and you have a boyfriend. Try to control your drool, okay?" I smiled and nudged her side with my elbow. I hoped it didn't come out sounding as annoyed as I felt. She did have a boyfriend, though. Captain of the lacrosse team. Probably why I watched him so closely around her. "But seriously. How do you know him?"

"That's Vincent. He was on our cruise this summer. We almost hooked up."

I raised my eyebrows. "Clarify, for the non-native?" I asked.

"We danced once after dinner, and he could barely keep his hands off of me. He asked me on a moonlight walk, and I know he would have at least made out with me. Seriously, he was this close to making a move, until Brendan 'happened to run into us' and told him I was only a freshman." Her voice was a cross between a whine and a groan. Lovely.

"And he's a...?"

"Junior," she sighed.

"And did Brendan also tell this guy that you have a boyfriend?"

She waved me off, still staring at the guy. "We were on a break this summer."

Hearing Julia talk about Rush like that, I wondered why she was even with him in the first place.

13

"That's random that Vincent and...."

"Sofia," she said.

"...Sofia were on the same cruise as you guys." I tried to hide my annoyance that Brendan hadn't mentioned any drop-dead gorgeous new-kid sibs with annoying names like Vincent and Sofia when he gave me the rundown of the cruise.

"Not really. Their dad just started working with ours." She waved her hand, then smiled briefly at me before continuing to stare at Vincent. "Or something."

Halfway down the hallway, the new girl—Sofia—stopped at a locker. No. Oh, no. My heart stopped. No way her locker was right next to Brendan's.

Of course, half a second later, Brendan stopped there too. The second he saw her, like every other guy at this school, his jaw fell open. Drool might as well have been pouring out of his mouth. I'd never thought of Brendan as an imbecile that could be distracted by a stupid drop-dead gorgeous girl.

Guess he was.

But then something even worse happened. The girl leaned against the locker, popped her hip out to the side, tucked a tendril behind her ear, and flashed Brendan the biggest damn smile I'd seen on anyone all day. I recognized that smile. She was flirting.

Brendan smiled back and, finally, Vincent stuck his hand out and shook hands with Brendan. Brendan's face looked wary for a second, but then he relaxed and smiled.

Julia was still buzzing as she watched them. I assumed that she hadn't dashed over there yet because she wanted to stick by me. I couldn't deny that I was grateful. "He's obviously going to be best friends with Brendan. So he'll be at the house all the time."

"So?" I grumbled.

"So at least I get to look at him," Julia giggled. "I'll see you after school."

"See ya." I squeezed her shoulder and she was off.

I walked toward my next class, slowing down a little as I neared Brendan. He always walked me to class when he saw me. But as I got near him, the smell of that girl's perfume overwhelmed me. Apparently it was putting him under some kind of spell—he didn't even look at me. So I sped up instead of stopping.

When I looked back over my shoulder one last time, Vincent's eyes met mine. I didn't want to—I swore I didn't—but I full-on smiled, letting it reach my eyes. And, oh God, he smiled back and flashed the most perfect dimple I'd ever seen.

Whoa. Suddenly, the hallway felt scorching hot.

I couldn't stop, so I turned back toward my class, trained my eyes on the black and white tile floor, and sped the hell up.

$$\Omega$$

For all of American History class, I tried to focus on our teacher's lecture. History wasn't normally that bad, and I

LEIGH ANN KOPANS

reasoned that American History could be fun if I got Brendan to watch movies about the events with me. The Crucible, Gone with the Wind, Tombstone, The Grapes of Wrath. He loved that stuff. I mostly tolerated movies—hardly any attention span to sit through the two hours or more—but even I had a soft spot for Wyatt and Josephine's love story.

I sat there, flipping through the pages of the textbook and adding. Four hundred and thirty-six days from when Japan joined the Axis to the bombing of Pearl Harbor. Nine hundred and twelve days from Pearl Harbor to D-Day. Four hundred and twenty-six days from D-Day to Hiroshima. And twenty-five thousand, two hundred and twenty-eight days from Hiroshima to my own personal atom bomb arriving at Mansfield.

A cloud of cologne greeted me as soon as I stepped out of the classroom. I looked up, and there was Vincent, fiddling with a locker handle. He was having trouble with the thing, and I remembered how tricky the ones at Mansfield had seemed when I started here last winter. I paused for the briefest second, and then his eyes met mine. They were milk chocolaty brown with flecks of green, and had the thickest, darkest eyelashes I'd ever seen on a guy. They seemed to nearly touch his eyebrows when he looked at me.

Wow.

"Do you need some help with that?" I asked, my voice sounding way breathier than I intended.

"There's a trick to them, isn't there?" He grinned, and that dimple was...

Wow.

I reached over to grab the handle. He didn't move at all, so now I was about half an inch from being pressed up next to him. I wiggled the handle side to side quickly, then wrenched it upward. Like clockwork, it popped open.

"Thanks," he said, smiling down at me. I forced myself to break my gaze with him, and when he swung his bag up to rest it on the edge of the locker and started to stack his books inside, I saw it. A lacrosse patch, right there on his bag.

I hate lacrosse players.

The fact that lacrosse was as big at WHS as football was in a Texas town hadn't helped my case back home. Carson had been the team captain, and everyone loved him. Breaking up the school's poster couple by supposedly sleeping with Carson had only painted a target bigger than Texas on my back.

"Okay, well, I've gotta go."

"Wait," he said softly, smiling at me still. "I didn't catch your name."

"Ashley," I mumbled, looking down at my shoes.

He stuck out his hand. "Ashley," he said. "Pretty. It suits you."

Holy hell, those eyes were convincing. I shook his hand, and when I started to pull back, he squeezed it the slightest bit, then let go.

"I'm Vincent," he said. "Before you go...could you show me where the hockey field is?"

"You're trying out, huh?"

"Yeah," he said. "What's the matter? Is that, like, a popularity death sentence here?" he laughed.

The look on my face must have been way too transparent. I forced a smile. "No...uh, no. It's nothing." This guy was not Carson, I reminded myself. This guy was cute, and new, and not Carson at all. Not even close. He pulled a baseball cap out of his locker and tugged it down over his mop of curls. I spent two seconds wondering why anyone would want to cover up such perfect hair. When I caught myself, I blushed, blinked hard, and brought out the smile again.

"It's this way," I said. "Come on. I'll walk you out."

Ashley, there are only 10 types of Mathletes in the world.

those who understand binary and those who don't?

exactly.

CHAPTER THREE

pleased with each other from the first

I stopped by Brendan's locker after lunch. It was on my way to fifth anyway, and I hadn't talked to him all day.

I'd spent the whole last period taking deep breaths and trying not to worry about Aphrodite. I tried to remind myself that Brendan wasn't like other guys—he didn't care about looks more than anything else. And even if he did think she was gorgeous—because, of course he would—there's no way he would spend as much time with her as he did me. We were best friends. We lived next door to each other. We were both Mathletes, for Christ's sake. Or, I would be, next week. Brendan would only see her a few minutes a day, at his locker. No big deal.

No big deal.

I let out a huge sigh of relief when I saw him standing there, and when he turned to smile at me, that same old grin that told me he couldn't be happier to see me. My heart eased a little bit, and all the stress melted away.

Despite not being a lacrosse player, Brendan was popular as hell. When I first got here, I thought it was because of his money. But as I hung out with him and his friends, I realized that it was his personality. That kid could get along with anyone. And he truly did, too. He was friends with the popular guys, and even though he didn't really play sports, he could sling a ball with the best of them. But then, he was also friends with the less popular kids. Even the geeks.

Even me, who didn't really fit in anywhere or get along well with anyone. Who, when I first arrived at Mansfield, spent her days mired in self-pity unless Brendan came to drag me out. Who was a total beast when I was first adjusting to my meds. Brendan didn't care one bit. He patiently fed my mood with pancakes, vintage movies, or random park outings with Hamlet the Great Dane, depending on the context.

Brendan really had a good heart. Even though he was completely clueless about how hopelessly in love with him I was, he had a good heart. That's why everyone liked him.

Brendan told me about his horrible lab partner for Chem, and we laughed about the ridiculous sweaters the math professor we shared always wore. Then, New Girl Goddess rolled in. Of course, I knew before I saw her. Her perfume made sure of that.

"Oh, Ash! This is Sofia." He never broke his gaze away from her. If he hadn't said my name, I would have thought he didn't even know I was there.

"Sofia," I said. I'm sure I sounded suspicious. I couldn't help it. Saying her name made me sound like a pretentious Italian snake. It felt wrong on my tongue. Actually, I wished I could rinse and spit.

"You're...Ash?" the girl asked. Even though she was the same height as me, I swore she looked down at me.

"Ashley," I said, giving my smallest acceptable smile. "I'm Brendan's...neighbor."

"Yeah," Brendan said. "She's my...one of my and Julia's best friends. She moved in last year."

"Wow." Her smile was saccharine sweet. "That's funny! You never mentioned her the whole time we were on the cruise..."

I sucked in a sharp breath, and tried to hide my hurt. It was one week. Just one. Maybe one week wasn't a ton of time to tell someone everything about your life back home. Even about your best friend.

"And she wants to be on the team, too."

"Oh!" Sofia seemed to perk up. "Yeah. Obviously we're here at Mansfield Prep over any of the other Pitt schools so that we can get into the best colleges. B here told me that this is great for applications."

Ew. "B?" Brendan hated all nicknames. I knew because whenever Julia wanted to annoy the hell out of him she'd call him "Bren" or even "Denny." I had to admit, that one always made me giggle.

I watched for the look of annoyance to cross his face, but he just stood there like nothing earth-shattering had happened.

This was worse than I thought.

She flashed that stupid 100-watt smile at him again. "You're doing trials for you Mathletes team next week, right?"

Brendan stared at her with a dreamy half-smile. Gross.

"Yeah," I said. "Starting them. There are only a couple spots on the team, though." Maybe this girl didn't understand that Mathletes was just as important at this school as football and cheerleading were at others. Especially that it was just as important to Brendan. Getting into Harvard, Stanford, or, as a last resort, Carnegie Mellon for their amazing math programs was his number-one goal.

If Mathletes had been this cool at Williamson, I might have been okay there. Only four Mansfield Mathletes could go to State, and if we won, only two could represent at Nationals. This girl had no idea what she was getting into. Except my stomach twisted when I wondered if maybe she did.

"Oh, I'm not worried. I'm really good. We almost made it to State last year."

"Almost?" I said. Brendan had led Manfield's team to State, and they'd come in third.

"Wasn't my fault," she said, flicking a tissue-thin piece of paper out of the brand-new planner she carried. "Just brought these to the office for my records. See for yourself."

"That's awesome," Brendan said, finally finding some words. This was almost too painful. I glanced over his shoulder at the transcript. Straight As. Sofia had straight As, in honors classes. A better than 4.0 GPA.

"Yeah, awesome," I said. It looked like I'd have to jolt Brendan back to reality. "Speaking of Mathletes, we're still meeting after, right?"

"Um, yeah." Brendan finally looked at me. "And we're gonna need you."

"Well, I couldn't leave if I wanted to. You're giving me a ride home, right?" He'd given me a ride home every school day for the last half a year. Granted, we'd had the summer, but still. Had he really forgotten?

"Brendan, you're not going straight home after school, are you?" Sofia looked at him with huge eyes and a slight smile. I hated the way she said his name, like the n's were too hum-my. "You're coming with us to Custard's First Stand?"

"Custard's First Stand?" I asked, my voice going up a pitch. Most of the kids who hung out there were in middle school. Brendan nodded, looking at her like she'd asked if he wanted a million dollars.

I took a deep breath, fumbling in my bag for nothing and trying not to watch Brendan watching Sofia. "Okay, good," I lied. "I'm craving some soft-serve anyway. So, I'll meet you at the car, okay?"

"See ya, Ash," Brendan said, not even bothering to look at me. I rolled my eyes and tried to explain the twisting in my gut as anger instead of the top of an inevitable downward spiral.

CHAPTER FOUR

of a cautious temper

Custard's First Stand wasn't a half-bad idea. It was crazy hot outside and something made me want a big bowl of vanilla piled high with M&M's. I hopped out of Brendan's car and met him on his side, and we walked silently together up to the ordering window.

The breeze blew hot and lazy, swirling around my calves and where my hair touched my shoulders and back beneath the tank top I'd been wearing under my uniform shirt all day. I closed my eyes and stood there, feeling Brendan's presence beside me. For a moment, I could imagine that today had gone just like any other day, that my best friend hadn't been so gaga over the new girl that he had almost completely ignored me.

That I wasn't in danger of being completely alone all over again.

"Hey." A solid, round shoulder nudged into mine, almost knocking me off my feet. I opened my eyes and caught myself.

"Hey yourself. Watch what you do with that thing. You could hurt someone."

"You're right. Wouldn't want any unfortunate accidents."

"Ha ha."

"What're you thinking about?" Brendan asked in his teasing voice. "Pretty intense daydream to close your eyes and get yourself knocked over for."

I'm thinking about how I wish you'd look at me like you looked at her all damn day. "Oh, I don't know. That it's good to be back at school."

The gravel in the parking lot crunched under rolling tires. I looked up just in time to see the shiniest red Porsche possible pull in, and Sofia's ridiculously long legs stretch out. Vincent drove, and seeing his baseball cap dip just enough to cover his eyes made me wince. What a tool. Until he turned and looked right at me.

His eyes sparked, and tugged right at something else inside me. And the way one corner of his lips pulled up in a smile...okay. Now I got why Julia was all obsessed-at-first-sight. This guy was absolutely gorgeous.

It wasn't long before half the lacrosse team joined us. Apparently Vincent had just introduced himself to all of them, and they were already fast friends. Most of them brought their girlfriends, and some of those girls brought their unattached friends. So, basically, we were going to have a little replay of lunchtime, except after school, more expensive, sweatier, and without any bathrooms to retreat to.

Fantastic.

I didn't mind these girls, really, I'd just never gotten

close to them. It's not that Britt, Aubrey, Charlotte and Zoe weren't nice, or smart, or funny, it's just that I'd never quite fit in. My drama was way more depressing than their drama. I couldn't bring myself to give a shit about lacrosse games or who was dating who after the hell I'd gone through last fall. By the time I'd been at Mansfield Prep for a few months, they'd given up on me.

Everyone had, except Brendan.

Which is why it bugged me so much that he hung on Sofia's every word. She was just like them. Exactly like freaking Kaylie Mitchell, who'd made my life a living hell at Williamson. Brendan had always wanted to hang out with me, not the stock pack of popular girls. And yet here he was, fawning over their newly transplanted queen bee and everything I was trying to forget from my old home.

The girls all sat on one side of the two picnic tables we'd dragged together, and the guys on the other. I reflexively sat across from Brendan, all the way on the end, and watched as all the girls leaned in toward Vincent like seedlings to the sun. He chatted with them, leaning forward and asking their names, leaning in close to say things quietly in each of their ears. The giggles were copious.

"So, what do you think about this guy?" Brendan asked, leaning forward and flicking his head toward Vincent. Just then, a tan, toned arm with perfectly painted nails rested on Brendan's forearm. "Space for me?" Sofia's sickly sweet voice interrupted the words I was about to say. That I thought Vincent was obviously very full of himself.

Sofia started chatting with Brendan again, flicking her hair back and pushing her chest out. Suddenly, I itched to leave the table, get up and walk anywhere. But even I knew how weird that would look, so I just looked down and pushed the M&M's around in my melting custard, watching the colors bleed and swirl into a weird shade of reddish-greenish-brown. Between the oppressive heat outside, and the melting point of custard, I figured this would be warm soup in a few seconds under eleven minutes. Ugh. Now I didn't even want the custard.

I was about to excuse myself and wait behind the car where no one could see me starting to unravel when Vincent's voice jerked me out of my pity party.

"So, hey. Which one of you lucky assholes is Ashley's boyfriend?"

The whole table went silent. A couple of the girls laughed nervously, and I shot them a grateful look. I wasn't some kind of freak or something. I just wasn't that interested in going out with anyone. Except Brendan.

Vincent quirked his eyebrow, and that slight smile was there just enough to bring out his dimple. His eyes sparkled playfully at me.

Holy hell, was he ever beautiful.

Brendan cleared his throat, and everyone turned to look

at him. "Ah...Ashley doesn't have a boyfriend."

Wow. And I thought this conversation couldn't get any more awkward.

"Well, that's weird,"Vincent said, leaning back in his seat and giving me a searing look. My cheeks blazed red-hot. I knew by that way he was looking at me exactly what he meant. I wasn't weird—the other guys were weird for not wanting to date me. Vincent held my gaze for two more seconds, and everyone at the table stared. Hell, the whole custard place stared. Then he went back to talking with the other guys at the table. A couple minutes later, he swiped the napkins from the table and stood up to throw them out. "Let's get going, okay, Sof?"

A breath of relief rushed out of me. I didn't know what it was about Vincent that made my stomach curl into a ball of tension, but I did know that getting away from him would relieve it.

CHAPTER FIVE

no feelings could be strong enough

That Sunday morning, I relished the opportunity to sleep in. My urge to crawl under the covers and sleep all day had been steadily intensifying since our first day back, actually.

I blinked my eyes open drowsily from the most wonderful daydream—Brendan and I holding hands, and him kissing my temple, during some sunrise from the water tower. He didn't tremble, wasn't scared. Wasn't focused on his fear of heights, or the next math exam, or anything but me.

That's how I knew it was a dream.

Still, I wanted to revel in it, and I turned my cheek to the side, rubbing it against my pillow.

That is, until a deep, thundering bark woke me up out of a deep sleep.

I groaned, rolled over, and pushed up the blinds from the window over my bed, blinking as the sun's rays careened recklessly through the slats. Blinded, I didn't see anything until a giant, wet nose attached to a black and white mottled snout huffed steam against my window.

"Goddammit, Hamlet," I groaned, but rolled out of bed,

stepped into a pair of jean shorts and threw a T-shirt over my camisole. I fumbled in the bottom of my huge duffel bag for some flip-flops. Poking my head out the front door, I noticed two things—Aunt Kristin and Uncle Bruce's cars were both gone, and a pair of giant black and white paws followed by a matching tail swished around the side of the house.

Of course the damn dog would want to play a game of chase.

"Hamlet!" I called behind the house, looking up and down the row of houses that stretched down the street. Back in Williamson, I lived in an old farmhouse, standing all on its own for miles. I could scream bloody murder from my driveway there and no one would hear it unless they happened to be passing by. Here, two kids laughing too loudly in the front yard playing hopscotch would wake half the street on a Sunday morning.

There were also a lot of roads around here, and that seemed to sense that the only thing bigger than he was that were willing to play chase with him were the cars.

Why couldn't Brendan keep his goddamn dog in check?

I tripped around the side of the house. The grass, dry from weeks of scorching summer sun, was sharp against my toes and ankles, but wet from dew at the same time. I cursed myself for not taking the time to put on real shoes, and I cursed Hamlet even harder as my heels slipped off the stupid cheap foam-and-plastic sandals and onto the grass below. I rounded the corner of the house and blinked my eyes into focus. That ridiculous giant dog, sitting square in the middle of my backyard holding two of Uncle Bruce's brand new, glowing yellow tennis balls in his drool-dripping mouth.

No matter how cranky I was at being woken up, I couldn't help but laugh. The damn dog was smiling at me.

"Is Brendan ignoring you today?"

Hamlet pawed the ground, and I looked over at the Thomas's driveway. Julia's car was gone, but Brendan's car was there, and so was his mom's. Meaning at least two grown people around who could walk Hamlet, and no one who was.

I trudged over to Hamlet, whose shoulder reached my waist, wrenched the dog-slobber-slick tennis balls from his mouth, and tossed them across the yard. He launched his massive body after them, and I stared after him, feeling sad that he only had this tiny yard in Pittsburgh to sprint across. The fluorescent yellow tennis balls glowed in his mouth as he galloped toward me, and when he was about twenty feet away, I realized he wasn't even close to stopping.

"Hamlet!" I shrieked, when his giant muscled shoulder slammed into my side, knocking me over. Before I knew it, I was staring up at the hazy blue-purple summer sky, and the damn dog was huff-panting over me, threatening to drop his drool on my face any second. I hooked my hand into his collar and hoisted myself up.

I hadn't even had the chance to get any food into me, and

I wavered on my feet from the lightheadedness when I stood. Luckily, I steadied myself against Hamlet. And then looked down to see my T-shirt coated in drool.

"Aw, Hamlet! You are the grossest!"

The dog freaking grinned at me. Like he was gloating.

"Kristin and Bruce are not going to be happy about you being in the house," I grumbled as I led him to my front porch with me, "but I don't trust you not to run for a second. And I'm not going after you again."

Finally, huffing and puffing, I made it to our blue-painted front door, pushed down the handle and...

"Oh, shit," I yelled at the rocking chairs and little glass table that lived on the porch. "Shit. Locked out."

I reached under the mat for the spare key, and found a key-shaped outline on the concrete, but no key there. That would be, I realized, because I'd grabbed it when I went for a run the other day, stuffing it beneath my sneaker's insole—and left it there. Locked inside the house.

I surveyed the situation. Giant, runaway-prone dog. Slobbery shirt, muddy shorts. Aunt and uncle gone. Starving. Locked out. I only had one choice.

I craned my neck up to the Thomas's house. My eye automatically went to Brendan's window. Every single time. Once in a while, I'd see his thin silhouette changing shirts, his hands running through his hair to unconsciously re-mess it when the shirt was down. Then my heart would trip and I'd have to take a deep breath to keep myself from daydreaming about being in there with him.

Yeah. I was definitely pretty far gone.

The light in his window was on, and so was the one in the hallway below it, so at least I knew he was awake. I glared at Hamlet and yanked on his collar. "Come on. And don't you dare pull me over again, you mutt." I ruffed the top of his head with my other hand and he gave me that goofy happy dog look again, and trotted back to his house alongside me. Like he was just out for a stroll to retrieve me, instead of me being the one to take him back home.

I opened the heavy glass door to the Thomas house, but when I raised my fist to knock on the main door, it pushed open the slightest bit. Hamlet nosed it the rest of the way open and barreled in, his nails skittering against the polished hardwood floor.

"Hello?" I called up the stairs, and waited a second or two. I was about to turn around and go home, wait on the porch or something, when my stomach growled. Then I remembered the cabinet full of junk food in the Thomas's kitchen—a studier's paradise. It didn't make any sense, but after a summer full of home-baked muffins and cookie bars from my mom, there was something about the processed, packaged goodness of a strawberry frosted Pop-Tart that made my mouth water.

I traipsed into the kitchen, which was still, quiet, and lit only by whatever summer morning's sunshine filtered through the curtained windows. The countertops were as pristine as the floors, which was insane considering that at least one teenaged boy was living in the house at any given time. The only thing that I saw there was a wineglass. Must have been left out from the previous night. I could imagine Hamlet propping his paws up there and knocking it over, into the built-in range top that it sat next to, so I moved to pick it up and put it in the sink. As I got closer, I noticed that it had a fresh water ring around the base, and the liquid in it was cold and damp to the touch.

Someone had poured it this morning.

A voice echoed from the upstairs, a lazy, low, yet loudly feminine cadence. Brendan's mom. I hadn't seen her yet, and I was excited to say hi, so I grabbed a shining foil pack of Pop-Tarts and walked back around to the stairs. But as I got closer, I heard her uncontrolled tone interspersed with a calm, quiet one—Brendan. Then, a high-pitched, crazy-sounding laugh, and Brendan saying, "Come on, Mom."

I made it halfway up the stairs and just barely saw Brendan closing a bedroom door behind him, leaning against the wall next to it, and blowing out a breath. He didn't look like my carefree Brendan. He looked stressed. Exhausted. Sad.

"Hey, what's going on? You okay?" I couldn't mask the sudden concern in my voice. I'd seen Brendan in intense moods, when he was concentrating on math or one of the old westerns he loved. When he was waiting for his favorite lines to come up in Tombstone. But that intensity was excited. This was completely different.

Like I'd flipped a switch, his face changed. With a grin, he pushed himself off the wall and came toward me. "Ash! Hey! What are you doing here?"

"Well, I was trying to sleep in. But Hamlet had other plans."

"Are you kidding me? I'm so sorry. But at least you got breakfast out of it," he said, raising his eyebrows at the crinkly wrapper in my hand.

"Yeah. Breakfast and a wet shirt. And muddy shorts."

"Oh, geez. Did he..."

"Steal Bruce's tennis balls? And make me throw them? And then tackle me on return? Yeah," I laughed. "But it's really no big deal. I'll just borrow some of your mom's stuff and..."

I headed for the door of her room, but Brendan darted out in front of me. "No, don't...I mean, it's not the best time to....I mean, she had a late night. Haven't you unpacked your own clothes yet?"

"Um...no, not really. But also, I locked myself out." I suddenly felt embarrassed, and stared down at my muddied feet. At least I'd given myself a pedicure before I rolled into town. "It was...I went for a run and...the key..."

"Oh, geez." He rolled his eyes and smiled at me. "C'mon, slugger. I'll get you one of my old shirts."

A few minutes later, I'd changed into Brendan's Mathletes shirt from his sophomore year—the one from two years ago, when the back said "member" where it now read "captain"—and a pair of his darkest boxers that I'd fished from one of the drawers at the back of his huge walk-in closet. I think they actually must have been before his latest growth spurt, because no way would they fit him now. But that only got me thinking about Brendan and his boxers, and exactly what parts of Brendan were up against which parts of the boxers, and...

I blew out a breath. I had to get a hold of myself. This would be a very long year if I didn't.

I still hadn't figured out what I wanted to do about this year. I wasn't clueless—a summer full of five-day stretches where I felt like I'd die if I didn't talk to Brendan soon was enough to tell me that I was crushing on him pretty hard. I also knew that he was the worst person in the world for me to be head over heels in love with. Because he was my best friend.

Brendan was the first and strongest tie I had to this place, and I wasn't about to do anything to screw that up.

When I first came here, everything had felt so empty. I didn't know my way around town. I didn't want to leave my room, I was so depressed. So Brendan had brought photos of the town and tacked them on my wall. He told me stories of things he had done there.

Soon, his Pittsburgh became my Pittsburgh.

Including Pamela's café. The first time we'd walked through the heavy glass door that rang a tinny bell, and stepped into the cramped diner whose air filled with the servers' shouts and the smell of staling coffee, it was like I could breathe again. Between the cramped space, the board games everywhere, the trivia cards randomly slung on the tables, the raised voices and the bustle and browning butter underneath pancake batter, it was just like my house. Just like home.

There was plenty wrong with having three little triplet siblings underfoot and a mom who was too exhausted from keeping up with them for the past six years to spend much time with me. They were always breaking something of mine and I hardly ever spent any time with Mom. But when we would cuddle up on the couch together for movie night—when I would always pick the movie and she would always fall asleep—something about the particular clutter and chaos and soft side of my mom was home.

No matter how much I loved home, though, nothing could make me stay there after the first semester of sophomore year. Nothing.

No, I couldn't go back there, which meant that I couldn't leave here, which meant that if I was going to confess my love for my best friend, next-door neighbor, and popularity lifeline at Mansfield Prep, I'd better have a damn good reason for doing it. And the only reason good enough would be if I knew, for sure and for certain, that he loved me too.

And not in the offhanded, "love ya" way we got off the phone every now and then, or when I did him a favor and he wanted to thank me. Or the "Oh, I love you" as he unwrapped and snarfed down a Snickers bar after not having eaten for six hours. Neither of those things would cut it. Nothing less than him taking my hand, looking me in the eye, and saying, "Ashley, I love you," and then kissing me would do. And maybe threading his fingers through my hair. And possibly throwing me down on his bed and having his way with me.

In other words, I'd have an unrequited crush on Brendan forever.

I snapped out of my daydream of being tossed onto navy blue sheets that smelled like Brendan's aftershave to see Brendan staring at me expectantly. "Ash?"

"Hmm?"

"The clothes are okay, right?"

"Oh. Yeah. Um, I'll wash them when I get home and bring them back by tomorrow."

He grinned. "Don't worry about it. So," he said, plopping down next to me on the floor, "What do you wanna do? Narrate your summer for me?"

I snorted. "Not much to narrate. Same old, same old. Sunblock's embedded in my skin..."

"Even though you still got quite a tan," Brendan said, nudging my knee and nodding his head toward my bronzedup legs.

I nodded. "At least two deadly spiders in the bunk, four bed-wettings, six twelve-year-olds caught making out behind the camp shed."

Brendan laughed. "Normal summer."

"Normal summer," I agreed. "Although I did learn how to really use the camera."

"That's what you say, but I still haven't seen any pictures."

I motioned for his tablet. "Here, asshole, I'll show you."

I navigated to my photo account page and let him sit there swiping through the pictures while I fiddled around on my phone, taking the time to look up and be satisfied when he oohed and ahhed every few seconds.

A couple of people had asked me the problem with me and Brendan. As in, why weren't we going out yet. I didn't know, really. Maybe he was too shy, or maybe I was. He had a lot of friends, and I had...well, not that many. I'd never really had close friends even before I was chronically depressed. Because of that, I'd had trouble being interested in casual conversation; after the incident, it had gotten even worse.

But with Brendan, it was different. I didn't know why, but he just got me.

We spent a lot of time together, but we were in different grades, and he was always at Mathletes practice. That was one completely, beyond-awesome thing about being at this school. I don't know if it was because of the proximity to Carnegie

Mellon, or just a weird quirk, but being a Mathlete here was actually pretty cool. Not like being a lacrosse player, but not like being a theater nerd, either. So this year, I was planning to up my cool factor and my closeness-to-Brendan factor by summarily kicking ass at math and testing onto the team for my junior year and his senior year. The year he'd be captain. The year he'd win State.

"So you made all these with one camera?

"Made them?' Well, there are different styles, different post-processing treatments, yeah."

"Like, in the computer?"

"Yes, in the computer."I grinned. "This one's called Lomo. It's supposed to look a little faded and the colors are supposed to be kind of weird."

"And it's also supposed to be blurry?"

"Yeah, I guess. What do you think of it?"

"I think I like the ones where the image is clear and the colors are true much better. Bright and sunshiny, and beautiful. It reminds me of you." He cleared his throat. "I mean, when I think of your summer. At camp."

My smile was so wide, I thought my cheeks would break off, crash into the floor and embarrass me in a totally new way. But when I glanced up and saw him still looking through the photos, I breathed a sigh of relief. He hadn't even noticed.

He shook his head, smiling and setting the tablet on his desk. "Look at you and your incredible brain. How do you keep it all in there?"

"Oh, come on, Mr. Math Genius," I scoffed, reaching out to push him playfully on the shoulder, then instantly berating myself. Any time I touched him, I worried about three things· one, I'd blush and he'd see it, two, he'd think I was trying to flirt, and three, he'd think I was comfortable with just being friends.

I was definitely not okay with just being friends.

"No, but seriously, Ash," he said, looking up at me. "I'm good at math, and I have a head for science. I get good grades otherwise, because I'm too damn stubborn not to. But you and that brain of yours...you're like fast and talented at the math stuff and the art stuff."

"Yeah, well," I said, drawing my knees to my chin, "It's the same brain for both things, you know. It's all 'brain stuff.'"

"You amaze me," he said, still smiling that same stupid smile.

I looked down at my feet, and rested my chin on my knees. "You think I'll make the team?"

"Ashley, are you kidding me? Yes. Yeah, you'll make Mathletes."

He reached behind me and started rubbing my shoulders. "I can't imagine the team without you."

I let myself fall to the side and into him, closing my eyes and letting the warm shocks of his touch run through my muscles. "Aren't you worried about people starting rumors?"

"About what? Me playing favorites?"

I really meant about us being together. At that point, I wouldn't have minded the rumors at all, actually. Maybe they would have forced Brendan to finally make a freaking move.

"Yeah, I guess," I said, still staring at my shoes.

"Nah. Everyone knows you're my favorite. And everyone knows that you're good at this stuff, Ash. And fast. What would the team do without you?" His voice lowered as he looked at me. "What would I do without you?"

That was it. I couldn't take any more. I had to make a decision about what signal to send to him, and I absolutely couldn't make it now, even if it meant staying locked out of the house. I was chickening out, just like every other time I hung out with Brendan and I thought I saw something in his eyes that may have meant he felt the same way.

May have.

I stood up, too fast probably. "I've gotta be back. Kristin wanted to take me to lunch." Kristin did not, in fact, want to take me to lunch, but it was the only excuse I could think of.

"Okay," he said, wearing that stupid smile that confirmed exactly how oblivious he was. Dude was crazy smart when it came to school, but when it came to people? He was dumber than a ton of bricks. "See you in the morning."

Riding to school with him was awesome, even though it made my stomach flip. "Bright and early," I said.

CHAPTER SIX

apt to expect too much

It was only the second week of Junior Honors English, which was basically the next lowest form of hell before we would descend into Senior AP English the following year. I'd seen the reading list for AP, with such delights as Moby Dick, Notes from the Underground, and Middlemarch. So you'd think that our Junior English professor would let us read some lighter stuff.

No chance. She plunked down a shiny new copy of Mansfield Park on each of our desks on the first day.

"I'm not trying to be cute," she said, her sentences punctuated with the thunk of each book on a desk. "Okay, well, maybe I am. I do love that our school shares a name with my very favorite Austen novel. But that's not why it's my favorite. Compared to Pride and Prejudice, which you'll read in AP next year, Mansfield Park is mature and nuanced, studded with deeper social issues than all the rest of Austen's works put together. We'll be having a quiz next Wednesday about the major themes and character arcs, so I'd suggest reading it more closely than you would, for example, the newspaper. Or your fashion magazines."

Britt raised her hand. She had been the rare freshman Mathlete, was freakishly good at every other subject, stunningly gorgeous, and incredibly popular. Yes, she was one of those girls. "We don't get the newspaper."

Mrs. Crawford rolled her eyes and, without looking back, said, "My point exactly, Miss Harding."

Some of the guys in the back of the class snickered at that last name, just like they did every single other time anyone said it. Including themselves. This was going to be a long year.

I'd heard enough about Mrs. Crawford to know to take her seriously, so I'd spent Saturday afternoon after breakfast with Brendan marking up my copy with theme, major plot points, and some interesting character stuff.

On quiz day, most of the kids had buried their noses in their books in the five minutes between arriving to class and the bell ringing, as though the text could be absorbed through their eyeballs in that span of time and then magically translated by their brain into quiz answers when the time came. Britt was one of them, and Vincent leaned across the aisle and rested his elbows on her desk, pretending to look at her notes with her, his gaze flicking down her shirt. I rolled my eyes, and then leaned back in my desk and closed my eyes for a moment of peace and quiet before bell rang.

Just as I was imagining the next shot of the river walk I'd like to attempt from the fire escape of one of the old restaurants in downtown Pittsburgh, my ponytail flipped up and around in a circle. I sat straight up and turned slowly to see Vincent, who slouched back and smirked just enough to let a dimple show in the expanse of his ridiculously flawless skin.

I caught my breath against the annoyance of some guy I didn't know, gorgeous or not, flicking my hair around like we were best friends. I cocked my head and raised my eyebrow.

He leaned down in his bag and pulled out his copy of Mansfield Park. It was one hundred percent flawless—unmarked and free of dog-ears—like it was pure luck he'd remembered to bring it to class today. "Ready for this quiz?" he asked. "I hear Crawford's a hard-ass."

I quirked an eyebrow. "Are you ready? Looks like you didn't prep."

"Looks can be deceiving." He tapped the cover of the book. "We read this at my old school. I'll get a perfect score, mark my words."

He'd read Mansfield Park when he was a sophomore? And I thought this school was nuts. I smiled. "We'll see."

Mrs. Crawford handed the papers back and we got to work. Twenty-five minutes later, I'd thrown down three different main thematic threads in the work and bitched for four paragraphs about why Edmund Bertram really had to be such a clueless dickheaded milquetoast when all the rest of the characters were really deep and interesting. I of course had already completed the first page, which had been regular multiple choice.

"I'll take your long answers," Mrs. Crawford said, pacing the front of the room. "You'll do me a favor by grading one another's multiple choice right now. Please pass your tests one seat forward and mark off any answers that don't match what I read here."

True to his word, Vincent got a perfect score. We handed the tests forward just before the bell rang. I didn't know why, but I let myself hang back to walk out into the hallway with him.

"I'm very impressed," I said.

He laughed. "By what? I told you I'd get a perfect score."

"So you just really love Mansfield Park, then?"

"Obviously." He smiled, but I couldn't tell what kind of smile it was. It looked completely genuine, yet vague. Like there was no real anchor between his expression and the meaning of smiling. Like it was his default when he didn't want people to know what he really thought of something.

At least it was a damn beautiful smile, though. I had to avert my eyes to keep myself from enjoying it too much, or I'd probably crash into the wall or something.

"So, you and Sofia," I said as we walked. "Are you, like, Fanny and William close, or more like Henry and Mary close?"

"Huh?" he said, looking at me with a furrowed brow.

I knew he had heard me. I got suspicious about that

uncracked book all over again. "Mansfield Park?"

There went that smile again. Totally chill, totally relaxed, totally in control. Totally disconnected.

He laughed again. "Well, let's just say we're close enough. We grew up moving around a lot. Most of the time, we were the only people we knew at a new school. So we've hung out more than most siblings, probably. And I know her well enough to know that if I ever called her Franny she'd kill me."

"Fanny."

"Yeah," he grinned, "That's what I said."

I knew something about that wasn't right, but my drive to bring up another topic of conversation was way too strong to let me push something less important.

"So it looks like Brendan and Sofia got friendly pretty fast on the cruise," I said, wondering how I could have thought that something that forward could ever sound like a casual ask.

"Okay, see? That's where we're not close. Because I do not get involved in my sister's love life. Line drawn. Right there."

"Who said I was talking about her love life?"

"Is there any other reason you would bring that up?" he asked, his grin now turning playful. "Whatever. The point is, I don't know anything."

We were most of the way to the lunchroom before I realized that we'd walked the whole way together. There were two interesting things about this. First, girls' heads turned for

Vincent like the boys' heads turned for Sofia. Second, Vincent was only looking at me.

"So, this Mathletes thing,"he said.

I almost jumped when he spoke; I was too busy thinking about why he was walking with me. Way to look like an idiot, Ash.

"Tell me about it. It's pretty cool, here?"

"Yeah, and if you get on the team and we go to State, it's really good for your college applications. Like, basically guaranteed to one of the better schools."

"And that's why everyone's so obsessed?"

"Yeah, pretty much." Except me.

"What about Brendan? He seems cool."

This, I could hear in his voice. He was saying that Brendan seemed too cool to be a Mathlete. I shrugged. "He just loves it. That's it. And, yeah, he wants to go Ivy League. So..."

"Okay, so show me the ropes?"

"You want to join Mathletes?"

"Why not? I'm good at math, and it's cool here. And you'll be there, right?"

My cheeks blazed red as I dipped my head in a single nod. "I will be there."

"Then so will I," he said with a smile. This one seemed genuine.

CHAPTER SEVEN

all favourable to tenderness and sentiment

For the next few weeks I sat in Mathletes practice, but I wasn't really there. Solving equations and problems was so soothing that it was like a drug to me, and sometimes I used it that way. I could handle the drills during the Mathletes practices themselves. Sofia spent them flirting with Brendan the entire time, dragging her flower-perfume cloud through the room, asking questions that, judging by the speed with which she scribbled down the answers to the problems on the written practice, she damn well knew the answers to herself. I could barely stand it.

Brendan had put me to the task of doing drills at the boards with the underclassmen while he floated around working on individual writtens with the veteran members of the team, who didn't need that kind of practice anymore. This was good for two reasons· One, it kept me too busy to watch Brendan standing so close to Sofia for an entire ninety-minute practice, and two, it gave me a chance to show off my mathematical prowess. In my best daydreams, Brendan saw me working out a complicated calculus problem or geometry proof, dragged me home after practice, and pulled me down onto his bed with him, recounting highlights from my performance during our own private one.

Now, however, my focus was in a different place. Don't freak the hell out and either scream at Sofia or sink back into depressionland. Or both. My dry-erase marker squeaked against the whiteboard as I jotted down the main steps in my strategy for finding area with a Riemann sum. "Guys, we're finding area using a series of rectangles, which is theoretically infinite in this case, right?" I waited for most of the underclassmen to look like they got it. "Okay. So we're actually using the revised formula for area, length times height. The limit as it approaches infinity of the sum of i equals one to n of f of xi times delta x. So n stands for...?"

"The number of rectangles," everyone answered.

I beamed. "Good. Good, you guys. And then, the xi will be equal to..."

"A plus i delta x," a kid named Mohinder answered immediately.

"Okay," I said. "Yes. Excellent."

Brendan looked over at me. I turned and gave him a little thumbs-up, and he smiled. And for a moment, the math centered me, and gave my mind somewhere else to focus besides on Brendan and Sofia and the particular chemistry that everyone could see between them.

It worked outside of practice, too. Each step of a problem was one more thing I could control. See Sofia walking in the hall, dream up a proof to solve. See Brendan smile and hug her, state the givens. Watch her laugh and touch his arm, state the theorem. For every five seconds that passed, work another step. If I got as far as solving it, duck into the bathroom and take a deep breath. And come up with something more difficult for next time.

So help me God, if they ever kissed, in front of everyone, I might end up solving the freaking Hodge Conjecture. At least then the Millennium Prize people would give me a million bucks and I could take a nice, long vacation.

Too bad solving those damn problems didn't get me any steps closer to solving my love life. Every day that Brendan got cozier with Sofia was a day he stepped further away from me, and left me dangling at the edge of the black hole of depression that he'd been the one to drag me out of in the first place.

Brendan was my lifeline, and I had no idea how I'd handle things if I lost him.

By five weeks into the year, we'd whittled down the twenty kids interested in being Mathletes to the eight we'd need to compete in regionals with quizzes, drills, and the general pain in the ass that was twice-weekly practice.. Even if it was kind of a big deal at our school, Mathletes wasn't big enough anywhere else to warrant an invitational competition, and so we'd had the AP Calc teacher come in and proctor our test for us, and that was that.

At least, I thought it had been. Until the next week, when the team had been narrowed down to ten for the regional tests next month – eight official team members and two alternates. Sofia sauntered up to the front teacher's desk where Brendan sat, with her Calculus textbook in tow, to ask him question after question about theory and strategy and God knew what else.

This was getting ridiculous—she could so easily find the answers to all of them on her own.

I was supposed to wait for Brendan to drive me home, so I couldn't leave. But I couldn't take it anymore. How close Brendan and Sofia sat all the time, how much they talked. They hadn't been out on a date, I knew that much. They hadn't kissed yet, according to Julia when I grilled her at lunch, and, being his sister, Julia would know.

Besides, Brendan would have told me. He told me everything, a truth I kept repeating to myself even though I felt it slipping away, day by day, through my fingers. He was just too preoccupied with school, and college applications, I told myself. He'd been out to Stanford, and up to Boston, too.

I stared at the two of them sitting way too close. And every day they got closer until I wondered when she'd start sitting on his lap. Not to mention the secret smiles they shared.

The thought made the air in the room go stuffy. I could barely breathe.

I pushed my books aside and jumped to my feet. "I'll find you in a few minutes, okay?"I called to Brendan.

"Sure," he said, bending his head back over Sofia's textbook, so close to hers that they almost touched.

A couple of weeks ago, he would have asked me if I was okay. Now, though, he barely looked at me. The edges of my vision started to get a little fuzzy. I rolled my eyes, mostly to tamp down the nausea that churned my stomach. Thank God I had my camera with me. It would give me an excuse to get out of there.

Not that Brendan was asking for one. I mostly needed one for myself, since I felt so lame, letting him upset me this much.

The stairs to the roof were at the back of a narrow alcove that also led to the janitor's closet—not the same stairwell we used to get to classes, which was probably why so few students had ever found that passage. Only a single flickering fluorescent light illuminated it, and the dull bluish glow was comforting, somehow. Maybe because it reflected my mood.

I made it up to the top of the roof and breathed in the cold. I was so on edge, I felt every whisper of the breeze like a tiny electric shock on my face, and when I breathed it in, down my throat and into my lungs, which were suddenly having some trouble getting enough air.

I sat down at the edge of the roof on the gravelly surface, grateful for the feeling of the stones digging into my bottom. If there were a thousand pebbles per square meter, and this rooftop was thirty by twenty meters, there were six hundred thousand pebbles up here. Approximately three hundred of which were currently digging into my butt. Lots of tiny pieces to make up the whole surface, reminding me that there were lots of little problems in the world, and mine weren't the only ones. I let my feet dangle over the edge, trying to force my breaths to their lazy swinging rhythm, trying to focus on the arcs they made in the sunset light. But all I could see was the memory of Sofia, hanging on Brendan's arm. Nudging her way into Brendan's life and onto the Mathletes at the same time—the only two things in the world that I really wanted.

My heart started pounding, and my lungs felt impossibly empty. I couldn't get enough air into them if I tried. Panic attack. Fuck.

This hadn't happened since I first moved here. Since the last time I felt completely alone.

A sharp whistle pierced the still air of the night. A tall figure in a baseball cap covering a mop of curls stood in the middle of the parking lot below. Vincent.

"Hey, Ashley! What're you doing up there?"

"Uh...photography project." I struggled for my original excuse, focused on getting normal-sounding words out. "Grabbing some sunset shots."

"Could you use some company?"

Before I had a chance to think about what I was doing, I nodded. I didn't know whether he could see it from that far below, or whether he assumed my answer was yes, but he smiled. I could see it from all the way up there on the roof— holy hell, that grin was beautiful.

"What's the easiest way up?" he asked. I returned his grin, thinking of all the harder ways up. Would he have climbed the wall like Peter Parker?

"Second door on the left," I shouted. I had to find more air to raise my voice, and I felt a little better then.

"The janitor's closet?" he asked.

I nodded, exaggerating my movement so he could see in the waning light. "Go through the door in the back of it, it leads to a stairwell. It'll take you up here."

He swung the door of the Porsche open, traded his huge lacrosse bag for a smaller one, and headed toward the school.

Waiting for him, my head spun at the easy way he said my name. How affectionate he sounded. I thought of all the other girls he could be hanging out with right now, or how he could have gone for burgers with the team.

I noticed that the stars had started to poke through the deep blue canopy of sky, and my heartbeat slowed. I pulled my DSLR out of my bag, along with a mini-tripod Brendan had bought me for my birthday. The sunset had brightened to an insane show of watermelon, tangerine, and orchid streaks, a last image of a quickly fading summer. I tilted my head back and took a deep breath in, glad for the sharp cold of the air, but regretting that there would be no fireflies.

The familiar creak of the roof door told me he was coming. Moments later, he plunked down next to me, like we'd done this every night for weeks.

"How was practice?" I asked.

"Oh, you know. Just another hour of jocks on a field."

I raised my eyebrows. To every other kid who played lacrosse here, the sport was what they ate, breathed, and slept.

"What?" He laughed. "There's more to life than lacrosse. Like this sunset. Probably why you're up here."

I wasn't about to tell him why I was up on that roof. Probably sucked enough having a sister in high school with you, without everyone talking about her. Plus, he didn't need to know any more about my crush on Brendan than he already did.

And I decided I didn't want to tell him, considering the way he was looking at me right now. Like I was pretty. Like I was worth looking at.

"Uh," I stammered, blushing at the thought, "What's in the bag?"

"A Snickers bar, if you want it." He smiled.

Could this guy read my mind? Those were my total weakness.

"Split it?"

"Absolutely," he said, tearing the wrapping, handing me half, and taking a bite. "Damn, that's good. My favorite since I was a kid."

I don't know why that made my heart jump a little bit, but it sure did.

"Okay. What else?"

"Ah. Most important. You're not the only one interested in capturing this beauty." He pulled out a sketch pad and drawing pencils.

"You draw? Seriously?"

"No, I just keep these around to make it look like I do. Seriously, Ashley. Yes, I draw."

I normally hated being scolded in any way, even jokingly. But something about the way he looked at me made me smile when he said it.

We sat there for a few minutes, Vincent scratching at his paper and me fiddling with settings and taking test shots. The only thing nicer than the camera Brendan had given me was the lens his parents had found to go with it. As easily as they spent their money on stuff they didn't need, they still did their research, that was for sure. This lens easily cost as much as the camera it fit on, and the vibrancy of color and its sharpness showed it.

I flipped through my shots of the sunset. It really was stunning here, in the cradle of the mountains. I leaned over to see what Vincent was getting. He was turned slightly toward me, staring as his pencil scratched.

"What are you doing?" Thank God it was so dark out, because I knew my cheeks were blazing red by now.

"I said I wanted to get up here to do a sketch of the beauty. I could have gotten shots of the sunset from the parking lot."

Whoa. He certainly knew how to lay it on thick. The trouble was, between that dimple and the way his eyes sparkled when he looked at me, I mostly believed him.

A vague panic rose up within me. Vincent was certainly cute, but he could also bring out the pretty words when he needed to. Something about that was weird. And no matter how fabulous Vincent was, he was not Brendan. He couldn't understand me like Brendan could. Nobody else would ever be able to do that.

Besides, I had no idea what to say to this cute, new, already-popular guy calling me a "beauty." I gulped, shoved the camera into my bag, not even bothering with the lens cap, and said, "I've gotta go."

I was already four long steps away, mostly to the door, when Vincent said, "Hey! Do this again some other time?"

I don't even know what I mumbled before I banged my way through the door, then pounded out the front steps to the school. I walked up to Brendan's car just in time for him to be getting there as well.

"Sorry it took me forever. She's really..."

"Behind?"I asked.

"Dedicated." He peered at me for a moment before continuing. "Did you get some good shots?"he asked.

I had no idea.

HEY ASHLEY, LOOK... ////////// OCTOP!!!!

hahaha, Vincent, that is so lame.

YOU JUST WISH YOU'D THOUGHT OF IT.

CHAPTER EIGHT

no hope of a cure

That next Saturday morning at Pamela's, Brendan had missed half my jokes, and had started at least two conversations completely out of the blue by telling me about some dumb-shit thing Sofia had said.

I swore "Sofia" was sounding more and more like a curse word every day.

My rational brain tried to convince me that my sinking back into depression was due to the lack of sunshine over the past couple weeks. But I knew it was more than that. I'd lost my only friend at Mansfield, and all I wanted to do was skip school in favor of hiding under my covers every single day.

The need to sleep, sleep, and sleep some more wasn't a good sign, and every time I took an extra Xanax, it was even more painfully obvious.

After another infuriating Saturday morning breakfast with Brendan, I sat on the couch, staring into space, debating over which stupid movie to turn on for way too long. I even felt too down to do my math homework.

Kristin settled herself down next to me on the couch, and leaned back. "Doing okay?"

I let out a long breath, and tried to blow away some of the sadness with it. No dice. "Not the best. I'm having kind of a tough time." I was grateful that Kristin knew me well enough to know exactly what that meant.

"Is this a meds thing, or a tough week thing?"

I smiled and made sure to look at her steadily when I answered. "Just a tough week thing." A few tough weeks, all horribly mashed together.

"Come with me to the mall, huh? Help me pick out something for Bruce's birthday."

I stared out into the empty living room, and into the already-darkening sky out the windows, and nodded slowly. "Okay. That might be good."

She patted my knee. "Good girl."

I nodded, holding back tears. I always appreciated the way Kristin knew what my coded language meant, and did what she could to help me out without pushing me too far. She was better at it than Mom, even. Not that Mom had had much of a chance to deal with the spiral of depression-fallout that had come from Kaylie Mitchell making my life a living hell at Williamson High.

The mall was bustling and crazy. The newly frigid air must have driven every giggling preteen and weekend-stir-crazy parent to the mall, because it was packed. I did a quick headcount in my immediate area, and multiplied it to fit the square footage of the mall's first floor that had been posted at the entrance. A couple hundred more people, and this place would literally be over capacity.

The air inside was heavy with the grossness of so many people breathing the same air, and I could almost see the germs floating through it as people coughed and blew their noses. Disgusting. The only thing worse than feeling down would be staying home from school with a sinus cold.

I helped Kristin pick out a new case for Bruce's e-reader and I got him a nice pair of gloves, since forecasters were predicting one of the coldest winters Pittsburgh had ever seen. Kristin ran into one of her friends, and gave me some cash to grab coffee for both of us, if I'd rather skip their chatting. I shot her a grateful look and headed toward the coffee shop.

On my way there, I passed one of the kiosks that seemed to explode with tacky merchandise for the entire three months before Christmas. It sold custom-printed shirts, bags, and hats—so cheesy. But one of the shirts caught my eye. Printed on it in bold letters was "Do Not Drink and Derive." I pointed to it and said to the girl at the register, "That's a good one."

"What?" she said, looking up from her cell phone.

Of course she didn't know what it meant. "How much for that shirt?"

"Twenty."

I went to pull out a bill, until I realized that the last thing

I needed was one more geeky math shirt. I could have probably made a quilt out of the stack of them that I usually wore as pajamas now.

But just as I was about to turn away, I remembered. Sadie Hawkins was two weeks away. Girls gave the guys they were asking a matching shirt to wear to the dance. Whenever I had thought about asking Brendan before, I'd started shaking and promptly forgotten about the idea. But this would be a great excuse. Hey, I found these shirts, I'd say. Now we have to go to Sadie. Because who else would understand them? And where else would we wear them? He'd laugh, and agree, even though he was always saying how stupid school dances were, and hadn't even gone to prom last year—he'd hung out watching movies with me instead.

But this would definitely work.

"Do you have a small and a medium?"

I walked away with my ticket to a date with Brendan finally in my hot little hands.

CHAPTER NINE

she did not seem to have a thought of fear

The next morning, I practically bounced down the stairs. I'd spent all of last night thinking about how I'd ask Brendan. I'd carefully folded the shirt in a variety of combinations, trying to see which one would be easiest to casually whip out of my bag and hand to him. I finally decided on rolling it up, because then I could hold it in one hand, and it would take him no time at all to unroll it to look at it, and laugh and smile about it. It would be less like he was unwrapping a present and more like he was reading a note casually passed to him in class. More like friends and less like boyfriend and girlfriend.

Right. Because that was exactly what I wanted. Smooth move, Ashley.

Whatever. This was going to be easy. It was Monday, a Mathletes day, and I'd meet Brendan after his last class, walk to the auditorium with him, and help him set up. That was when I'd ask him.

"Mathletes tonight, right?" Aunt Kristin asked as she passed me the milk to pour on my cereal. I couldn't chew fast enough this morning, even though I was half-dreading going to school. I answered through a mouth full of shredded wheat, too anxious to care.

"Yeah. Brendan's driving me home, though." I couldn't believe the little smile that crept across my face when I said it. Even I knew I looked smug. But between the mad performance I was about to give at Mathletes practice tonight and that awesome shirt, he wouldn't be able to resist.

My stomach churned a little more with each class bell that rang. I even avoided Brendan at lunchtime, hiding out in the library instead. I wanted to give his buddies—one of whom was hopefully not Sofia—the chance to do all their stupid talking and back-patting then, instead of at the beginning of Mathletes, which is when I wanted to catch him.

Also, I was feeling pretty sick by that point. But whatever. In the back of the library, I whipped out my compact and spoke into it, practicing how I'd sit, how I'd hold my hands, how I'd bat my eyes, how I'd smile. I even practiced swinging my backpack around to my side, unzipping it without fumbling, and pulling out the shirt design side up.

I so had this in the bag.

At the end of my last class, I tried to look casual and pack up my stuff quietly ahead of the bell. I knew it annoyed the crap out of Mrs. Helmsley, but I didn't care. Thank God there was no one in this class I typically walked the halls with. I stopped by my locker to slide my History and English textbooks inside, and to swipe on some lip gloss, checking the little mirror right inside the door and admiring the cute sweater I'd picked that morning.

I strode down the hall at a fast clip. I seriously felt like everyone I passed was stepping out of the way. Like I was Moses and all these kids were the Sea of Reeds. The universe was smiling on me, that was for sure.

Brendan stepped out of his classroom—he had Biology last period. It was like he was moving in slow motion. I didn't know if it was because I wanted to ask him, or because he just looked that good, but his jeans and his light blue T-shirt fit him particularly nicely today.

When his eyes met mine, that smile that made me all melty spread across his face, and I had to command my heart to stop wanting to fly out of my chest. When I reached him, though, instead of sweeping me up in a bear hug like he normally would, he just slung one arm around my shoulders. He didn't press a kiss to the top of my head, like I'd envisioned he would so many times last night. Like he did at the beginning and end of every day. And then, he looked down at me and said, loudly enough for everyone to hear, "Hey, kid."

Kid? Kid? My self-confidence sagged around my ankles. I may have been a class below him, but Brendan had never cared about that. What the hell was going on?

We walked to the auditorium for practice, him making small talk and me trying to swallow hard and hold back tears.

I tried to tell myself it was no big deal. We'd get to the auditorium, I'd help him set up, I'd mention how I'd found a whole bunch of new practice tests. We'd sit down and I'd show off by working one that, as far as I knew, he'd never seen before.

It was going to be fine. Just fine.

I pushed open the swinging doors with the arm I didn't have swung around his waist, and my heart stopped, jumped out of my chest, and rolled down the long carpeted aisle. Clunked against the wooden front of the stage.

I smelled her almost before I saw her. Never had I thought I would hate the smell of flowers so violently.

Sofia.

She wore a blue flowered dress that was a little too swingy and a lot too low-cut for the frigid mid-October Pittsburgh wind that howled outside the school's walls. And the only thing perkier than the cleavage bouncing out of the top of it was her hair and her smile.

"Brendan!" she squealed as she skipped toward the back of the auditorium to meet us. Brendan dropped his arm from my waist and stepped forward, away from me, to meet her. She jumped at him, throwing her arms around his neck. Even though he looked a little awkward doing it, he put both arms around her waist and she lifted up off the ground a little.

The same way he always hugged me. Except today, when he hadn't.

She linked her arm with his and walked with him to the table and chairs someone—I'd be willing to bet she—had already set up for our second meeting. I heard her blabbing about how she'd been concerned about how some of the team members would approach some question, and shouldn't we do more trials to time people, and we should probably also do drills for speed, shouldn't we?

Brendan knew all that. But the way he was looking at her, you'd think he didn't. He was watching her with all the fascination of someone who was hearing this stuff for the first time. Someone who hadn't led the team to State last year.

It was like Sofia was preaching the freaking Mathletics gospel, and he was buying every damn word as the God's honest truth.

I trudged down to the front of the auditorium and settled in the chair next to Brendan. Sofia was in the seat across from him, and kept reaching across to touch him on the forearm.

"You know, I'd never actually thought of it that way before," Brendan said to something Sofia had just been chattering about. Probably it was as insipid as the tone of her voice.

I was suddenly having trouble getting air into my lungs again. And the auditorium, which had seemed so large when we first walked in, was shrinking around me. This couldn't be happening now. Could not. And if I could get this one thing done, it wouldn't happen again, I was sure of it.

"So, Brendan," I said, steeling myself. "I know that school dances are seriously lame, but sometimes something's just too good to pass up." I reached back to swing my bag around, just like I'd practiced a thousand times.

"Are you talking about Sadie?" Sofia piped up. God, I wished this Sadie Hawkins shirt was a mallet so I could beat her over her squeaky little head with it. "Can you believe that Brendan ever thought those things were tired? Don't worry. I'm making him go with me. I'd never miss a tolo."

Tears flooded my eyes. No way was this happening. No way had she asked him to Sadie Hawkins before me. No way had she found the one thing I would get the guts to do to tell Brendan how much I liked him and stomp all over it.

I must have looked like I didn't understand what she was saying, with the blinking and all, because she lowered her head and spoke a little more loudly and slowly, and her smile got just a little bigger. "In California? We called them tolos. Girls asked the guys? Well, anyway. I told Brendan there was no excuse for missing one of the best dances ever—not even studying for math."

She looked absolutely giddy with her own brilliance. The room spun around me and I wanted to vomit.

Then, I heard the telltale sound of the auditorium door swinging open.

Vincent strolled down the aisle, his arm wrapped around

Britt's waist. She stared up at him like a puppy dog. "So, are we doing this Mathletes thing or what?" he said, grinning. He sidled up to me and nudged his shoulder into mine. "I heard you're the up-and-coming star."

"I was just telling Ashley here about tolo, and how fun it is, and how me and Brendan wouldn't miss it for the world," Sofia squeaked.

Me and Brendan? Were they a couple now? I studied Brendan. He was shuffling around a bunch of the papers containing competition questions on his desk. If they were together, he was certainly doing a poor job of being excited about it.

"Aw, a tolo?" Vincent said. "I loved those! Too bad guys can't go without a date."

By this point, a couple more kids on the team had started to trickle in.

"You'll take me, right, Ashley? Don't let the poor new kid be left hanging at home."

I should have made a joke about how he could have found any girl in the school he wanted to take him. But damn me, I looked up into those warm, soft eyes, and they looked at me the same way they had a week ago on the roof, like I was really beautiful, like I was something to be enchanted with.

And just like that, the shirt I'd envisioned handing across the table to Brendan a hundred times got passed into Vincent's hands instead. "Why not?" I said shakily. "And I already have a shirt."

"Aw, sweet!" Vincent said as he unrolled it and read it for everyone. "Do not drink and derive." The entire little crowd cracked up. Obviously everything that came out of Vincent's mouth was inherently more hilarious than anything I could have said. Britt stared at me with deadpan, murderous eyes, then mumbled something about the ladies' room and stalked out through the side door. It was just a stupid Sadie Hawkins— she could cut in on a snowball dance if she wanted to, anyway.

Then my gaze caught Brendan's. It was moving between Vincent, the shirt, and me. His expression was a perfect cross between realization, sadness, and—did I see a little embarrassment? He knew that shirt was for him. And he knew I was going to ask him. And he knew what a damn big deal that was. The only question was — what would he have said?

CHAPTER TEN

bickerings and jealousies

I busted through the double auditorium doors to the hallways, only then realizing how much I'd loved the little island of Mathletes practice in an otherwise empty sea of velvet-covered auditorium. The hallway was a salmon run, a frenzy of kids not really thinking about where they were going or why. Voices and conversations flowed around me like water, individual words droplets splashing against my skin.

And then a whole spray of them hit me in the face.

"Can you believe that whore Ashley Price is the one who gets to be making out with Vincent on Sadie night?" Britt's voice was distinctively sharp among the dozens of others around me.

If I could have, I would've stopped dead in my tracks. It wasn't the "making out" or even the "Vincent" that stopped me. It wasn't even the fact that I'd never wanted to go to Sadie with him in the first place.

It was the words "whore" and "Ashley" in the same sentence. It knocked the wind out of me.

I shouldered my way through the crush of kids to my

right, leaned against the wall, turned to the side so that no one could see me and so that I could catch my breath. Even through my gasps, I could hear the rest of what they were saying. "Hanging all over Brendan since the day she got here...then going after the guy we all want? Like he's more interested in her than he is in us? Like she even stands a chance?"

It had been a long time since I'd had to deal with this kind of shit. Eight months, to be exact. Hadn't been trash-talked about, not in broad daylight at least, since I left Williamson.

I wasn't going after Vincent at all. Of course I was stunned a little bit every time he looked at me since I met him weeks ago—those warm eyes and thick lashes were almost too gorgeous to be real. Never mind the fact that they focused on me with interest. I was pretty, just as pretty as some of the other girls, but I didn't dress as nicely, and didn't run with the giggly boy-baiting crowds. Never attracted that much attention from any guy.

Until now.

I'd always thought no one cared that much about me being close to Brendan—although even thinking about the girls saying I was hanging on him made me bristle, since I never did that. Even being hopelessly in love with him, I knew the difference between acting like a guy's best friend and throwing myself at him.

Besides, one of the reasons I'd always loved Brendan was that he didn't act like the other popular, rich guys around those girls. He didn't take girls out on fancy dates, and never bought expensive clothes. And he didn't look like the famous actors in magazines. He was just Brendan. With his warm smile and floppy hair and his slightly skinny frame and broken-in jeans and incredible brain and uncannily complete understanding of me.

And, I reminded myself as I watched him walk out of a classroom and down the hall with Sofia, his interest in the drop-dead gorgeous new girl.

Either way, Brendan was the one I cared about, and Sadie Hawkins with Vincent was not worth the trouble it would apparently cause. He was cute, but not cute enough to elicit the word "whore" being spat at me for the next eight months, and probably another visit to the psych ward. I had to figure out a way to un-ask him. But first, since my pulse was already racing and I was breaking out in a sweat, I had to get the hell out of there.

The rush of students had thinned considerably in the time it had taken me to catch my breath and screw my head on straight. Still, I plowed through the middle of the hallway like that was the only way to get through. Maybe it was. Just ten more steps till I reached the outside air.

Six steps to outside. Two.

And then, echoing off the walls, someone shouted, "Hey!

Ashley! Ashley Price!" Even raised, the voice was baritone and rich, soft and strong at the same time. Like velvet. I turned over my shoulder, against my better judgment, which was telling me to just get the hell out of there. Vincent was jogging up to me, his curls swaying against the bottom edge of his perfectly broken-in baseball cap just the slightest bit.

I turned back around and kept going. Outside was a shock of smoky cool brightness. The sun scorched my eyes and my field of vision, and I relied on memory alone to propel myself in the right direction to eventually hit the little car Kristin and Bruce sometimes let me take to school, if Kristin didn't have much planned.

"Hey, Ashley!" Geez, this guy didn't let up. His footsteps scraped after me against the gravel. Reluctantly, I slowed down. Anyone could see, in this instance at least, that he'd literally been chasing me. I reached the first line of cars and slowed until he caught up with me, then tented my hand over my eyes to look at him.

"Hey."

"Hey yourself."

Wow, his teeth were white. And those lips...

"Well?" Why had he tried so hard to catch up with me if he had nothing to say?

"That's it. Just...hey. I don't know."

I gave him a weird sideways smile, shook my head, and kept walking.

"Hey! Wait up!" Vincent caught up with me again as I hoisted my bag over my shoulder, grunting. He held out his hand. "Let me."

I rolled my eyes, but my shoulder did ache from the four huge textbooks straining the canvas. I held the strap out to him, and he smiled as he took the bag.

Suddenly, I felt a lot lighter.

Vincent said, "I just thought, you know, since we're going to the dance together, we could talk. Get to know each other. Or I could at least walk you to your car."

"Yeah...about that...maybe I should give the other girls their fair shot at you."

Vincent laughed, almost a snort. "Am I a target?"

"Well, to them you are. And I know you don't know me that well, but I really am not a fan of putting myself in the path of shooting arrows. Especially when they're that sharp."

"What are you so worked up about? It's just Sadie Hawkins. Just one night."

"Look, Vincent. It's not you, okay? You're..."not Brendan. "You're great. It's just that...everyone wants to go out with you. Every girl here wishes that she was the one taking you to Sadie."

Brendan would have shrugged it off. He would have pretended that wasn't true. But Vincent just cocked his head a little to the left, smiled, and said, "Yeah. But you're the one I wanted to say yes to."

I started to hyperventilate a little. This was no good. Not at all.

"Look, are you having second thoughts?"

"No...I mean yes..."

The look of shock on Vincent's face would've made me giggle if I wasn't so completely freaked out.

"I mean...no." I don't know what came over me then, but something about the way he looked at me made me feel so damn confident that I touched his shoulder. "No, don't take that the wrong way, just...there's only one person who knows what I'm about to tell you. Can you keep a secret?"

He stood up straighter, and a serious look swept down over his face. "Absolutely."

"I left my old school because...well...everyone heard that I slept with some guy."

"So?"

"Well, 'some guy' was the captain of the lacrosse team..."

"...and he had a girlfriend?"

I nodded and swallowed hard. "Yeah. The head cheerleader."

He leaned back against the wall and raked his hand through his hair, blowing out a low whistle. "Shit, Ashley. How'd you get caught up in that?"

I felt my face screw up, and suddenly Vincent looked serious again. "Did he...you know...force you?"

"No...no! That's the thing. Nothing happened."

"Wait. Like...you didn't sleep with him?"

I shook my head, stared at my shoes, tried to keep the tears from filling my eyes. "Didn't even bat my eyes at him."

"Okay, so where did the rumor come from?"

"His girlfriend's best friend. I wouldn't help her cheat on a math final."

"And for that, she got you burned so bad you had to leave the school?"

The tears spilled out now—I watched a couple fall through the air and darken the floor at my feet. "Yeah. Tore my textbooks out of the spine, superglued my locker shut. Slashed my tires. Egged my house. Spray-painted it, too. Stole my homework and used it for toilet paper. Stuffed my clothes in the toilet during gym. Harassed me online. Made a website. Hijacked a billboard."

"Are you kidding me?" Vincent stood up again. I could barely see him through all the tears pooling in front of my eyes. The lump in my throat blocked any words from coming out, so I just looked him in the eyes and nodded. I think that was the first time he realized I was crying. It must have been, because he stepped forward and wrapped me in his arms.

Even though they were warm, and he smelled so, so good, I stiffened. "It's...it's okay," I said, standing up and hastily wiping my eyes with my shirt sleeve. "It's just that...I don't know. I already don't have a lot of friends here, you know? And I have a lot going for me here, academically. Mathletes, and a few friends at least. And really nowhere else to go if I screw this up. So...I appreciate you saving me in there. Really. I do."

"What," he said, "you didn't mean to get me that geeky math shirt?"

The smile on his face betrayed him. He knew that I'd really wanted to ask Brendan.

"Look," he continued. "I know it wasn't meant for me. But I think you're great. Okay? And I don't want you to miss out on the fun. And I really don't want to miss out on a night with you." He reached down and picked up my hand.

I smiled, and sniffled. I should have felt completely embarrassed, but for some reason, I didn't. Why was I spilling everything to this total stranger? Was it those eyes? That dimple? The way he smiled at me?

Whatever it was, I was in trouble.

"So I promise you," he said, "that for the next two weeks, until Sadie Hawkins, I won't so much as look at another girl, if that's what worries you. No sitting next to them at lunch, no driving them home, and absolutely no carrying their books." He looked at my bag, still slung over his shoulder. "Do you think that'll avert the vitriol?"

I sniffed again. Vincent reached out one finger and touched my chin, lifting it up so that I looked at him, then dropping his hand. I nodded gratefully. "Yeah." I said. "Yes. That's...you don't have to. But thank you. I mean...it's just a few weeks, and then you can..."

"Hey. Hey. If there's one thing you should know about me, Ashley Price, it's that I don't believe in playing by the rules. Besides, do you think I'd offer if I didn't care about you? Or if I really wanted to date anyone else?"

Oh, God. Did this mean we were dating now? "You mean, go on a date," I said, immediately biting my tongue.

He shrugged, and smiled again. "Sure. Whatever. Go on a date. Or another one after it. Or a lot of them." Then he turned and walked to his car.

I didn't know what to say. "Thank you," felt weird, and "see ya" felt too casual. So all I managed to choke out before he disappeared behind the flashing windows was, "Uh..."

And he just smiled back at me, not seeming to mind at all.

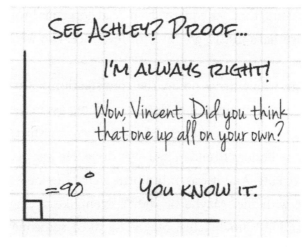

CHAPTER ELEVEN

'never' is a black word

Somehow, I arrived home without ever remembering driving along the roads or stopping at the lights.

There were two things my brain was having serious amounts of trouble computing. First, that the drop-dead gorgeous new girl was literally all over Brendan. There were two options; either someone else had finally realized how amazing Brendan was and gone for it, or there was something else going on.

Second, that her equally drop-dead gorgeous brother was trying so hard just to go out with me, once, two weeks from now.

The whole drive home, the conversation with Vincent repeated itself in my mind. He had saved my ass in there. And he looked at me, in my eyes and not down my shirt, like no other guy besides Brendan had ever done. He was decent. He was very cute. And it was only a little weird that he wanted to go out with me. Maybe he didn't even like sitting at the popular kids' lunch table. Maybe he liked someone a little quieter. Someone like me.

The only question was, did I like someone like him?

Really, I didn't know much about him. Hardly anything at all. I knew I liked Brendan—I knew I liked his easy, oblivious smile, the way we were together, the way he smelled. But how much of him did I like because he was familiar? Because he'd rescued me? Because he'd been the lives-next-door best friend that I'd never had living in farm country, because he'd been my ticket to everyone liking me at Mansfield? Brendan was the person who helped me start over.

He also happened to be perfect for me.

"It's just a dance," I said under my breath. I trudged up the front steps and into the house, which was cluttered but not dirty, like always. A problem of people with too much money and too much time on their hands—shopping. The living room was full of random department-store bags containing things like brand-new comforters and napkin rings, and yet another black cardigan or pair of silver earrings for Kristin.

I stopped in the kitchen to grab a soda, and a note waited for me on the kitchen counter. It was in Kristin's scrawling handwriting. "Out late. Frozen pizza in freezer." I wrinkled my nose. Pizza was okay, but the cardboard crust made the frozen stuff completely inedible for me. Kristin meant well, but she never paid much attention to things like that.

I traipsed through the open living room area, pulling out my phone and checking the texts for the homework questions from Brendan I knew would be there. Every day last year I'd had to field his questions clarifying the assignment. Nothing. I scrolled through to make sure. Nope. Seriously? Nothing? It must just be that he didn't want to bother with it the first few days—even though he was a little bit of a slacker, he was smart as hell, and always caught up.

My limbs buzzed with some weird feeling I couldn't name. Antsiness, annoyance, I didn't know. I just knew I didn't want to sit still.

I dropped my backpack with a thud at the doorway to my room, and kept walking toward the bathroom. Without even pulling up my hair, I cranked on the cold water, bent down, and splashed my face with it. When had it gotten so hot in the house? Or was it just a weird bubble of heat around my whole body?

Either way, that water felt good. I leaned forward, planting my hands on the sink and staring in the mirror. Water dripped off my eyelashes, my nose, and my bottom lip. I wiped the water from my lids and leaned in even more.

I'd always thought of my hazel eyes as a mess of colors that couldn't make up their minds to be one thing or another, but now that I really paid attention, the light brown flecked with green and a little blue and ringed with dark brown on the outside was mesmerizing. Like a kaleidoscope. My lashes were dark, thick and pretty, and combined with the careful makeup I'd applied there, they looked mysterious. Like something a guy might want to lose himself in. Suddenly, I could see why Vincent looked at my face, instead of scoping out my chest.

I leaned back a little then and pressed my fingertips to my cheeks. They had thinned out over the summer, I realized now that I really looked at them, leaving what appeared to be a higher cheekbone. Even though my face was tanned golden and sprayed with freckles by my summer in the sun, I definitely looked more grown-up than I had the last time I stared in this mirror. The summer had changed me.

I mean, hell. I was pretty. Pretty enough for a guy like Vincent to really, really notice me. To be excited, instead of annoyed, when he got stuck going to Sadie with me.

Pretty enough for a guy like him to pursue, even.

Staring in that mirror, imagining how Vincent had been looking at me in the hallway, my eyes trailed down my neck, which I stroked with my fingers, and down to my shoulder. My bra peeked out of my tank top strap a little. It was actually a little sexy.

If I was Vincent, would I really want to go to Sadie with me? If I didn't know about my crazy crush on Brendan Thomas? Or even if I did know about it?

Probably.

Would I want to kiss me?

Hell yeah.

I caught my bottom lip between my teeth. I was ready to laugh at myself for even trying to pull a purposefully sexy look, but it actually worked. I really did look sexy. A totally new feeling for me. I kind of liked it.

But how would it look if I actually tried to kiss the guy? You know, give him the signal, lean in, or maybe even grab him to make out in the hallway?

Something in my stomach quivered. I leaned forward and let my eyes flutter closed. I tried to imagine Vincent's deep brown eyes looking into mine, communicating something that would be just for the two of us. Something that told me he knew me in a way no one else did.

I got closer and closer to the mirror, watched my own lips part in anticipation. I closed my eyes all the way...

...my breath pushed back on my face from the cold glass...

And there, before my daydreaming eyes, I could only see the flop of Brendan's hair, could only feel his thin fingers brushing down my neck.

I leaned back and slammed my hands on the sink, throwing my head back and growling in exasperation.

"Get the hell out of my head, Brendan." I wiped my face with the towel, leaving a trace of lipstick that I knew Kristin would be pissed about. I dried my hands on it, too, then chucked it in the laundry bin.

One last check of my phone. Zero messages.

"Or at least send me a text, and give me a good reason I should keep you in my head at all."

I crossed the hall to my room in a huff, fished out my calculus textbook, and worked the problems at the back of it until my brain felt numb.

Okay Ashley, I have an equation for you. Here:

$$\text{let } f(a) = \sqrt[n]{e^x}$$

Ooo, ok...

$$\lim_{t \to \infty} f(a) - \frac{i}{f(t)} = \frac{d}{dx} f(v)$$

$$\lim_{t \to \infty} f(a) - \frac{i}{\infty} = \frac{d}{dx} f(v)$$

$$\sqrt[n]{e^x} = \frac{d}{dx} f(u)$$

$$\lim_{t \to \infty} f(a) - 0 = \frac{d}{dx} f(v)$$

$$\left(\sqrt[n]{e^x}\right)^n = \frac{d}{dx} f(u)^n$$

$$e^x = \frac{d}{dx} f(u)^n$$

$$\int e^x = \int \frac{d}{dx} f(u)^n$$

$$\int e^x = f(u)^n$$

...you are so immature.

CHAPTER TWELVE

as fearful of notice and praise

I went through a week and a half of walking through the halls of Mansfield Prep being Vincent Cole's Date to Sadie Hawkins. I couldn't stop rolling my own eyes at how ridiculous that was. Instead of envying me, those girls should have all been holding me up as a role model for how to be more assertive. Even though I technically hadn't asked Vincent—he'd accepted my sloppy invitation to someone else. My invitation that was too late.

Every time I saw Brendan in the halls, in fact, my footsteps echoed off the shining tile—too late, too late, too late. It was a refrain that didn't make any sense. Just weeks ago, we'd been so close to being together. That morning on the water tower, the way he looked at me through the brightening fog...

Too late, though. Because even then, when I'd been imagining feelings in his eyes, he already knew Sofia existed. Had already spent that whole damn cruise with her. Had probably been thinking about her while he was looking at me like that. What exactly had they done under those stars together?

Vincent, on the other hand, was thinking about me. Only

me. Just like he'd promised. A promise I hadn't even asked for, but he upheld it like his life depended on it. Not only did he not carry any other girls' books, or lunch trays, or backpacks. He didn't make eyes at any other girls, talk to any other girls, or walk beside any other girls.

None of the guys here had ever wanted to hang out with me. Probably the combination of math, the camera, and that being around me was pretty much all depressing all the time. Unless they loved a girl who randomly stared off into space and couldn't hold a conversation particularly well, they weren't gonna want to go out with me.

All signs pointed to Vincent being exactly the kind of guy I should want to be with—the kind of guy who wanted to treat me exactly like I should be treated.

Which is why it was a total mystery that, whenever I saw him, I tried to duck out of his line of sight. Every time I saw that golden mess of curls, chiseled jaw, and strong, wide shoulders, my heart sped up. And not always in a good way.

Instead of letting it stop me in my tracks, for the first few days, I made my feet speed up right along with my heartbeat, only feeling calmer when I caught a glimpse of Brendan. Being near him was certainty. It was my safety in this school that I'd always been too scared to find my own place in.

That kind of faded when, every day, I ran into Brendan talking with Sofia. Or walking with her. Or carrying her books.

So the next week, when Vincent stepped up to my lunch table and looked at the empty seat beside me with a question in his eyes, instead of looking away, I smiled. When he talked, I listened. And when he offered to walk me to my car, I didn't say no.

Every day, Vincent walked a little closer to me, smiled at me a little bit wider. Every day, I smiled back at him a little more and wondered when I'd see Brendan a little less. Every day, more eyes followed us. And every day, I cared less.

A full week after I accidentally asked Vincent to Sadie, I'd almost started dropping the "accidental" part when I thought about it. I'd asked Vincent to Sadie. Vincent was cute. Vincent thought I was cute.

Brendan was barely freaking looking at me, and, for the first time since I'd met him, he was making me feel worse instead of better.

Three days before the dance, Vincent sidled up to my locker as the last bell rang. Crazy how the guy always seemed to find some noise or event to announce his arrival. I'd planned to head out to the water tower that afternoon, since the woods surrounding it had begun to edge themselves with autumn gold. The camera bag just barely fit into my locker, and apparently it was tougher to wrench out than it was to squeeze in. Vincent's voice, low and velvet, breezed in over my shoulder.

"Need some help with that?"

I looked back at his face, just a foot away. Close, but not too close. I couldn't even find fault in how close he was standing. His face looked like patient understanding, didn't set me on edge at all. I needed that. Needed to feel like someone really wanted me for a change.

I gave him a grateful smile and stepped to the side. He had beautiful hands—not too big, and not too small, strong fingers. Seriously, he could be a freaking hand model if he was so inclined. I watched as he patiently fit them between the bag and the walls of the locker—was it weird that I was so focused on his fingers?—and shimmied the bag, hefting it out of its metal bounds so carefully I would have thought it was a bird's nest with just-laid eggs.

"Can I carry it for you?"

I nodded and smiled again. "Just be careful. That's my baby."

"A junior girl at Mansfield who calls tech, I'm guessing, her baby?"

I smiled, and patted the camera bag he'd just slung over his shoulder. "Just the DSLR."

"Yeah, that camera. I meant to ask. You on yearbook or something?"

"Nah. I'm not into deciding who gets immortalized in the popularity handbook every year. I'd rather hunt down beauty outside the school walls."

"Well, from my experience, not enough people are

looking for beauty inside the school walls."

I turned to him and raised my eyebrows, with a smile playing on my lips. "Okay."

"I'm just glad I found you. I mean, it. I mean…you know." That gentle smile on his face, that look that said he wasn't actually stammering or having trouble getting words out, didn't match his confession. I knew that he knew the difference between "you" and "it." But hell, those words were beautiful. .

"So, what were you thinking for dinner? Before Sadie?"

My panic must have been evident on my face, because he immediately jumped in with, "I mean, if you don't have anything planned, it's cool."

Oh, thank God. My car was in sight. "I guess I…I mean, it's very casual, right? So we could just…"We reached my car, and I clicked the alarm off. He laid my camera bag on the floor of the backseat, and I could swear he peeked in it one more time as he did. Then he reached up and opened my door for me, helping me into my seat with the other hand.

"Hey,"he said, "you have a lot on your mind."

I had no idea what he was talking about, but I wanted to see where this was going.

"Let me take care of dinner. Okay?"

I was raising my eyebrows again. Even though I had no idea about the exact expression on my face, he laughed.

"Nothing big, nothing fancy."

I nodded. "Promise?"

"Promise."

$$\Omega$$

I'd meant to get up in the early in the morning on the day of Sadie Hawkins to go for a run, pick my cutest pairs of jeans, concentrate on a shower and makeup. But I just....didn't. Vincent was picking me up at six, and I only really rolled out of bed at three.

Mansfield Prep had a uniform, one we all bought from the same place, and so no one really would have noticed me wearing my dirt-cheap clothes my mom had found on the clearance rack of the discount superstore for most of my life. It was one of the reasons I didn't go to that many parties— these were the kind of kids who noticed which stitching patterns on the pockets of which washes of jeans equaled "designer."

Sadie at Mansfield Prep wasn't fancy, but I had some idea of what the other girls wore from watching Julia get ready for last year's. She had dragged me to the store with her after grabbing her mom's card from her purseand obsessed over a pair of pristine, dark jeans with silver stitching. They hugged her in all the right places, as opposed to my beaten-up worn ones, which hung instead of clung. I looked ruefully at my small stack of jeans. One pair was nice and dark, and I'd almost never worn it. When I unfolded those, I remembered why—I'd bought them my own freshman year, and two months later, promptly gotten the curves every girl who started freshman year on the thin-as-a-stick side dreamed of.

Those jeans clung to my hips in a way that would make any guy look at me. I knew it even then. And that wasn't anything I'd ever wanted—I'd only ever cared about whether Brendan was looking at me.

A few weeks ago, that was still all I cared about. But Brendan wasn't taking me to Sadie. Vincent was. Or, I was taking him.

But he was definitely taking me out to dinner. No one could argue that.

I gasped and my eyes flew open wide at the realization. He'd volunteered to take care of dinner so that he could say he'd asked me on a date. Was this one more attempt at keeping new gossip away from me?

If it was, it was working. Both to keep the gossip away, and to make me like him.

I imagined a perfect pre-Sadie dinner—a picnic at the park, watching the early autumn sunset, feeling the air chill as the sun dipped below the horizon. There would be crackers and cheese and fruit. The guy would offer me his coat, and sit right down on the ground not caring about damp grass or dirt. I pictured Vincent there. I'd never seen him even close to dirt, or dirty or sweaty or otherwise disheveled in any way. But I supposed it could happen.

Right. Vincent. Taking me to Sadie, now, technically. Where I had to wear cute jeans and shoes. Right.

The dark pair of jeans fit exactly as I'd remembered. When I combined them with the T-shirt and a pair of fabulous heels on I'd snagged from Aunt Kristin's closet, and some big flashy sliver earrings I'd grabbed from her costume jewelry box, I had to admit it. There, in the mirror with my leg popped out to the side and my hand on my hip, I looked good. Even with the geekiness of my shirt.

Mathlete sexy. It was something I could get used to.

I walked down the hallway and back again, watching the sway of my hips in the mirror. Not too bad. I somehow managed to look like I knew what I was doing in those heels, and not really be in any pain. It felt good to have control over something, even if it was something as stupid as that.

Surprise number five kajillion of this year, crazy as it was already. For the first time in a long time I felt comfortable in my skin again. I liked it. I liked feeling like the old me, that I was strong and desirable just as I was. Strange how everything that had happened last year had made me forget it.

$$\Omega$$

I carefully heel toed my way down the stairs, to test the stair factor, and also because I was starving. Aunt Kristin was standing in her yoga pants and sports bra, throwing frozen strawberries in a blender with protein powder and spinach leaves. I made a face. She always swore you couldn't taste the spinach, but the weird greenish-brown color alone made me want to puke.

She looked up, gave me the once-over, and grinned.

"Are those my new Adrien Abelle heels?" Her eyebrows pushed up, but she was still smiling.

I looked at her sheepishly. "Um, yes? For Sadie? If it's okay?"

"Sadie's tonight?" I could almost reach out and grab the excitement from her words as they floated on the air toward me. "You never told me," she said, her eyebrows drawing in.

"Yeah, well, it's not really a big deal. You know."

"I don't know, first dance of the year? When I was at Mansfield it was always a big to-do. Not dress-wise, obviously, but still. Set the tone for the rest of the year."

I rolled my eyes before I even realized I was doing it. Thankfully, Aunt Kristin was more like a teenager sometimes than an adult who knew everything about what I should be doing and who I should be doing it with. She threw her head back and laughed. "Point taken. So, where's Brendan taking you for dinner?"

A burn flared in my chest and shot straight up to my cheeks. I looked down, memorizing the grain of the leather against the careful lines on Aunt Kristin's shoes. "It's not Brendan."

"What do you mean, it's not Brendan, aren't you guys

kind of...you know..."

"A thing?" Heat crept over my face as I rummaged through the fridge and grabbed the first thing my hand fell on to eat—carrot sticks. Great. I focused all my energy on opening the zip-top bag they'd been relegated to, but it wouldn't come open. "No,"I mumbled, "there's this girl..."

"Oh, Ashley. Honey. I had no idea he had a girlfriend."

"She's not his girlfriend," I said, a little too forcefully, as my fingers scrabbled at the godforsaken strips of blue and green plastic that had somehow joined forces to keep me from eating this snack I really didn't want. "She's not...she's just some stupid new girl, they're not...whatever." I threw the bag down on the counter, blew my hair out of my eyes, and stood up straight, looking at Aunt Kristin.

"So, it's okay if I wear these?"

"Yeah. And the jeans...that's a good look for you. Your dad might think a little too good, but coming from your younger, funner aunt...a good look."

I pushed my hip out to the side, feeling the stretching tightness of the denim against it. It was definitely a close fit. I turned to walk back upstairs, swaying a little more with my steps.

"When are you picking him up?"Kristin called after me.

"Oh, he's getting me."

"Really?"

"Uh huh. And taking me to dinner. Said he'd be here at

six."

"Wow. That's...not common. For Sadie. You're supposed to pick him up. We used to bring a picnic."

I wrinkled my nose. "Isn't that kind of sexist? I don't even know what to put in a picnic lunch."

Kristin laughed. "Everyone should know what to put in a picnic. Boys and girls."

I shrugged, anxious to get back upstairs, to be alone, no matter how easy Kristin was making this whole thing. "He wanted to deal with dinner. I don't know."

"And who's 'he'?" she asked, smiling a sly smile.

"Oh. Right. Vincent. His name's Vincent." I told her his name like I would have read an item off of a menu—with mildly interested casualness and zero excitement.

"Will I like him?"

I laughed. "I guess we'll see." I was still trying to figure that out myself.

CHAPTER THIRTEEN

nothing could be more obliging than your manner

Vincent arrived at exactly one minute before six o'clock. I knew because I was watching our driveway through my bedroom window, holding the curtain back from the edge just a bit. And Vincent, apparently, liked to do things in style. Instead of his usual spotless Porsche, he'd hired a freaking limo.

He stepped out and leaned against the shining black side of the car. He looked perfect, as usual. He turned around and leaned over, using the tinted windows outside as a mirror, and ran his fingers along the fringe of curls at his forehead. He took the chewing gum out of his mouth and carefully wrapped it in a paper, which he stuffed in the trash can hanging on the back of the passenger's seat. Then he looked at his watch, nodded, picked something up off the passenger's seat, and walked up the driveway.

My stomach twisted. I pulled away from the window, closed my eyes, and took deep breaths. I was going to a dance. With a guy. Who was not Brendan.

I rolled my eyes. That sounded ridiculous even to me. Brendan was Brendan. Just a guy. Just a stupid guy, who I knew liked me—or used to. Or did he really think we were just best friends? He was just Brendan. Just one guy.

Ω

The doorbell sounded, sharp and short, and my feet carried me to the stair way more excitedly than I would have thought.

Vincent stood in the foyer holding a single pink rose. And looking like a freaking supermodel. The shirt that would have been comfortably baggy on Brendan closely hugged his muscled, six-foot frame. Underneath the shirt was a perfectly pressed orange oxford collared shirt, which perfectly matched the color of the font in the tee.

I smelled the strong mint of the gum he'd been chewing just beneath the scent of his cologne—musky, woodsy, and strong. He smelled like guy, one who had tried to get ready for a nice date. The only thing Brendan ever smelled like was dryer sheets and sometimes, if he'd just gotten out of the shower, that green soap he used. And vanilla. He always smelled a little like vanilla. Warm and comforting and familiar and...home.

And I was going to Sadie with Vincent. Vincent. Who had hired a limo, and managed to look gorgeous even in a stupid T-shirt.

The flecks in his eyes seemed to sparkle when he looked up from his conversation with Aunt Kristin to me. "Wow,

Ashley. You look great."

"Easy for you to say," I joked. "You're wearing the same thing."

He laughed, and even then, those damn eyes seemed to bore a hole into me. He was looking at me like he'd been waiting to see me for years. Like he was amazed.

"You brought me flowers?" I asked. "Like the limo wasn't enough?" Oh, shit. Now he'd know I was watching for him out the window.

A split second after I realized it, a look of happiness-bordering-on glee lit up his face. He shrugged, though he still didn't do too much to hide his obvious pleasure. "You don't like it?"

"No, uh...I mean, it's nice. It wasn't necessary..." I trailed off.

"I just want you to feel special. It's not a crime, is it?"

"Special" hadn't been part of any vocabulary I had used when thinking about myself since...ever, really. The cutest boy in school was standing here, in our foyer, pulling out all the stops for me and a stupid dance.

Nobody else had ever made that kind of effort. Definitely not Brendan, and there was no reason to think that he ever would. I just needed to let it go. Have fun. I was a normal high school kid going to a normal high school dance. There was no reason for all this drama and angst.

I took a deep breath and looked down at the rose Vincent

held out to me. I couldn't help but raise my eyebrows.

"Oh. I know it's not a corsage kind of dance, but I really hate not being able to bring a girl flowers," Vincent said, holding out the rose. Aunt Kristin stepped back and looked at me, unable to hide her expression of pleasant shock.

"I know yellow roses mean friendship," Kristin said, "and red mean love. What do you think pink means?"

I shrugged and turned to grab my bag, when Vincent said, "Admiration. And gratitude. I asked the florist."

I scoffed. "You're the one taking me to dinner."

His eyes smiled down at me. "You're the one letting me. I'm just really glad I was there that day."

"Okay, well," Kristin said with a nervous laugh. "I'll just...get back to my show," she finished lamely. "Back by when?"

"Midnight for sure, Mrs. Harris," Vincent said, still looking at me.

I turned to make eye contact with Kristin. "Probably ten, though. It'll be closer to ten."

"Midnight's fine. I'll see you then, sweetie." She grabbed my hand and held on as she looked at me. "And have fun."

Ω

On our way out, Vincent left his customary half-foot of distance between us. Enough to keep me comfortable, and close enough to send me the signal, loud and clear, that he liked me. Yep. Flower, once-over, limo. He definitely liked me. And the flutter of excitement in my stomach about just that fact was not unpleasant at all.

Vincent made some motion through the front windshield. While it was a limo, it wasn't so stretch, and the space in the back was pretty tight. When he ducked in after me, the scent of his cologne filled the air. It wasn't choking, but it did catch me off guard. His grown-up cologne was just one more thing about him that made this all feel very grown-up.

But thinking of the way my hips curved in these jeans, and the warmth that ran through me when Vincent's leg smooshed up against mine in that backseat, I suddenly felt some pretty adult feelings myself.

We rode for a few blocks, staring out the window.

"What are the autumn leaves like in Pittsburgh?" he asked.

"Oh!" My voice suddenly filled with a kind of warmth I didn't hear from myself too often. I remembered last year tromping through the woods, trying to catch the perfect macro and then, later, landscape shots of the beautiful Pennsylvania fall foliage. But then I remembered. That was at home.

"Well, here it's fine. But up at Tioga..." There was that wistful tone in my voice again. I cleared my throat, and glanced over at him. "The national park near my parents' house, Tioga, has the most incredible foliage. But I guess you won't be seeing that." I forced a chuckle.

His eyes burned into mine again. "Who knows? Maybe I will."

I caught his gaze for another second before turning to look out my window.

We rode another fifteen minutes in silence until I noticed we were headed toward downtown. I realized I had never asked him where we were going to dinner.

The car slowed, and I looked at Vincent curiously. He popped open the door, stepped out, and reached a hand in to help me out. "Dinner." He smiled. I looked up at one of the tallest buildings in Pittsburgh.

"Where—?"

"Just follow me." He still held onto my hand, fingers closed, like a gentleman would have held onto a lady's a century ago. We stepped into a fancy lobby with a marble floor and giant chandeliers dripping with thousands of crystals. A cellist and pianist played in the corner of the restaurant, populated with tables lit by candlelight and adorned with wine buckets.

The patrons were in all kinds of fancy dress, the women in precarious-looking heels, even crazier than mine. But none of them were wearing jeans. I looked down at our shirts, tugging on mine, and flushed. I suddenly wanted to get out of there. Badly.

"Vincent, I had no idea..."

"Hey," he leaned down and whispered in my ear. "My dad knows someone who knows someone. They reserved us a spot all to ourselves. We're perfectly fine, dressed just like this."

I tried to smile at him, but it didn't change the fact that I had to walk past all those people eating in their fancy clothes. Of course they all stared at me.

I hated being stared at.

"Would it make you feel better if we ate out here?" he asked.

"No, let's just...get to our table."

We arrived in a small back room with a table set for two. There was a long buffet with about five main courses, three salads, and twenty desserts lined up, waiting for us.

"I didn't know what your favorite was, but I know we have to get going soon. So I had them make a bunch of stuff, so we could eat and go."

"Why did you bring me here?" I asked. I couldn't find anything malicious in his face, since he just looked at me in that way he always did—like he was just so, so happy to be with me.

"I just wanted you to feel special. I don't know. No one else is doing this. I want to stand out."

I smiled. "Well, you certainly accomplished that."

His face fell a little bit. "It's too much, isn't it?"

Well, shit. I may not have been instantly head over heels

for him, but he was still a good guy who treated me well. I didn't want to make him feel bad. "No, no. It's awesome. Really, Vincent. It's great." I craned my neck to look in the buffet trays. "Hey, is that mac and cheese?"

"Yeah, I think so." He grinned. "That's what I asked for. Fancy place, normal food."

I laughed. "Okay, so what else is there?"

His shoulders relaxed. Thank God. I'd broken the tension. "Uh...hot dogs, I think. French fries?"

"Well, now you're talking." We grabbed plates and dug into the spread. I ate one bite of everything, because there were just so many choices—including one bite of every dessert. It might have been normal food, but hell if that wasn't the best mac and cheese I'd ever tasted. It made me seriously wonder what kind of expensive-ass cheese was in this.

After twenty minutes of eating and laughing with Vincent, we both stared at the last bite of dessert—old-fashioned cheesecake with cherry topping. He picked up his fork, poised it over the top, and looked at me.

"I'll let you have it," I said. He dug in, loading his fork with a big, dripping bite, and had the fork almost to his mouth. I leaned back in my seat. "Even though it's my favorite."

His eyebrows flicked up and he gave me a little smile. Then he turned the fork around, and leaned toward me.

I knew I was supposed to move, to lean forward to meet

it. I don't know why I didn't. That didn't stop Vincent, though. He kept leaning forward, propping his elbows on the table between us and cupping his left hand under the fork to catch any drips.

"Vincent, I can't eat all—" But at just that moment, he took advantage of my open mouth and shoved the cheesecake in.

I couldn't help it. I laughed. It was so rich and good that I might have even made a little noise at the taste of it. Right before something gooey dripped down my chin.

"You just have a little—"Vincent leaned in a fraction of an inch more, swiped his thumb across my chin, and held his hand there for just a moment longer than he had to, staring at the place where the topping had been. His face turned dead serious, and my stomach flipped.

Half a second later, I swallowed the bite of cheesecake, gave a slight laugh, and looked away. "Um, wow. That was—"

"Good?" Vincent asked, his face still serious. "There's definitely more, if you want."

"No," I said, suddenly very focused on his lips, "I think we ate every single bite of dessert."

"I wasn't talking about dessert." Vincent's eyes burned into me. For a moment, I thought there was a hunger there, but then he went back to how he always looked—satisfied. Patient. I cleared my throat.

"Dinner was awesome," I said, getting up from my seat

and locating my bag. "But you didn't have to do anything this fancy. Really."

"You like simple. Got it. I'll keep that in mind for next time." He flicked his eyebrows up at me again, got up, and turned to open the door for me before I could say anything.

And the crazy thing was, I wasn't even sure if I wanted to.

ASHLEY, YOU LOOK SO $\frac{TAN\ C}{SIN\ C}$ IN THAT T-SHIRT.

You're kidding me, right? That one's too easy...

COME ON, JUST SOLVE IT.

fine... $\frac{tan\ c}{sin\ c} = \frac{\left(\frac{sin\ c}{cos\ c}\right)}{sin\ c} = \frac{1}{cos\ c} = sec\ c$

...are you drunk, Vince?

NOPE. YOU'RE MY SEC C SADIE DATE :D

you're cute.

CHAPTER FOURTEEN

of a cautious temper

Mansfield Prep wasn't very far from the restaurant. On the ride over, I leaned back in my seat, and Vincent did the same. Just like on the way to the restaurant, his thigh pressed up against mine. Unlike on the way to the restaurant, the space between us was filled with my memory of that bite of cheesecake, and how Vincent swiping his thumb across my chin had felt less like a hygiene move and more like a proposition. Or, the way he looked at me now, a promise.

He leaned his head back on the headrest, then turned it to me. "I had fun tonight." His voice was quieter than normal, more gravelly. There was something about the way he said the words, a little breathlessly, like it was a secret between us, that made me look at him.

His gaze was so focused on me. Again, I laughed and looked forward to break the tension. "Night's not over yet. We still have some dancing to do, and some geeks to make jealous."

That smile came back. "Exactly which geeks are you talking about?"

I laughed. "Um, all of them? Our shirts are awesome. 'Do

not drink and derive?' Come on. Who's not going to be jealous?" I swallowed a lump in my throat that had risen there independent of any specific thought.

A seasoned Mathlete would have cracked up, but Vincent just sort of shook his head and gave a vague smile. He must have gotten the joke, but I guess it just wasn't hilarious unless you lived and breathed math.

Now that we'd had dinner together, instead of thinking he looked slightly too formal and way ridiculous, I appreciated how the collared shirt Vincent was wearing framed his face. His absolutely stunning face.

Like he knew what I was thinking, he looked forward and smiled.

We were both quiet for the next few minutes, until the limo slowed. Vincent leaned forward and tapped the glass in front of us. "Just wait for us out here." The super faint outline of the limo driver's head nodded.

Vincent held out his hand, palm up and fingers relaxed, to me. "Ready for this?"

I smiled. "That depends," I said. "How good of a dancer are you?"

Ω

Vincent dropped my hand as soon as he helped me climb out of the limo, and I glanced around at all the other kids getting out of their cars—their everyday cars. Granted, they drove makes that my family couldn't pay for if they sold the whole farmhouse, but they were still the same cars they drove every single day to school.

"Hey, Ashley!" a high, perky voice called out across the parking lot, echoing against the shining marble walls of Mansfield Prep's columned walkway, and bouncing back to my ears like a freaking banshee.

Sofia bounced toward me across the parking lot, her stretching-to-eternity, thin-yet-perfectly-curvy legs encased in skinny jeans, wearing a pink and green paisley shirt and the craziest stilettos I'd ever seen. She walked on them as confidently as a runway model would. And, behind her, she dragged Brendan. He looked like an adorably confused puppy. I hated that look and loved it at the same time.

"Hey, Ash," he said, smiling in that same confused way.

"How'd it work out?" Sofia asked, looking at Vincent.

"Perfectly. If that was dinner every night, you wouldn't hear a complaint out of me." Vincent stepped close and nudged his shoulder into mine, smiling down at me.

Brendan looked at me curiously. "Didn't you bring a picnic?"

"Well, uh..." I cleared my throat. "It was picnic food. But it was..."

"Gruyère mac and cheese, man. It was epic. At Seviche, that restaurant downtown. Simple food, incredible view. You should think about it. I'm sure your dad basically designed the place, right?"

"Uh...maybe. Yeah. I don't know." Brendan looked down at where his hand connected with Sofia's, like he just realized he'd been holding it. He drew it away from hers and used it to run back through his hair, which was perpetually flopping in his eyes. Half the time I thought he kept it that way just so he could push it back like that when he needed something to do with his hands.

The thump of a bass wafted from the auditorium. Vincent gestured with his chin toward the school. "Sounds good. Who did they get?"

"Tommy and the Last Kisses," Sofia said. "Britt's dad knows their publicist and convinced them to stop here on their way cross-country from Philly."

"I thought they sounded familiar." Vincent looked down at me, checking for recognition. I had no clue. He shrugged. "First dance, Ash?" Brendan's face fell. No one ever called me Ash besides him. But the way Vincent looked at me and reached for my hand...it didn't sound too weird. Brendan certainly wasn't trying, and that fact was quickly changing my attitude from sad to pissed off, and it looked like it could head into me not giving a damn. I smiled at him. "Sure." Slipping my hand into his, we started walking toward the school. I looked back over my shoulder and called, "You guys coming?"

Ω

Like most everything else about Sadie, I hadn't known a thing about the theme. We walked inside the school's ballroom—yes, Mansfield Prep had a ballroom, for donor's events—to see it decked out with chrome accents, pastel streamers, a huge jukebox framing the stage that held the band, and a make-your-own milkshake stand.

"Roadside Diner theme. Nice,"Vincent said.

"How did you figure that so quickly?" I asked, kind of impressed. It did look good, like the 50s sock hop scene had transported itself here.

"Oh, as soon as Sofia heard that they were doing a tolo, she got right on the decorations committee. She likes to be in charge of everything. Has a picture of what she wants, and she'll do anything to make it happen."

"Well, you're twins. Are you the same that way?"I asked.

"Nah. I'd rather be surprised by finding something that's already absolutely perfect for me." He gazed down at me, his eyes falling on the same spot where he'd wiped the cherry topping from my chin. My heart quickened again. The strings of white lights reflected on every surface ten times more intensely than normal. Including those rich brown eyes of his, sparked with gold. They were so bright, were looking at me so warmly, the specks of gold like little flames, that if I looked into them for too long they'd melt me, too.

I suddenly found Aunt Kristin's shoes desperately in need of a scuff check. I lifted one and examined it, brushing some mud from outside off the heel.

"Like this sorry situation, for instance," he said. He gestured toward the room and its empty dance floor, and a bunch of kids gathered along the walls in circles of three or four, talking. Dozens waiting in line for malts or sodas. "I'm pretty happy with it, because I don't care about any of those kids. I only care about you."

My cheeks blazed red. Thank God the lighting was dim. I didn't know what to say to that. I didn't even know how I felt about that. "But Sofia…Sof won't like this at all. I'm giving it about sixty seconds till she does something about it."

"What do you mean?"

"Just watch. You'll see what I mean." He pointed at Sofia as she and her chestnut hair bounced across the dance floor. Even I had to admit that paisley collared shirt looked good on her. How it was possible for a girl in high school to have such long legs, such a tiny waist, and such big boobs was beyond me. I knew by the way at least a dozen other guys watched her that they were thinking the same thing. She was like a freaking Barbie doll, and consequently the wet dream of every guy here.

My gaze turned to Brendan standing in the doorway where she'd left him. The look on his face was different. His mouth hung open and he kind of slouch-swayed to the music like all the other guys, but the way his eyebrows drew together just a bit in the center gave it away. It was the same look he got whenever he was trying to figure something out.

Of course he thought she was hot—everyone did. But he was also totally confused.

Sofia stood on her tiptoes to talk to the bass player. His eyes drifted from her face to a point below her chin and he got that same bemused expression guys always had when they were getting a free show. Which meant he was no longer thinking with his brain, at least not the one in his head. Which meant, at this point, he'd do whatever she wanted.

Damn, this girl was good. Sometimes, I wished I could control people like that.

The bass player nodded at her, walked over to the lead singer, and whispered something in her ear. She smiled, winked down at Sofia, and said into the microphone, "Okay, you deadbeats, whaddya say we really get this dance going?"

There was a halfhearted cheer from the crowd, mostly coming from the group of designer jeans and stiletto-wearing, $500-phone-toting girls Sofia had already started to rule.

"We're gonna snowball. One couple will start us off, nice and slow, and when we switch songs, they grab new partners. Girls ask the boys. Got it?"

Another cheer, and this time some of the guys joined in. Leave it to them to appreciate a situation where they didn't even have to find the balls to ask a girl to dance. Even I thought it was an okay idea, until Sofia walked to the dance floor hand in hand with Brendan, and that weird burning started in my chest. And it only got worse when the first song the singer played was a slow song. A very slow song.

I watched as Brendan let his hands curve around her waist, right where the shirt bunched into her jeans. I thought my eyes might burn out of their sockets. His hands sat there for the first few seconds, his palms flat, but as the song went on, they talked and laughed even more. Sofia went from resting her wrists on Brendan's shoulders to leaning her forearms there. Her face was just inches from his. The song swelled as it ended, and Sofia tossed back her head and laughed. Then she looked at Brendan with her eyebrows furrowed, and reached up and held some of the hair out of his face. He shook his head, letting his hair flop like normal back into his eyes. Just like I'd always liked it.

The singer finished crooning the closing notes of the song, then announced, "Okay, each one of our original couple, choose a new partner, and after that, it's all girls!" Her tone was way too chipper and enthusiastic for something so incredibly stressful. Still, I couldn't tear my eyes away from Brendan.

And then, he looked up at me, and mouthed, "Please?" while smiling that sheepish smile I couldn't resist. I rolled my eyes and headed toward him, but I couldn't wipe the grin off of my face. Sofia's eyes caught mine, and for a split second I could have sworn they shot poison at me. But then that smile, the impossibly peppy and unmovable one I'd seen since I hung out with her at Custard's First Stand, took over, as she extended one perfectly manicured nail toward the captain of the lacrosse team—Rush, tall and muscled and definitely Julia's boyfriend.

The interlude music was slow, and my heart jumped as I got closer to Brendan. He put one hand on my waist, but held out the other away from his body.

He wanted to dance with me like he'd dance with his mom. Or his sister. Or his best friend.

Just his best friend. Nothing more.

He smiled at me. That genuine, huge, heartwarming smile that made me feel right at home, even in the middle of this crazy, awkward, angsty dance floor, where girls were starting to pick new partners left and right, and dirty, territorial looks were a dime a dozen. Yeah, I felt right at home with Brendan, no matter what else was going on.

The only question was, why did I even still feel that way? Because the other thing I knew for sure was that his fingers didn't curve into my waist like they had with Sofia's. And he definitely wasn't anywhere close to hugging my body to his.

With a couple dozen couples on the floor, the interlude ended, and the singer started a fast, wild number with loud drums and screaming horns. And that's when Brendan's fingers finally dug into my waist.

A smile so wide spread across my face, I swear I must have looked like an idiot. But the same one was on his.

"Do you still remember?" he shouted over the scream of the horns.

"How could I forget?" I shouted.

For being so wiry thin, Brendan was also cut, and a lot stronger than he looked. We launched into the swing dance routine we'd picked up in one of the many fancy elective gym classes Mansfied prep offered last year.Brendan had saved me from the indignity of learning the routine with one of the only other girls who'd been stupid enough to take the class without arm-wrestling her boyfriend into taking it with her.

But when he pulled me to him, his hand was flat against my waist. His fingers didn't curve in and hold on like they did to Sofia's. Less curves to hold onto, I guessed, but still. I knew the difference.

By then, between all the kicks and twists and jumps and twirls and lifts, all the other kids had backed up, making a circle of floor around us, and were clapping in time with the music. God, no matter how tightly he was holding on to my waist, it felt so good for us just to hang out for a few minutes. No Sofia. No weirdness. No obsessing. Just moving, feeling, being.

When the song finally wound down in a three-round fanfare of trumpet, everyone applauded like crazy, and the singer cried, "Let's give it up for our swing-dancing couple in the center! Way to take it back to the '30s, you guys!"

I wiped the sweat from my forehead with the inside of

my wrist and beamed. But when I turned my face to Brendan's, his eyes were somewhere else. On Sofia, looking all mopey at the edge of the circle.

Vincent walked up and nudged his shoulder into mine, holding a drink in each hand. Brendan took the opportunity to drop my hand and head toward Sofia. The smile she flashed him must have blinded him, because he smiled and walked with her to the milkshake station without a glance back at me.

I spent the next half hour standing around talking with Vincent, then following Julia to the bathroom and listening to her angst about why her boyfriend wasn't loving every second of this dance. "I mean, that magazine said they love it when the girls take charge. Sadie is all about taking charge," she whined, touching up her lip gloss in the mirror.

Then, in a cloud of flowery air, Sofia walked into the bathroom and pushed into a stall.

This was my chance. Just to get a second alone with Brendan, to say hi. I didn't know exactly what I wanted to say to him, but I did know I wanted to say it without Sofia.

Brendan had stepped out into the courtyard, even though it was freezing. Sofia had spent the evening so far at the punch table with a group of girls, throwing glances at me over her shoulder. How she'd picked up so many girlfriends in the few weeks she'd been here, I'd never know. I couldn't imagine having that many friends in my whole life.

Brendan leaned against one of the stone pillars. If I stood

behind one just right, no one in the auditorium would be able to see me. Perfect.

It was starting to get pretty chilly outside. The wind had already begun to howl through the mountains that held Pittsburgh, and the air it swept in off the rivers was frigid. Even though I had on a long-sleeved shirt underneath the math tee, and full-length jeans with my heels, a shiver shuddered through my whole body. "Jesus, Brendan. What are you doing out here?" If he couldn't hear my teeth chatter from two feet away where he stood, it would be a miracle.

A song that was not fast, but not slow either, floated out into the courtyard. I peered inside to see how the other kids were taking it. Slow, with lots of wandering hands. Awesome.

I clutched at my upper arms, crossing my arms in front of me. "Oh, Ash." Brendan looked over at me with a soft smile. "Here, babe." He unbuttoned the paisley shirt that Sofia had given him—under which he wore a dark blue shirt with a very faded Superman logo on it—and held it out to me. I winced.

"You know how I hate DC comics."

He laughed, lazily, and leaned back against the pillar. He didn't shiver at all, though his arms were now bare. "Well, then don't look at me."

I couldn't not look at him if I tried. He wasn't beautiful like Vincent, but my God. There was something about the way his shoulders sloped down into toned arms, and the way his throat moved when he swallowed. And the way he smelled, which surrounded me as I pulled the cotton button-down over my own shoulders. Like his shampoo and dryer sheets and the grapefruit I knew he ate every morning, and a little vanilla— warm and comforting. I don't know how or why the stupid pink paisley shirt didn't smell like some perfume that Sofia had put on there, but I was grateful.

"What are you doing out here? You'll catch your death."

He chuckled. "You sound like my grandmother."

"I'm just worried about you," I grumbled, and shivered again.

Brendan pushed himself away from the pillar and walked over to me, where I leaned against the other one. He faced me and stepped in closer, so that our feet almost touched. His breath came in white clouds that warmed my face. It was all I could do to not close my eyes.

That is, until a split second later, when the smell on his breath hit me. Sharp. Alcohol. Not beer.

But I couldn't say anything. He was so close. Then, he reached out to rub my upper arms, and I swear, I could have shaken down to my individual molecules right there in the courtyard. I shook, but it was no longer cold. It was straight-up nervousness.

"You're freezing," he said, looking down at me with a slight smile on his face. With something in his eyes that I had never seen before. He studied my face, smiling bigger now, and dropped his hands, sliding his fingers down over my forearms and weaving them with mine. Warm waves ran up through my arms and back down my torso. He drew my hands toward him and put them around his waist. "Come here. Dance with me. You'll warm up."

"Um...okay," I managed to stammer before he swept me up in the biggest, softest bear hug we'd ever had. We swayed together there in the freezing air of the courtyard, to a beat decidedly slower than the song playing inside.

We'd sat close before, but never pressed up against each other front-to-front. We'd certainly never hugged for this long. Brendan leaned his chin on the top of my head, and before I could even compose myself from that, kissed it softly.

I couldn't breathe. I swore I would never take a breath again. Brendan hugged me even closer. "I love you, you know that, Ash?"

I closed my eyes. Those were the words I'd dreamed of hearing since the first week I met him. But something about this picture—Brendan in just a T-shirt in the frigid air, the sharp smell on his breath, and the way the "I" in "love" slurred just the slightest bit—it wasn't right. This was not right.

Sadie Hawkins was not normally a dance that people brought their own beverages to, as far as I knew—kids at Mansfield saved all their serious partying for prom, when punishments would have less weight, since it was the end of the year. But Brendan had come with Sofia. She was new here. And a bitch. A rich bitch. And probably a lush, too.

"Brendan," I sighed, "You're drunk, aren't you?"

"I don't think you can get drunk on three shots, Ashley." His voice went so soft, and husky at the same time, when he said my name, "Ashley" instead of "Ash," that I almost wanted to believe him. Almost wanted to believe that the way he pressed my body up against his, the way his hand moved up now and played with the hair at the nape of my neck, came from real emotions, instead of fuzzy ones. I knew about beer goggles, and I tried to tell myself that these were just stupid three-shot feelings.

"You, Brendan? Absolutely can. It's not like you're pounding down drinks every weekend like some of the kids here do."

"You were going to ask me, weren't you?"

I rolled my eyes. Why couldn't he stick to the topic? "Why does it matter? Sofia asked first."

Brendan laughed. "Yeah, she did. And she wasn't taking no for an answer."

I tried to figure out what the tone in Brendan's voice, the edge to his words, meant. Obviously, he thought Sofia was cute, from the way he looked at her. But the way he held me told me that he didn't only have eyes for her. Maybe. I hoped, even against my brain, which screamed at me that Vincent was the one I should logically be swooning over. Somehow, no matter how hard I tried, it kept coming back to Brendan.

"But you're having a pretty good time with Vince, huh?"

"Vince?"

"Yeah. He seems like a good guy." Again. The "d" slurred. Great.

I leaned back and looked at him, shaking my head a little bit. Once again, I had no idea what to say. What the heck was wrong with me? Since when had I cared about saying anything to Brendan?

When I looked out over his shoulder, my eyes met Sofia's. She was wearing the same damn shirt I was, now. And she was pissed.

Then I knew since when. Since he went to Sadie with stupid Sofia. Since he was no longer all mine.

"Dance the rest of this song with me, huh, Ash?" he asked, his voice still husky. And then I couldn't help it. I let his warmth wash over me, and stood on tiptoes, swaying with him there, and leaned my chin on his shoulder. And looked straight at Sofia, staring at me from the damn punch table.

Annoyance flashed through her eyes. She leaned in and whispered something in Britt's ear, and started walking straight toward us. She'd be here in ten seconds.

I stepped back, wrenching myself away from Brendan's bear hug, even with every fiber of my being wanting to stay there all night. I yanked my arms out of his shirt.

"Hey, what's up?" The softness in his voice was wearing off. I shoved the shirt into his waiting hands and mumbled something about needing to meet Vincent.

Sofia and I crossed paths, and I stopped for a second to avoid bumping into her. She plastered on the most fake smile I'd ever seen, and reflexively, I fake-smiled in return.

"He's a little tipsy," I said.

"That's just why I was coming out here," Sofia said. Her breath smelled like alcohol, too, but her eyes were clear and her voice was a little too perky for my liking, or for this conversation, for that matter.

"Are you okay?" I asked.

"I think Vincent was looking for you."

I locked my eyes with hers. "Are you okay?" I asked again, articulating each word. Brendan may have been acting ten kinds of confusing, but I wasn't going to let Sofia drive him home if she had been drinking too much.

"Yeah." She nodded, meeting my eyes, then looking at Brendan. The plastic smile came back. "You don't need to worry about him anymore, okay?"

I blew out a shaky breath. The only way she would say that, with so much steadiness and challenge in her voice, was if she knew I'd be tempted to step up to it. If she knew I wanted Brendan too.

And now that she was with him, now that she had staked her claim to him, at least tonight, I couldn't afford to do that. Not when I still had so few friends, and so many potential enemies. And considering her insta-popularity.

She could crush me. And then I wouldn't only lose

another school, I'd lose Brendan too.

I turned on my heel, stalked back inside, and I didn't even feel the cold. A blizzard could be going on, and I'd melt a bubble around me just from the heat in my cheeks, and the heat that burned in my chest.

I only made it a few feet inside before Vincent found me.

"Hey," he called. "Ashley!" His voice was equal parts relieved, happy, and concerned. His eyes danced. Did they do that for everyone, or just for me? Because whenever they were on me, I felt like they didn't look at anyone else quite that same way. He didn't grab me. Didn't step closer. Didn't pressure me at all.

"Wanna dance?"

My eyes narrowed at Brendan and Sofia, standing outside. She was saying something to him, playing with his hair again, or complaining about it—it was hard to tell. But she squealed, and smacked at his wrist for something, but then caught his arm and wrapped it around her waist. I rolled my eyes. I couldn't look anymore. Not tonight. Not when I knew Brendan wasn't even really himself.

Not when I knew that drinking at all wasn't his real self.

"Yeah. Yeah, I do."

CHAPTER FIFTEEN

powers of pleasing

Sadie Hawkins night ended as uneventfully as any high school dance night possibly could. I got bored, and kids started heading to after-parties, or whatever. Vincent must have understood by my body language or something that I didn't want to go, and he didn't ask. He walked me to the limo, let me in, laughed with me about how lame the Snowball and all the other games Sofia brought up throughout the course of the night to get people dancing were, and that was that.

The whole night, Vincent didn't dance with anyone else. Didn't talk to another girl, didn't bring another girl punch, even. One hundred percent true to his promise.

"I think you made your point, you know," I said, interrupting his calm stare out the window.

"What do you mean?"

"You can hang out with other people. I think the other girls have quit hating my guts for holding your hand."

It was true. I got a couple glances dancing with Vincent, but overall, no one had seemed to care that we were together.

Were we together?

With four words, Vincent broke my thoughts. "I don't

want to."

I laughed. "What do you mean, you don't want to? Don't tell me you're some kind of introverted, antisocial freak." Like me.

"No. No, I like partying just fine, hanging out with other kids. But I like hanging out with you way more. And if partying isn't your thing..."

He leaned over to me, reached his fingers out, and let them brush against mine. The warmth of his touch sent a calm through me, a steadiness I hadn't felt in a long time. My fingers reached back to tangle with his. Yes, something about this was nice. Solid. Adoring.

But it wasn't real, because I barely knew Vincent, and all things considered—dinner, limo, and gorgeous smile—I had no idea how I felt about him. The only thing I knew was that I still had feelings for Brendan. Despite Sofia, despite the drinking. Even despite him ignoring me.

I extracted my fingers from his and leaned back against the seat, staring out the window, plastering a smile on my face so I didn't look as shaken as I felt.

"Look, Ashley. I know."

"Know what?"

"About Brendan."

I looked down at my hands, my fingers folded together. Like they could be with Vincent's if I'd just let him. And there was really no reason why not.

"What about him?"

Vincent smiled that gentle, patient smile that brought out his dimple ever so slightly. "I know you like him. A lot. I could tell by the way you danced together."

Unfortunately, so could I.

"I can also tell that he likes my sister. Like, a lot. I'm a guy, okay? Even though it's my sister, and that's weird, I see these things."

I wanted to say that she didn't give him much of a chance not to like her, that she was always all over him. I tried to remember if I had even gotten a word in edgewise with Brendan at school since she'd first arrived at Mansfield Prep.

Then I remembered that Brendan was definitely his own person, who could have made time to hang out with me if he had really wanted to.

And as much as I suspected holding hands with Vincent wouldn't bring me the kind of thrill I'd always gotten bumping shoulders with Brendan, I couldn't think of any good reason not to give him more of a chance, either.

So instead of saying anything, I bit my bottom lip to keep it from trembling. I also happened to know from looking in the mirror the other day that I looked pretty sexy doing that. I immediately released it.

God, I was a mess.

"No pressure. Because honestly, I like you a lot. You're pretty, you're sweet. You're hella smart, and you always make me laugh. You can eat like nobody's business. And I love how much you love that camera of yours."

I stared at him. No high school guy should be this forthcoming with his feelings. He liked me. And he told me. And for the handful of seconds that I sat there thinking that, I realized how much I liked that.

I would have killed for Brendan to tell me how he felt in so many words. I'd pay to hear it.

"You know what I think? I think you're so afraid of the past repeating itself that you're afraid to live in the present. I know it sucks to get bullied. Okay, well maybe I don't know, but I can imagine. And I'm really sorry that happened to you."

"Yeah," I scoffed, as I bit my lower lip, holding back tears.

"Really, I am. Anyway, whether you like me or not is beside the point. Even though I want you to."

My cheeks felt warm, and I looked up at him. He gazed at me with a kind smile on his face. "The point is...you're a junior in high school. A new high school, where the same shit won't happen. Things won't be this easy ever again. Let yourself enjoy stuff, Ashley. Let me help you."

Just then, the limo pulled up to my house. I smiled at him. I wanted him to know that I appreciated him, even if I wasn't ready to be as close to him as he wanted me to be. There was just something about him that told me to keep him at arm's length. "Thank you," I said, "for tonight. For everything. It was fun."

Did I see some sadness in his eyes?

"Absolutely. I'll see you on Monday. Save you a seat at lunch. You will still sit with me even though Sadie's over, won't you?"

"Even though you can start letting the hundred and one interested parties take the seat now?" I tried to make my voice sound like I was joking, even though I totally wasn't. I wasn't sure I wanted to be with Vincent, but somehow I felt like my sanity right now hinged on giving him a shot.

"I told you, Ashley. I like you. I'm trying not to be weird, but...I just want to spend more time with you. If I don't freak you out, or anything." He shrugged. "I mean, it's school. It's a public place."

I laughed. "You know that's not what I meant."

"Most of your friends sit at our table anyway."

"You mean, Brendan and Julia?"

"Yeah." He smiled. He reached to the side and opened the door. "Ladies first."

Ω

The whole next day, I couldn't stop thinking about how Vincent had left me that night. The weirdest, most old-fashioned thing. He'd walked me up to the front door, thanked me again, lifted my hand, and kissed it. Then, he'd turned right around and left, throwing a smile and flashing his dimple at me over his shoulder.

I kind of liked it.

Maybe what weirded me out so much was that Vincent's words matched up with his actions. So far, at least. Whether it lasted or not, that wasn't something I was used to seeing. Not even from the person I trusted most.

Ω

I had Kristin drop me off at school fifteen minutes earlier than usual, texting Brendan and telling him not to worry about driving me. He replied back, "You sure?" but when I ignored him, he didn't send any more texts. I knew, because I manually opened the messages app every fifteen seconds just to make sure.

I'd tossed and turned the whole night before, and I still had no idea what to say to Vincent about his proposition. If that's what it was. Part of me wondered if the way he walked me to the door, and pressed his warm, soft lips to the back of my hand, and flashed those gorgeous brown-and-gold eyes at me, and murmured "good night" was only part of all my weird dreams.

I did a great job of skating through first, second, and third period, and the insane hallway time in between, dodging the four people I most did not want to see—Sofia, Brendan, Vincent, and Julia. I had no desire to talk about Sadie with them. Just better to let it go. Unfortunately, my good luck didn't hold out.

I finally ran into Sofia between third and fourth period when I slipped into the girls' bathroom. One of the stall doors swung open and almost whacked me in the face, and a split-second later, the telltale cloud of flowery perfume floated out from behind it.

"Ashley! Hey!" Her smile was a cross between the one I knew for sure was a fake and something that looked more genuine.

"Oh, hey, I was just—"I motioned toward the stall, but she hooked her arm in mine and strolled over to the sinks, then dropped it, pulled out her makeup bag, and started touch-ups while chatter about classes, school, electives, and gossip tumbled out of her mouth like an unstoppable waterfall.

As she talked, I stared at her mouth. I couldn't understand how someone could keep up with that much makeup, and wondered if that's what guys really liked. If that's what Brendan really liked.

I let my eye glaze over, taking in her eye makeup, perfectly plucked eyebrows, and shining earrings. I tried to imagine myself doing that every day. My fingers touched my cheek, feeling the zit there, as well as the complete lack of makeup. I thought of my freckles that had come out during the summer, and about my pale brows, and the fact that I'd only ever worn diamond studs since my eleventh birthday, when Aunt Kristin had taken me to get my ears pierced.

It took me a second to realize Sofia had stopped talking

to me and was staring at me, her eyebrows up.

"Ashley? Hello? Earth to Ash." She laughed from her belly, like it was the funniest freaking thing she'd heard all day.

"I'm sorry. What?"

"You mean, 'Pardon?'"

I fought hard not to glare at her.

"I was just saying that you could make it a little easier on him."

"Him...?"

"Vincent, silly! He's starting to mope, and generally be a pain in my ass."

"Mope about what?"

"Honestly, were you even paying attention at all?" She laughed again, as if someone not paying attention to her would be the silliest thing possible. "He likes you. He told me he told you, but I'm sure he didn't, or he did it in some stupid surreptitious way, because..."

"Oh no. He told me."

"And? Was he stupid about it?"

"I...no. I don't know. I don't think so. He told me he wanted to spend more time with me. That he liked me." I shrugged.

"And?"

"And...I guess that's it."

"I mean," Sofia shoved her lipstick back into the makeup

bag, and that into her backpack. "How are you not, you know, together? Have you seen him?"

Weird that a guy's sister would be talking about how hot he was, but when something was as obvious as that, anyone could talk about it without looking like a freak.

"I don't know." I shrugged, trying to disguise the fact that my heart was beating a mile a minute. Was it that obvious to everyone else that he liked me, too? Why couldn't I figure out how I felt about the guy? He'd done everything right, given me no reason to be suspicious of his intentions, but there was just...something. That extra something that kept me from grinning like an idiot when I heard he liked me, that made me want to dodge him in the hall instead of hoping I ran into him.

Sofia sighed. "I don't know if there's someone else you like, or what. But he's seriously acting really strange. Different. Normally, he'd take a rejection, like you've apparently given him—"

"I..."

She waved her hand at me. "And start thinking about the next girl. But with you, he seems...," she looked me up and down, "...determined. Anyway. Do you like him?"

She smiled at me, but she was putting me on the spot in a big way, and she definitely knew it.

Fake smile time. If I was ever going to perfect one, this was the time. I'd been so freaking worried about just getting through the school day after everything hit the fan at my old school, and I hadn't even bothered here.

I tried then, though, forcing the corners of my mouth up and feeling the crinkle at the corner of my eyes. It felt foreign and weird and slightly uncomfortable, like a Band-Aid I was just waiting to pull off as soon as the bleeding stopped.

"Yeah, I do. He's great."

Sofia's eyes flared the slightest bit in what looked like surprise. Then her lips curved up, too, and she leaned in to the mirror, daubing at her lip gloss.

"Well, I don't know if you've noticed, but most girls here would love to be in your position. And I'm sick of them asking me whether he's available, whether he really likes you as much as he seems to, blah blah blah blah. I know it's fun to lead guys on, but Ashley, seriously." She picked up her bag from the counter and hoisted it onto her back. "Maybe throw him a bone?"

My mouth dropped open and I scrambled for something to say. But she headed for the door before I could, throwing over her shoulder, "See you at Mathletes, right?"

$$\Omega$$

Lunch was there before I knew it. I remembered my Saturday promise to sit with Vincent, and my stomach twisted. When would I be able to tell what my own damn body cues meant? This could have just as easily been the stomach flu as nervous flutters.

I craned my neck, looking around for Vincent's mop of curls, and after a few minutes of trying with no luck, gave myself permission to hide in my usual lunch table corner for as quick a lunch as possible. Something about the promise of ducking out of my forty-minute lunch in under ten, and grabbing half an hour to edit photos using Mansfield's expensive editing software all by myself in the chilly hum of the computer lab, calmed the frantic beating of my heart.

Until a hand brushed the small of my back, and a whole different sensation took over my body. I turned to look Vincent right in the face.

"Hey, beautiful. We saved you a spot and," he lifted his arm, which I now noticed held a lunch tray with two plates on it, "I grabbed you a slice of pizza. You do like pizza, right?"

I had to admit, I was charmed. This time, the grin was genuine. "I do."

Vincent smiled and walked with me to the table as we chatted about our classes from that morning. "All these classes are so boring," he complained.

Sofia grinned and snatched a French fry off his plate. "Are you complaining about classes again? Quit bragging, no one wants to hear it."

"No one's more bored in classes than Ashley, so she'll understand," Brendan said, smiling at me. "Good to see you here, Ash. Joining the land of the lunch living."

He was right, I realized. I hadn't eaten lunch in the cafeteria for weeks. It was just one more opportunity to see Sofia fawning over Brendan that I didn't want. But now I realized the only thing that was worse. Seeing the same old Brendan looking at me the same old way, but not meaning it the way I'd always dreamed of.

Because, God, that look of familiarity, that Brendan who knew me and always accepted me no matter what, still made me feel weak in the knees. Nothing could change that. I didn't think.

Except maybe the absolute worst thing—that that look didn't make me feel safe and secure anymore. Now, it only made me feel sad. Gut-deep, heart-wrenchingly, might-need-to-go-home-and-weep-and-probably-up-my-meds-again sad.

"So I guess that means you already went through all these classes at your old school, too?" Vincent asked, handing me a napkin.

Brendan spoke up. "Nope. She's just crazy smart. Picks it up at light speed and spends the rest of the class doing God knows what."

"Brendan, please." Still, I couldn't help but smile.

"Composing the next great masterpiece in her head, that's what," he continued. "Sofia, have you seen Ashley's photography?"

"You take pictures?" Sofia said, cocking her head to the side and giving a slightly sweeter version of the same smile she'd flashed me in the bathroom. "Are they good?"

"They're amazing,"Brendan said. "She's really—"

"Wow, you must have a really great camera."

Nothing pissed me off more than when someone assumed my photography was amazing because my camera was. First of all, because that just wasn't true. Ansel Adams could have shot with a cell-phone camera and still produced museum-worthy work. Second, because Brendan had given me that camera. And just because Brendan was responsible for my psychological well-being in this place did not mean that he was responsible for my mad photography skills, the ones that I'd busted my very own butt working on.

"She's really good. I can't believe I haven't seen any of your new stuff, Ash."

That was because, in the seven weeks since we'd been back in the same town, he hadn't asked. "Oh, um...well, you did know about a few of the shots. That one we took on that foggy morning, and—"

"Hey!" Sofia interrupted, leaning forward on the table to show everyone, but especially Brendan, a shot of her cleavage. "B, tell Vincent what you were telling me. About Ashley."

Brendan's face lit up, and I bristled. Until he turned to me and said, "Yes. Ashley. Seventeen, next week. What do you want to do?"

Last year, Brendan had found out that I'd turned sixteen in the midst of the shittiness that was my life at Williamson and had been determined to celebrate, no matter how belated it was. I'd talked him into just a cake and movies in his living room with Julia, his mom and dad, and Kristin and Bruce, and the hand-me-down camera body as a present, but he had promised to do something more awesome this year. I'd forgotten all about it.

"Oh, same as last year," I said, fumbling in my bag for nothing.

"No, no, no. You're gonna be seventeen! Leaving sweet sixteen behind, that's a big deal!" From her tone and the look on her face, I suspected Sofia could muster enthusiasm about dust bunnies if she thought it would get her somewhere. "I was thinking a party, for sure, and..."

"A party? No." I looked up at the both of them firmly.

"But why not?" Vincent nudged his knee into mine and smiled. "Shit, Ashley, if anyone deserves it, it's you. Plus you've been here forever and hardly hang out with anyone."

I wanted to tell him that that was the way I liked it. That I was comfortable with just me and Brendan and my camera and not taking the risk of ever, ever going back to the way things were.

But then I remembered what he'd told me the night of Sadie. Let myself enjoy life. Teenagers enjoyed parties, and Sofia wanted to have one for me. I was a teenager, and Sofia was the most popular girl at school. Somehow. And Brendan would be there, and so would Vincent, who, I finally understood, actually just wanted to make me happy.

"I want to do it. I want to be in charge. It'll be my gift to you," Vincent said.

Oh hell, but his smile was gorgeous. I started digging in my bag more intensely now.

"Ashley doesn't like big parties," Brendan said. "She never wants to be the center of attention. It's just not her thing."

I looked up at him, ready to thank him, and immediately saw Sofia's arm twined around his and her chin resting on his shoulder. And him not trying in the least to shrug her off. My mood changed in a flat second from super grateful at his willingness to rescue me to completely pissed off.

"Um. I..." I still really didn't want a party, as much as I kind of wanted to shake whatever claim Brendan seemed to think he could make on my decisions like this. He was totally right—parties for me were not my thing at all. In fact, they were pretty much my worst nightmare. But who said that couldn't change? I shrugged my shoulders and smiled at Vincent. "Let me think about it, okay?"

The silence for that split second as Brendan looked at me, shocked, buzzed with the tension.

Sofia broke it. Of course. "Well! We should go, huh? You said you'd introduce me to the Mathletes practice drills you East Coast kids use." She flashed a grin at me and Vincent and shrugged. "What can I say? I'm clueless. I'm just happy he lets me try for the team." She turned a simpering look on Brendan.

"Even though I wish you'd try out for lacrosse. Those guys' girlfriends have so much fun." She hooked her arm in Brendan's, pouting slightly, and I fought the overwhelming urge to dive across the table full of empty pop cans and half-eaten pizza and rip her face off.

"Yeah." Brendan cleared his throat. "So, see you after school, Ash? Mathletes?"

This time it was Brendan I forced the smile for.

CHAPTER SIXTEEN

if one scheme of happiness fails

The Mathletes practiced in the auditorium so that we could set up the boards—the most badassed part of Mathletes, and the one I was best at. I loved the intensity of standing at a huge whiteboard opposite some other kid and ripping through an equation for everyone to see. Since we'd gradually weeded out the less impressive contestants, only having eight official members on the team made the pressure that much more intense.

"So, uh…" Brendan strode across the echoing auditorium stage, trying to raise his voice enough to silence the three underclassmen, two sophomores and one junior, who were playing some video game on one of their laptops, and the two girls Britt and Hannah, who were upperclassmen. I knew for a fact that Britt was only here for extra credit in her Calculus class—not that she wasn't good at it, but she didn't care about the Mathletes. And Hannah just wanted something to beef up her college applications. Locker-room gossip was that she needed to live up to her mom's expectations and attend Pitt and belong to the same sorority. That sort of shit drove me crazy.

Not getting their attention, he readjusted the position of the two huge rolling whiteboards we used for practice, pulled out all his dry-erase markers, and tested the ink on the board. He started scribbling an equation up there—a job the captain typically left for underclassmen. He seemed to realize this in the middle of writing it, because he turned around, opened his mouth, clamped it shut, cleared his throat with his fist to his lips, opened it, said, "Uh, guys..." then shut it again. Then he turned back to write more equations.

The cloud of flowery perfume floated up around my head to meet me as I took a seat. I hadn't even seen Sofia sitting back there, but now she unstretched every fabulous inch of her body from her seat and strode up to the stage like she was running the show.

And, it appeared, she thought she was.

"Hey, losers!" Her tone was full of contempt, but when everyone looked up at her, she grinned that stunning grin that apparently made everyone forget what a bitch she was.

Sure enough, Britt and Hannah snapped to attention and looked at her like they were ready and willing to be her freaking slaves. And the boy geeks just started concentrating extra hard on not drooling.

"Brendan is our captain. And I am so excited to be a Mansfield Mathlete. I want to offer myself," she raised her eyebrows and strode across the stage to touch Brendan's forearm, "as his right-hand Mathlete. To do anything he wants." She was always touching his damn arm. Presumptuous, and possessive. Did I see his eyebrow raise? Or was it just at the "anything he wants"line?

"So,"Sofia continued. "What do you guys do first here?"

"Um." Brendan cleared his throat and moved his arm from underneath Sofia's. I couldn't tell whether he was dropping it or moving it away on purpose. "Let's start with some drills at the boards."

"Okay," Sofia bubbled. "I'll write the problems up there, and..."

"You don't have to do that."

"Really, it's fine. I'm still getting used to things, and then they can concentrate on getting them right. I'll just watch today. You keep the practice problems...?"

"In my bag," Brandon said, giving Sofia a slight smile. I rolled my eyes. Maybe she thought she was doing him a favor, or maybe she wanted to be in control of something. But she bounced over there like he said he had a dozen cupcakes and a bottle of champagne in the damn thing. She pulled out a whole thick stack of papers and plunked it down on the black stage.

"Oh, hey, actually we'll start with the easiest short forms to warm up, since it's only really our second meeting since getting the team together. Just the ones on the purple paper. You've got the whole stack there."

Sofia plunked her bag down next to the stack and swiped

some of the purple papers off the top. She transcribed problems on the boards in nearly perfect handwriting. The girls, being more senior members, were used to the form and got through each one faster, in less than a minute; the boys took a little longer.

I wasn't a natural match with anyone but Brendan. When both the girls and the boys had gone through five problems each, his eyes flashed at me. "Now I want to show you what I expect you all to be doing at the end of the semester. Right before State. Because, with my secret weapon, we are going to make it."

Pride swelled in my chest even as my cheeks turned red. If he wasn't talking about me, I'd eat my shoe. He knew how fast I was.

"Sofia," he said, and my heart stopped. No way he was talking about her. "Grab the pink pages. Those are the competition-grade ones. Those are the ones Ashley's about to do and show you all how she can totally kick my ass."

I beamed and hoisted myself out of the seat and strode toward the stage steps. I basically freaking bounced up there. I knew I didn't look like Sofia, but hell if I didn't feel like her, all bouncy and feisty and gloating.

It felt surprisingly good. Maybe I needed to channel my inner bitch more often.

"Why don't you just have huge copies of these or something?" Sofia complained as she copied the problem on the board.

Brendan laughed. "We're not as rich as your old school, apparently. And even if I wanted to use our funding for it, it's more fun to do it this way, don't you think?"

She half smiled and repeated under her breath, "More fun. Right." Obviously this was a girl who hardly ever had to write anything out by hand. Even though her symbols were all off, her spacing weird, and the curlicues on the ends of the integral symbol that opened the problem way too flowery, I knew before she was done writing it out how to solve it. I watched Brendan's face for the same recognition. It took him a few seconds longer, but he got it too.

We shared a glance and a grin, each held up three fingers, pulling each one down in unison as we mouthed "three, two, one..." then lunged at the boards with our dry-erase markers. The pungent scent of the ink and the mad squeaking filled the air for thirty seconds before I stepped back, fully confident when I shouted, "Pi over four!" I knew I'd completed the work faster than Brendan. But he stepped back at exactly the same time, raising his arms triumphantly and turning in a slow circle, his hair falling in his face.

I hadn't seen him look so damn happy since that last Saturday before school started.

"Haha, yeah, okay, but let's see who's right," I said, my hands on my hips. And checking the other four teammates. Mildly interested in our little competition, they were all copying the problem in notebooks and trying to sketch an answer for themselves.

"Nah, it'll take these clowns forever to get something." Brendan grinned. "Sof, what do you see for the answer to this one?" She flipped all the way to the back of the packet, then looked at me, her mouth wide and her eyes popping open. "Pi over four. Well," she said, "I guess we know who the smartest girl at this school is."

"No, no, I just have a good tutor." I tilted my chin up at Brendan, remembering all the tricks he'd taught me last year for working the problems speedily. Thinking about all the time we'd spent together, and all the trash talking that had turned into gentle pushing around that I was always wishing would turn into something else.

"Oh, whatever, Miss 'I-don't-like-to-be-the-center-of-attention.' You totally owned that! Look at you!" She smiled like the freaking Cheshire cat, but there was an edge to her voice that I knew was something other than friendly.

"Okay, that was awesome." Brendan cleared his throat behind me and my little impromptu stare down with Sofia was broken. I wasn't confused at all about her, even if Brendan was. She was just waiting for me to completely screw up so she could move in for the kill.

I wasn't really worried that what she thought about me would affect what Brendan thought about me. Was I? We were best friends. I didn't think anything could ever change that.

"Let's move on to the writtens," Brendan continued. "I liked your work at the boards, and I know that's the part of the competitions that gets filmed and everyone cheers for, but the writtens haul in more points than anything. Okay?"

After a fast bathroom and water break, we each took separate desks, plunked down in the attached chairs, and began scribbling when Brendan started the timer.

"Look, Brittany, do you want to get into Columbia or not?" Brendan said, when the girls started whining. I smiled as I ducked my head. He could pull out the authority when he really had to. I hoped it was the competition with me had made him feistier, and not Sofia's general stupidity.

Damn. I really hadn't realized just how much I hated that girl until Mathletes.

We all bent our heads over the fifteen written questions. The point for these wasn't to show work, but just to see who could complete it with all the right answers the fastest. Brendan slapped his down first, then, as I was walking up to Brendan's desk to put mine down, Sofia slapped hers down in front of me.

I guess I'd been operating under the assumption that she didn't really know what she was doing, even though I knew she'd been on the team at her old school.

I guess I'd been assuming wrong.

Brendan raised his eyebrows at her, a smile playing at the

corners of his mouth. He bobbed his head as he ran his finger down the sheet of paper, then looked up at Sofia. "Perfect," he said.

She beamed, then squealed a little. It made me want to rip her throat out.

"Well, I think we have a contender for first chair here, team." Brendan called down to everyone else in the chairs. The girls shrugged and went back to their test. They didn't care what position they were, as long as they could stick this whole delightful experience on their resumes. The three boys wore expressions that ranged from "I can't believe a girl is beating me" to "raging hard-on." I guess a girl as hot as Sofia knowing her way around a math test was like a geek fantasy.

I guessed right, because for a split second, Brendan was looking at her the same way. Freaking fabulous.

As much as I wanted him to be mine, he never had been, and I'd never tried to change that. Still, I knew that no matter how hard I tried to swallow that damn lump in my throat, I couldn't hold back the tears burning at the corners of my eyes.

"I'm just gonna...use the restroom. Again. We're almost done, right? I'll meet you in the parking lot," I mumbled as I stooped down, picked up my bag, and started heading up the carpeted aisle to the back doors.

I knew I was dragging my tennis shoes along the ground. I stared down at the laces, focusing on the crisscross pattern, trying to make myself concentrate on anything other than the weird aching in my chest. I knew I was pouting. I didn't care.

Something small and glinting silver skittered away from across the red carpeted aisle and under a seat. I knew from the color that it wasn't a mouse, thank goodness, or I would have seriously lost it. I hesitated for another second, but kept walking. And it happened again. The white rubber of my shoe's toe box hit another silvery something. I raised my eyes to the sloped red-velvet carpeted aisle and saw the whole thing dotted with silver. I bent down and picked one up, squinting at it in the dimmed lights, already turned down by the janitors.

They were chocolate Hershey's kisses. I looked at the other kids, packing up their stuff and passing their papers forward to Brendan. "Did one of you losers do this?" I tried to keep my tone playful but I was really kind of freaked out. This was the weirdest thing I'd seen at Mansfield Prep in a long time. Ever, actually.

But at least it stopped the tears. The weirdness of Brendan and me and Brendan and Sofia and what was right or wrong, normal or weird, up or down was momentarily erased by an auditorium aisle full of artfully arranged chocolate spaced a foot apart in a repeating diamond pattern.

Stepping around the chocolate, I walked all the way up the aisle and out the auditorium door. I followed the trail, continuing through the breadth of the hallway, past the band

and choir rooms, woodshop, and all the downstairs classrooms. The pattern of silver dots continued up one stairwell around the turn, and down the wide first-floor hallway.

They were hard to tell apart from the metallic-specked white tile of the floor, so I was actually kind of surprised when the pattern stopped abruptly halfway down the hall. Right in front of my locker.

I quickened my steps and then, from around the corner, stepped Vincent, scaring me half to death. I clutched my chest and squeaked a little when I heard a cough from behind me. The whole Mathletes team had followed me up into the hallway.

"Vincent, what the hell...?"

He just smiled that patient smile and stepped toward me, holding out an envelope.

I took it from him as my stomach flipped and dropped. "Seriously, what is this?"

He laughed. "It's not a bomb or anything. Just read it."

I looked down at the envelope and back up at him what must have been at least three times, then slid my finger under the flap and opened it. Inside was a square of heavy cream cardstock that said·

"Now that I've kissed the ground you walk on,
Let me treat you like a princess on your birthday."

My brain told me to roll my eyes, but my heart flopped around in my chest. And, damn me, a smile took over my face. I must have looked like an idiot. Yet here I was, standing in a chocolate-studded prep school hallway, holding a romantic note from the cutest guy in school. A guy who really liked me, who was begging me to let him throw me a party.

Yeah, okay. Of course I was smiling.

"What do you think?" He stepped even closer to me, but still didn't touch me.

"Just a small party?"

"Small. I swear."

"Like, less than fifty people?"

"I was thinking less than a hundred."

I rolled my eyes, still smiling. Then I looked up in his. God, they were on fire. They set my insides on fire a little too. I sighed. "Fine. Yes."

"She said yes!" Vincent pushed both his fists up in the air and turned a little circle in a victory dance right there in the hallway. The Mathletes exploded into applause, and someone even let forth a wolf whistle. I laughed and, without even thinking, stepped forward and hugged him around the neck, standing on my tiptoes a little to do it.

"Really?" he said in my ear, so low only I could hear it. I stepped back and dropped my arms. I shrugged.

"Sure, why not? Remember? You said it'd be good for me.

Enjoy stuff."

He smiled and slung his arm around my shoulder, letting his forearm dangle off of it. We walked back toward the crowd of Mathletes. It didn't feel too bad, walking arm in arm with this guy. Not too bad at all.

Until I saw Brendan, staring at me like I'd just punched him in the gut.

But something like defiance rose up in me. Brendan wasn't my boyfriend. He was still paying attention to me. Why did I even have a problem with Sofia touching his arm?

I shouldn't. It was stupid. So, from that moment on, I was going to stop caring about any other girl touching Brendan's arm or kissing his cheek.

Instead of dropping my arm from around Vincent's waist, I curled my fingers around it, looked Brendan right in the eye, and said, "Vincent, do you mind driving me home today?"

There was obvious satisfaction in his voice when he said, "Not at all."

And even though everything in me screamed that I didn't want a party, that all I wanted was Mathletes and pancakes and foggy mornings and light-switch games, there was a small part of me that screamed something else. Namely, how sweet Vincent had been the last few weeks, and how good he smelled, and how kissable his lips looked right that second.

So I stretched up on my toes, leaned in to him, and

planted a kiss low on his cheek, right at the corner of his mouth. Then I tried to ignore the low noise Brendan made when Vincent turned the slightest bit, pressing his lips against mine for a brief second before pulling away and smiling.

Then we walked out the doors hand in hand. And I didn't even think about looking back.

Ashley, there's something I need to tell you.

What?

Well, I've discovered something. Irrefutable proof, actually.

Ok...

See, girls = time × money.
and we know time = money.
so girls = money × money = (money)^2
and since money = $\sqrt{evil}$
I then posit: girls = ($\sqrt{evil}$)^2
so therefore, girls = evil.
Brilliant, right?

...I'm not talking to you anymore.

CHAPTER SEVENTEEN

a good deal in love

Vincent ran around a lot that week, passing out fliers for a party that was supposed to be under a hundred people.

That first day, I snagged one off the top of his pile, teasing, "Why are we not texting these? Don't you care about trees?"

"I do," he said, "but this is more colorful. More fitting for a princess. Besides, Sofia is texting."

I stared down at the quarter-sheet-sized pink paper, which was just Vincent's handwriting photocopied. "Hey, this is next door to me. Brendan's house."

"Yeah." Vincent shrugged. "He said he wanted to throw you a party, but I offered first. Said it was the least he could do. And it saves me from cleaning up, so...anyway. Gotta plan. I'll see you later." He ducked his head down, smacked a kiss on my cheek, then flashed that damn dimple. I couldn't help but smile.

"It is gonna be chill, right?"

"Absolutely. You're the birthday girl. You asked for chill, and chill is what you'll get."

I made my way to the cafeteria, where I'd promised Julia I'd have lunch with her.

She sat bent over her Algebra textbook, and looked at me with forlorn eyes. "Will you help me here?"

"Yeah, but isn't that due next period? Why didn't you have it done last night?" I tried to keep the scolding out of my voice, but it was a pet peeve of mine when kids stressed over their homework the period before.

She sighed, and put her head down on her arms right there at the table. "I would normally ask Brendan to help me, but he's been spending all his time with Sofia. In his room."

My eyes practically bugged out of my head, and I had to swallow hard to get more words out. "Studying what?"

"Math, they say. But they're mostly quiet. And you know what's going on when two people are mostly quiet."

I stared at her. "They're in there making out?"

Julia looked at me. "Please. Do you think I care enough about Brendan to snoop on him while he's in his room with a gorgeous girl 'studying'?"

"No. But maybe you care enough about me?" I tried to sound like I was teasing but really the panic was rising in my voice at a crazy rate.

"Hey, what are you so upset about? It's not like you like him or anything."

It's not like I was ballsy enough to show or tell anyone I liked him, no.

"I mean, you have Vincent fawning all over you." Julia practically sighed as she said his name. "Why are you worrying about what my stupid geeky brother is doing with his new bitchy girlfriend?"

The use of the word "girlfriend" made my stomach do flips, and I felt my face getting hot. "You think she's a bitch?" I tried to tone down the glee I knew was in my tone.

Julia snorted. "I know she's a bitch. How else did she manage to climb the social ladder at Mansfield Prep faster than an acrobat on crack?"

I shrugged. "I don't know. Money?"

Julia stared at me. "Seriously? You think just because a kid's rich she's the queen of Mansfield Prep? Then check out Henry Green. Tons of cash and still gets stuffed in his locker like twice a week. No, there's something else. She knows how to talk to people, how to make them feel good. Or something. Doesn't change the fact that I'm hoping she'll get me invited to all the best parties. It's my turn to have hot guys fawning over me," she pouted.

I leaned over and kissed her on the cheek. "Thanks, honey." For the next few minutes, I guided her through the problems giving her so much trouble.

As I stood up to leave, she let her mouth drop open in mock shock. "What, you're not going to grill me about my classes and how hard I'm studying?"

I laughed. "You're a big girl. You can take care of

yourself." When she still looked shocked, I laughed again. "Next time, I promise. Tomorrow."

Julia smiled knowingly. "If I didn't know better, I'd say you were mega distracted by that guy."

I furrowed my eyebrows, confused. She'd never refer to Brendan as "that guy."

"Hello. Vincent? Seriously. Since when have you been such a space cadet? He must be really taking over your brain."

I forced a laugh. I think I sounded like a barking seal. "Yeah. Must be. I'll see you later Jul, okay?"

CHAPTER EIGHTEEN

a little amusement among ourselves

The party was that Saturday night. I'd convinced Kristin and Bruce that I didn't want to make a big deal out of anything, and thankfully, they had listened to me, just bringing my favorite almond-mocha cake out at the end of cooking my favorite dinner Friday night. They had tickets to the opera on Saturday night anyway, she said, and when I told her my friends were planning something, a look of happy relief swept her face.

"Brendan and Julia are taking you out?"

"No. Um...Vincent."

"Vincent?"

"He wanted to throw a party for me."

"Why?"

I shrugged. "I don't know. Is it so crazy that someone would want to have a party for me?"

"No, honey, you know that's not what I meant. It's just that you normally don't like that sort of thing."

What was it with all these people trying to tell me what I did and did not like? What I was and was not supposed to want? Yeah, I felt a little jittery at the idea of a hundred kids from school, most who barely knew me, standing around and staring at me as I blew out the candles on a birthday cake. But maybe Vincent was right. Maybe I did need to branch out.

But I couldn't say any of that to Aunt Kristin. Maybe because I didn't want to talk about it, and maybe because I didn't really believe it myself. "Anyway, I'll be out late. But it sounds like you will, too."

"Speaking of that, I need to duck upstairs to get ready. You'll be okay?

I waved my phone. "Yep."

"All right. While you've got that thing on you, call your mom, too. Okay? She's been texting, checking up on you through me. I tell her you're great, but it's not the same as hearing from her."

I gave her a halfhearted smile. If Mom wanted to talk to me, she could just call me. But I really didn't want to have that conversation now. "Will do."

Ω

I spent the rest of the day getting ready for my birthday party. Even thinking those words felt so weird. Especially because I knew nothing about it, aside from Vincent's promise to treat me like a princess while at the same time keeping it completely chill. I stared at that closet, wondering how a chill princess would dress at her birthday party.

I thought about Brendan saying I didn't like parties, and

Aunt Kristin. How I didn't like being the center of attention. I looked down at my broken-in jeans, plain flats, and graphic tee. I definitely looked like someone who didn't enjoy parties.

What would happen if I spent tonight trying to be someone no one thought I was? I wondered how much of me was really me or how much of me was trying to conform to what I'd already made people think I was. I wondered how much of that was keeping me away from who I could be, like Vincent said.

Okay. So maybe I'd try to look like a chill princess who loved birthday parties. Maybe I'd actually try to have fun.

Half an hour later, and surrounded by piles of clothes, most of which I'd accumulated in the ten months that had lapsed since I'd first moved here, I stood in front of my full-length mirror and admired myself. I'd found a pale pink lace skirt that puffed out from my waist, making me look like I probably had more hips than I actually did, and stopped a couple inches above my knee, which made my legs look longer than they actually were. I'd snagged a gold-brown wrap top from Kristin's closet and dug out some bright gold flats that I'd always been too scared to wear with anything for fear I'd stand out. Tonight, that's what I wanted to do. I really did feel exactly how I wanted to—understated, pretty, a little fancy. I popped my hip out and did my little lip-bite thing.

I wondered if this outfit would inspire Vincent to finally make the move and try to really kiss me—hands-in-my-hair, biting-my-lip kissing. One thing I knew for sure—I was ready to feel, just for this one night, what it felt like to be wanted, looked at, admired, by a whole house full of people.

$$\Omega$$

I was just spraying on some perfume I'd found in Aunt Kristin's room that was light and fruity, instead of the heavy and musky stuff she usually wore. Something seemed weird to me about wanting to smell like a fruit basket, but I knew perfume was something people wore, and I didn't want to smell like a freaking flower truck like Sofia.

The doorbell rang, and even though I was expecting it, I jumped half a foot. I swiped on one more coat of lip gloss and felt my stomach flip as I imagined the look on Brendan's face when he saw me. Wow, Ash, he'd joke. You clean up nice. And I'd roll my eyes like I didn't care what he thought.

I skipped down the stairs, feeling jittery all over. When I reached out for the door handle, I realized my whole arm was shaking. Get it together, Price.

Vincent wore dark jeans, a simple brown button-down with cream stripes, and the most gorgeous-smelling cologne I'd ever smelled on anyone. I seriously fought the urge to lean into him and press my nose into his neck, and my lips to his Adam's apple.

It felt foreign to me that I didn't know anything about where Brendan's parents were or what they were doing this weekend. It was amazing how seven weeks of not hanging out all the time could change my relationship with the people next door. I craned my neck out the front door and looked at the Thomas house.

Oh, my God. How had I not noticed the prep going on all day? The porch was covered in pink streamers, and every single light in every single room shone bright against the darkening night. Dozens of paper lanterns lined the walkway. Music thumped and crashed from the living room, coming from what sounded like a live band—had Vincent really hired a live band?—and through the side window I could see tables filled with food and at least three fancy cakes.

My mouth formed an "o." "Wow. That is...wow," I said, setting my teeth in a weird half-shock, half-smile expression. Vincent held out his arm for me, and I took it, telling myself to enjoy the way his bicep felt beneath my fingers. Birthday princess. Think birthday princess. Try to be special, Ashley. Try to act like you think you are.

I took a deep breath and smiled up at Vincent. "So, I guess we can just walk over?"

We crossed the lawn and had almost made it to Brendan's porch when Vincent stopped and held me out at arm's length. "Thank you," he said, grinning down at me.

"For what?" I asked. "Thank you. This is very sweet."

"I know it's not your thing. I guess I just wanted to do something awesome for you, and parties are how we do awesome in Hollywood."

"No, this is great. Really. I'm...I'm doing what you said. Trying new things. Exploring my options." And for the first time when I said it, when I talked to him and looked him in the eye, instead of my stomach turning, my heart fluttered a little. This felt exciting. Nice. Certainly, gorgeous Vincent looking at me like I was a supermodel didn't hurt.

"Well," he said, turning and holding his arm out to me again, "let's get in there."

Ω

A car door slammed behind us before we made it, and three lacrosse players stepped out of their Lexus, popping the trunk and hoisting out something huge, metal, and heavy. . It took two of them to carry it and the other one to shut the trunk behind him.

"Is that what I..."

"Hey, guys!" Vincent called. "Thanks. It can just go in the kitchen."

"Is that a...keg?"

"Yep," Vincent said, looking pleased with himself. "Is everything okay?"

I tried to keep my face calm. "Yeah. Yeah, totally. Just, when you said 'chill party,' I thought..."

"Yep. Everyone can have a little something to drink, get nice and relaxed, have a good time. Everything will be quiet.

And very, very chill."

"Chill," I repeated, a bit numbly.

"Hey, you aren't worried, are you? It'll all be fine. Trust me."

We climbed the steps and the music started to drown out his voice already. If the level of chill was related to volume of the band, this party was going to be the exact opposite of chill. Vincent swung his arm around my neck, just like he'd done the last week, resting his forearm on my shoulder. "Birthday girl's here!" he crowed to the room full of kids from Mansfield Prep already filling Brendan's living room, which at least someone had had the good sense to move most of the furniture out of.

The smell was the first thing I noticed. Pungent, rank, and sharp, alcohol was definitely in the air. Even though I almost never went to parties, I still recognized the scent. And ever since that night at Sadie, when the alcohol made Brendan do and say things he probably wouldn't have otherwise, I was pretty sure I didn't want that smell near me again.

The band, complete with guitar, bass, drums and horns, struck up a version of "Happy Birthday." Everyone in the room joined in the singing and applauded for five seconds before the band launched into another song.

Everyone went back to dancing, and the room felt sweatier by the second. Vincent let his fingers trail along my upper arm. I wanted to feel excited about something like that, attracted to him, happy that he was paying attention to me. But the horns screamed in my ears and the drums vibrated through my body in place of the attraction I desperately wanted to be there.

Why couldn't I happily join the crush of sweaty bodies on the dance floor? Why couldn't I smile and scream and dance and hold onto Vincent's hand? Was it because it was too hot, or because the room reeked of alcohol? Or was it something else?

"I think I need some fresh air," I yelled in Vincent's ear, and he walked me back to the kitchen, where a bunch of kids were examining bottles of alcohol and digging through the cupboards for shot glasses.

Hal, one of the asshole kids on the lacrosse team, squirted a dollop of whipped cream from a can onto his wrist. "Hey, Vince! We're starting whipped cream popping in the living room in five. These rich bitches love it," he said, giving me a sideways wink. Gross.

He slapped his forearm at the elbow. The little pile of whipped cream went sailing in the air in a narrow arc above his head, and he caught it expertly in his mouth.

"Gettin' better, man!" One of the other guys clapped him on the back and looked up at the ceiling. I followed his line of sight to see at least six dollops of whipped cream stuck to the ceiling.

"Oh my God," I breathed. If this is what the kitchen

looked like, I could only imagine how the rest of the house was doing. I just hoped Brendan and Julia had enough notice to prep all the expensive antiques in the house in the same way as they had prepped the furniture. All the Thomas's poor couches and chairs were probably huddled together in one of the back rooms, covered in plastic tarps and utterly terrified.

"Hey, hey, guys. What are you doing?" Vincent dropped my arm and strode over to the counter where two girls were mixing some combination of liquids in a pitcher.

"For the shots, Vincent, duh. Hal missed six times and he's gonna miss a lot more when we change locations."

"Shit, you guys, just...just be careful, okay?" Vincent scratched at his jaw and looked around nervously. At least he seemed mildly concerned about Brendan's house.

Vincent turned to me. "Ashley, I don't want you to worry about any of this."

"But I..."

"No, seriously. Seriously. It's your birthday, okay? Pretend you didn't see this, go sit out by the pool. I'll deal with it and bring you a drink in a second."

I looked him and the guys eyeing the bottles again. "Just a pop. Okay? No vodka or whipped cream or...whatever."

"Of course. Whatever you want," he said, flashing me that smile that I knew was designed to calm me, but didn't.

I let my gaze drop and headed out to the back.

CHAPTER NINETEEN

her curiosity was all awake

The backyard was strewn with the same magical paper lanterns as the front , but the scene out there wasn't quite as magical. The beautiful blue pool had a couple kids bent over it, throwing up. All around the pool, there were couples stretched out on chairs, in various stages of making out and undress. From the deck, I could see and hear it all, and smell a little of it too. Not a pretty sight.

I was getting ready to turn to go back inside, maybe find Julia and figure out how to deal with this mess, when a voice startled the hell out of me from the side of the deck. "Hey Ash!"

Brendan.

"Hey, where have you been?" I asked, crossing over to the deck and looking down over the side, where Brendan was fumbling around in an outdoor storage bin for something.

"Just trying to find some stuff to clean up this mess. But since they don't have anything called 'Puke-Be-Gone' for the pool, I think we're just gonna be stuck calling the professional cleaners for that, too."

"Too?"

"Yeah. We already have the carpet guys coming tomorrow." He shook his head as he climbed up the deck and wrapped his arms around me, enfolding me in a big, sweet bear hug.

For a second, I froze. Brendan hadn't hugged me like that since before I'd left for the summer. Since before he'd met Sofia. He drew back and spoke, looking me right in the eye. "Happy birthday, Ashley. I'm sorry this party is so...you know... high school." As soon as his breath hit my face, I realized where warm, fuzzy Brendan had come from—the air between us now had the same weird musky-pungent scent as that inside the house. He'd been drinking, too.

He must have known the look on my face, because he said, "Just had one shot. It's like the price of admission through the kitchen. But I swear that's all I had. Okay?" I nodded.

"Sit with me?" I asked. "Make our stupid high school classmates getting out of hand and ruining this party not suck?"

He laughed and followed me to the chairs on the deck. One girl was still throwing up, and I winced.

"So you're not mad at Vincent?" I asked cautiously.

"Not really. I mean, it sucks that he did this, I guess. But I assume you said it was okay. Besides, I don't think one guy can really control the force of that many kids with alcohol on the brain. But I heard they were bringing the keg. I even had carpet cleaners rented and ready to go for tomorrow."

"So what are you stressed about? You're the one who let Sofia talk you into doing the party here." And the one who let Sofia ruin the perfect balance of our friendship and made me agree to this whole thing anyway.

"Sofia, yeah. And Vincent, and Julia. Anyway. I didn't know they'd bust into Mom's cabinet." He blew out a breath, raking his fingers back through his hair. "I....have no idea how I'm going to deal with that."

"Well...how much can it be? Maybe I can grab a few bottles of Kristin and Bruce's..." I trailed off. They never had more than a bottle of vodka, and maybe one of bourbon lying around. They would definitely notice if one went missing.

Brendan looked up at me, his eyes suddenly seeming very tired. Old. "It's...a lot. Mom drinks a lot, Ashley."

"Like...like enough that you're worried about her?" I found myself choked up. I knew what he was going to tell me, what I should have known and was too dense until now to put the pieces together to figure out.

"Yeah. It's bad. A lot more than she used to last year. I don't know if Julia notices, because it's mostly me taking care of her. It got a lot worse this summer, when Dad was gone on so much business. Maybe because he was gone, I don't know. But he's still always gone, and I'm pretty sure he has no idea how bad it is. He's only home on nights they would normally party anyway, you know?"

"How bad is it?"I asked quietly. A lump rose in my throat. Not so much because I was worried for Brendan's mom—she'd never been around much and I wasn't close to her—but because no kid should have to take care of their parent. Not for that reason.

"It's...she needs a drink to get out of bed some mornings."

"Oh, shit. Like most people need coffee."

He nodded, staring down at his hands, which were folded together in front of him.

"Shit," I repeated. He nodded. It seemed like the only thing we could really say that would accurately sum up the situation. "Shit, Brendan."The lump in my throat hadn't gone away, but I didn't want to cry. Didn't even really know why I would. "Why didn't you tell me?"

He buried his face in his hands and leaned forward for thirty seconds, a minute. He didn't say a word, and every second of his silence was excruciating.

He sniffed hard, once, then sat up again. "I don't know. I didn't want you to worry about it? I still wanted you to be my friend, I guess? I didn't want to lose you. You're...you're my best friend, you know? I didn't want to lose you."

I leaned into him, resting my chin on his shoulder from behind, without even thinking. Close but not smothering. Letting him know I was there for him. Because if there was anything I knew about who I was in this place, it was that I had been miserable here eight months ago, and Brendan had been here for me. Wherever, however he was miserable, I wanted to be there for him, too.

"Shit, Brendan, you couldn't get rid of me if you tried."

He started to laugh, and then all of a sudden, he sat forward and turned back to look at me. His breath warmed my cheek, and if he hadn't just told me his mom was an alcoholic and he was basically taking care of her and his whole house all the time, it would have been the perfect time to kiss him. But it wasn't. It so wasn't. I sat up straight again, and breaking contact with him was excruciating.

"What do you do? When that happens, I mean?"

"Sometimes I bring her a drink. Sometimes I don't. I bring it to her more often than not. What can I do? A lot of times she throws things at me if I don't. Or cries. Or both. If I don't, she comes downstairs and messes shit up looking for more to drink anyway. And then I get myself and Julia out of the house every morning." He hung his head. "Plus, I make plans to go to CMU instead of Harvard, so Julia's not left here all by herself to deal with it."

"Oh," I said, my voice barely above a whisper. "That's why you quit talking so much about Harvard."

"Or Stanford, or MIT. Yeah. That's why."

Not to stay here for me. Not for a long shot. Of course not. God, how could I have been so stupid? How could I have ever thought that?

"How long has it been like this?"

"Since Paris last year. When Julia and I went to visit my grandmother for the summer. Dad was traveling a lot, I guess, and we were gone, and she was lonely. That's what she says."

He shrugged again, and sniffled, which totally caught me off guard. I sat up and looked at him just as he swiped at his eye, then stood up, brushing his hands off on the fronts of his jeans. He stared at the back of his backyard, hard.

"I never understood him and his goddamn cars and his goddamn glass garage. I'm gonna have to Windex that whole goddamn piece of shit motherfucking thing now."

"Wow, I haven't heard you swear that many times in one sentence in, like, ever." I stood up next to him, and laughed a little, hoping at least my smile would transfer to him. "Hey. Hey, you okay?" This was one time I wasn't going to think about whether Brendan liked me or whether he liked Sofia or whether he was just obsessed with Mathletes and clueless. I grabbed his hand. He squeezed it, and if he wasn't so upset, I seriously might have swooned.

"Yeah, I just....I'm sorry your birthday sucked so much. I knew you wouldn't like this." I bristled, but held on. I couldn't ever get too mad at him. After all, he was right. I totally hated this crap.

"B!" warbled a voice from just inside. "There you are!" The screen door banged open and Sofia's flower-cloud and hair bounced out through it. She was wearing a tiny shirt and a tight jean skirt, and wobbling significantly on spiky heels that made her just about Brendan's height.

Brendan dropped my hand as Sofia rammed into his side and I tried to get over my supreme annoyance of that, the fact that she had interrupted us, and why she ever thought it was okay to call Brendan "B."

The party raged on from the inside, the band playing ever louder. I marveled at the miracle of all the kids coming to puke back here, in the high-hedged backyard, and thanked God for the fact that no one had dragged any tacky red plastic cups out to the front yard, or deposited their vomit there.

Just then, Sofia lurched across the deck, dragging Brendan with her, and managed to instruct him to hold her hair before she vomited over the side. Awesome.

"Hey Vincent?" I called. I craned my neck back just in time to look through the window and see him knocking back a honey-colored shot with two other guys, then licking his wrist. I rolled my eyes and tried to tamp down the anger in my chest. Did he seriously break from cleaning up the mess of alcohol in the kitchen to...contributing to the mess of alcohol in the kitchen?

Happy freaking birthday to me.

"Vincent, I think we need you out here."

He banged out the door too, and saw Sofia, still sputtering over the edge of the deck.

"Oh, Jesus Christ, Sof. Really? I think someone needs to take her home," Vincent said.

"You think, genius?" Brendan's voice ripped through the air, stronger than I'd ever heard it.

"Well, be my guest."

Sofia moaned over the banister. "Brendan, take me home," she whimpered.

"Can't you just crash upstairs somewhere?"

"All the beds are taken," she moaned. "Besides, I want my stuff. Brendan?"

Vincent looked at Brendan. "You can go ahead, bro. I'll take care of stuff here."

"Oh, I...I really should not leave the house. Not with it like this. You'll have to do it. She's your sister."

Vincent flexed his jaw, standing up straighter. "Dude. If I take her home like this, no way I can leave her there. She's so trashed, I wouldn't feel okay with her being there alone."

"Which is exactly why I can't take her. I can't leave Julia here with all this shit to clean up, can I?"

Damn Sofia. If she hadn't felt the need to get drunk off her ass we wouldn't be in this situation.

But, after all, it was my birthday party. Of course it was all about her. That made perfect freaking sense.

Vincent threw his hands up in the air. "Dude, I got here first, remember? My car's blocked. At least give me your keys. Yours is in that garage, right?" Vincent tilted his head up to indicate the huge white garage that stretched out behind the pool and opened to the street behind. "I'll take yours, and I'll bring it back in the morning."

Brendan dug in his pocket and pulled out a key chain. "Take my Corolla. There on the left. Okay?"

"What, you don't trust me with any of the sweeter rides?" Vincent smiled that mischievous smile that I'm sure was really cute when the situation was not annoying or gross. Unfortunately, it was exactly that right now.

"No. The sweet rides are my dad's, not mine. And besides, on that upholstery? Not with her like this." I grimaced as Sofia lurched back toward me, and I wrapped my arm around her bony waist to support her. The flower cloud was now replaced by a vomit stench, and I wrinkled my nose. I couldn't believe I was actually wishing for those flowers back. Brendan, on her other side, turned his head away. "C'mon. We'll walk her back, you get the car started."

Vincent started to pull away, but Sofia nearly fell down again, so he motioned for Hal, who had come out to the backyard with his own drunk girlfriend and was washing the whipped cream off his wrists in the pool, which was probably a healthy percentage vomit now. This night probably could not get any grosser.

Brendan glared at him. "Can't you see that he's drunk, dude?"

"He's just starting up the car. I can't leave her, you said that yourself."

I had to admit, there was something kind of hilarious

about all these problems being caused by Sofia's complete lack of ability to restrain herself. Or, it would be hilarious if it wasn't all so gross.

Sofia stood there, moaning, waiting for the car to pull out. After a few minutes, I heard an engine revving, and we slowly started down the deck steps.

The crazy thing was, I knew what Brendan's Corolla sounded like. It was a little rattly from that tailpipe we'd rammed into the concrete parking space barrier and never told his dad about. This was a loud, low purr.

Brendan must have heard it too, because all at once, his head snapped up and he let all of Sofia's weight drop against me. Hal sat in the driver's seat of a car. But it wasn't the Corolla. "No fucking..." he muttered, then sprinted toward the garage at full tilt. "No fucking way!"

But he was too late. He was almost to the garage's side door, his arm reaching out for the knob, when the revving got louder. So fast I couldn't believe it, the car lurched backward, shattered the glass into a million twinkling crystals on the lawn, and shot across the yard, straight into the swimming pool.

Brendan stood frozen, his hand still on the garage door's handle, staring at the garage-wall carnage and the giant bubbles breaking the surface of the swimming pool's water. An anguished squeak-whine escaped his gaping mouth.

Sofia was the first to scream. Either she hadn't been quite

as drunk as she was pretending to be, or the sound and the splash woke her up. I followed it up with a hearty, "Jesus Christ!"while she staggered toward the pool.

There was just one problem with this whole picture, aside from Brendan's dad's prized Ferrari dying a slow, bubbly death in the swimming pool that probably cost half as much as the damn car did. Hal still hadn't surfaced. Five seconds later, no sign. Not even little bubbles.

"Oh my God," I moaned, realizing what I was going to have to do. I ran to the edge of the pool, kicked off my flats, and dove in.

The shock of frigid water seemed to slice through my skin and thicken my blood. I forced each movement of my muscles as I practically felt my body temperature dropping. Hal sat in the driver's seat, eyes wide, and I thanked God he was conscious. I swam down to him and tugged on his wrist, pulling him out of his shock and helping him snake his way out of one of the open windows. His hand scrabbled at mine as we both swam back up to fresh air.

My head broke the surface, and I gasped and sputtered. I glared at Hal, who was gasping way harder than I was, and made it to the side to see Brendan standing in the grass, gaping at the bubbling pool, about ten feet away from Sofia, who just sat on the grass holding her head. I could still hear the glass shattering, like it was on a loop in tiny microphones in my ears. After I made sure Hal made it to the side too, I hauled myself out of the pool and surveyed the scene.

I don't think I could have made up a bigger disaster if I tried.

Until I looked up at the deck, and saw Brendan's dad just standing there, taking it all in, looking like he was going to puke himself. His mouth dropped open once, twice, three times. His face progressively turned from pale, graying green to bright red, to purple. I rarely heard Mr. Thomas talk—rarely saw him, as a matter of fact—but I assumed the choked high-pitched sound that came out of his mouth next was not normal.

"Is everyone safe?"

"Dad, I..."Brendan said in a low whisper.

I wasn't sure if I was imagining the giant vein popping out of his neck, but I swore his voice got even quieter. "Is everyone safe, Brendan?"

"Yes. Yes sir, Ashley pulled Hal out, and he was the only one in the car." Brendan's voice was so quiet, like it was tiptoeing around landmines of his father's rage.

I was surprised Brendan didn't turn around and puke, as terrifying as his dad's expression was.

Then Mr. Thomas's line of sight connected with Sofia, sitting on the lawn, and Vincent, slowly stepping back toward her. "Sofia? Sofia and Vincent Cole are here,"Mr. Thomas said as the strange plum hue slowly left his face, leaving an odd pattern of white and red blotches. My arms trembled. I wasn't sure whether it was from how wet and frozen I was, or from outright fear.

"Yes, sir," Vincent said, lowering his eyes to the ground. "Yes, sir. It was my idea. A birthday party for Ashley. My father was entertaining, so we couldn't use our house and I really only wanted to have a small get-together. It seems that some kids broke into Mrs. Thomas's liquor cabinet, and I was in there trying to clean up, and Sofia wasn't feeling well, so Brendan gave me the keys to his car, and I asked my friend to start it for me, because I didn't want to leave my sister. She's...not feeling well."

"As you said."

"Well, it was poor judgment, sir, because this kid really wanted to mess around in your Ferrari. I'm so sorry."

I had to give it to Vincent. He had balls to be talking to Mr. Thomas like this when he'd basically just drowned Mr. Thomas's baby. Even I knew how much Mr. Thomas loved that damn car.

But instead of crying, slamming things, or flying into a rage, Mr. Thomas just stared at the pool, licked his lips, and said, "Well, son, that's what insurance is for."

"Mr. Thomas, I assure you, I—"

"Vincent. Get your sister home, son. Most of your...guests...left when I arrived home and sent them away. So your car is free now. And Ashley," he said, turning to me, "You'd better go on home. I understand that this isn't your fault..."

Brendan sputtered, "She didn't ask for it, Dad, she didn't even want a party, she—"

"I'll speak to you in a few minutes."

Mr. Thomas cleared his throat. "As I was saying, Ashley, I know this isn't your fault, so I won't speak to Kristin or Bruce about this this time. As long as it doesn't happen again. Understood?"

Every bone in my body wanted to tell him that I had absolutely no control over whether it happened again, but seeing the terrified look on Brendan's face and hearing the occasional bubble that still broke the surface of the pool put me into a somber mood. "Yes, sir."

Without a word, Vincent walked over to Sofia, hoisted her off the grass, and started walking her toward the front door.

"I'm sorry I ruined your birthday," he murmured as he passed.

"Ruined my birthday" was an understatement. Vincent had promised me a chill party, talked me into it, and then allowed the whole thing to spiral into the least chill event I could imagine. "My birthday? You think that's all I care about here? God, Vincent! You're such an insufferable asshole." I'd never said anything with as much venom in my voice in my entire life. I looked over at Brendan one more time, then stalked over to the side of the house, grabbed a huge rubber trash can, and started picking up red cups from all over the lawn and chucking them in. Each one punctuated Vincent's stunned silence with a hollow, pinging thunk as it hit the inside of the can.

"Ashley. Ashley." Vincent's voice strangely didn't sound slurred or groggy at all. Still, I told myself he had to be at least a little drunk. If he'd just given Hal the keys to Brendan's dad's Ferrari so he could crash it into the pool and he wasn't drunk, I would have killed him. "Ashley, what are you doing?"

"I'm cleaning all this trash up off Brendan's lawn so that he doesn't have to do it all himself after you've gotten him into trouble and sent him into freaking shock, Vincent."

"Ash, it's fine. Forget about it, okay? I'll take care of it."

"No, no. It's not like anyone else is going to help him. Get the hell out of here, Vincent."

"Ashley. This wasn't my fault. I didn't bring the alcohol. I didn't ask anyone to. You have to see that. I'm not even drunk."

He could have been right. I'd only seen him do one shot. And his voice was steady, his eyes clear.

"You heard Brendan's dad. It's okay. But seriously. Get the hell out of here."

I looked over my shoulder at Brendan's dad standing over him. I couldn't hear his voice, but from the look on his face, it was most certainly not okay.

"So," Vincent said, "I'll talk to you tomorrow?"

"If you're lucky." I rolled my eyes and kept cleaning up, letting my anger drive my arms.

Ω

I spent the next half hour warming up and picking up red cups and other random trash around the house with Julia, whose face was frozen in the same terrified shock as Brendan's had been. We worked almost silently, spraying surfaces with all-purpose cleaner and straightening cushions. We were both waiting for the roaring to begin.

But we never heard a single shout from Mr. Thomas. Thirty minutes after he'd come home, Brendan stalked through the house, not looking at me or his sister, ran up the stairs, and shut his door. It happened so quickly I couldn't have called after him if I wanted to.

Mr. Thomas came in then, looking totally normal. "Ashley, I think it's time we all turned in. Thank you for your help."

I tried to make eye contact with him, and found I just couldn't. So I mumbled my thanks, or my acknowledgment, or something, and slunk home.

I locked the door behind me, hoping Kristin and Bruce wouldn't be home soon and notice the giant crane that was just pulling up to the house to pull the drowned Ferrari out of the pool. I flopped down on my bed face up, turned on my bedside lamp, out of habit, I was sure, and stared at Brendan's room. I couldn't believe it, but the light was on. Grinning, I reached up and flashed mine twice, and watched as he did his, too. Then we shut them out together.

I spent a long time that night staring at the ceiling, listening to the diesel-engine roar of the crane with the huge boom that had rolled into the Thomas's backyard, and the huge rush of water when it pulled the car out. The creak of the shining red convertible strained against the straps, and there was a weird crunch of metal as it hit the bed of the tow-away truck. I wondered why Brendan's dad hadn't completely lost his shit when some stupid drunk kid busted his garage and drowned his Ferrari at some stupid birthday party he knew I would never have asked for.

CHAPTER TWENTY

not if you were to give me the world

The sun had just begun to poke in through my blinds when the text notification on my phone screamed in my ear. I didn't know how I had possibly slept with the image of Mr. Thomas's plum-faced rage, immediately followed by the weird lack thereof, running through my head. What was worst was how quietly upset Brendan had been.

The text message tone screamed in my ear again. "What the—?" I muttered before finally grabbing it, swiping the screen and glaring against the impossibly bright light that assaulted my eyes. Just one message, five words from Brendan. "If you're up, call me?"

I groaned and sat up, wiping the sleep out of my eyes and willing my head to stop pounding. "Well, now I'm up," I muttered, punching in his name and pressing the phone to my ear with one hand and tying my hair back with the elastic that was always around my wrist with the other.

"Hey, Ash," he answered after the first ring. "We're still going to breakfast, right?"

"I mean, yeah. Sure, I guess. If you're up for it." Brendan and I hadn't missed many Saturday morning breakfasts, but he'd canceled yesterday's to get ready for the party. I hadn't been planning on him moving it to today.

"I know it's Sunday, but I'm in if you are."

"Are you even allowed to leave the house after last night? Is your dad still there?"

"No, he left again this morning. Can you meet me at Pamela's, though? I have some stuff to do in town right after."

I sighed, my head still fuzzy from sleep and putting together everything Brendan said. "Yeah, okay."

Ω

Kristin dropped me off with strict orders to call her as soon as I needed her. I smiled and brandished my cell phone in recognition as I stepped out of the car. Brendan was already there, standing on the sidewalk, fidgeting against the cold. As I approached him, we looked at each other for a hard second. I didn't smile. I didn't know what kind of face to make, after last night. After what I'd learned.

"Hey," I said, walking up to the sidewalk to meet him.

"Hey," he said, with a soft smile.

For the first time in weeks, something felt kind of normal.

We slid into our booth and the waitress brought us a pot of coffee. Brendan poured for us both, nudging it over to me without cream or sugar. I had to love a guy who knew how I took my coffee, no matter how weird he acted.

Finally, I asked, in a low voice, "What happened last night?"

"What do you mean? You were there."

I blew out a breath and shook my head, exasperated. "I mean, what happened with your dad? He should have been screaming and throwing shit and generally freaking out, but he was just so..."

"Not totally enraged? Yeah. It's because of Sofia."

"What the hell does that mean?"

Brendan sighed and looked down at his hands, which were folded together in the middle of the table. "Well, Vincent and Sofia, more accurately. Do you know why they're here? In town?"

"Because Mansfield Prep's such a good school. Yeah." Because they're hoping the name of the school will get them into college when they can't get decent grades?

"Well, yeah. But why they're in Pittsburgh in the first place."

I shook my head slowly, drawing my eyebrows in. "I guess I never thought about it? I thought it was just coincidence that you met them on that cruise, I....do you know why they're in Pittsburgh?"

Brendan leaned back in his chair and exhaled heavily. "You know Dad's a real estate developer, a property manager, right?"

"Yeah. Which is why he's always traveling everywhere,

checking on his properties."

"Right. Well, Sofia's dad is here looking to open up a Bertram, Crawford, and Cole office in one of a few cities. Buffalo, Richmond, or Pittsburgh. The office would be huge. Forty attorneys, at least. He brought the family here for a year to feel it out, find clients. And if he settles on Pittsburgh...."

I sat back too, then. "Then your dad would be home a lot more while they developed the property."

Brendan nodded and grabbed for the menu, even though he knew exactly what was on it.

"And be able to deal with your mom."

"Yeah, and maybe get her some help? I don't know." His eyes looked wet again.

"And let you go to one of the schools you really want to go to."

"Yeah, even though it's getting kind of late for that. But yeah. Ideally."

"Okay, but what does that have to do with your dad not completely losing his shit when Hal drove his freaking Ferrari into your pool?"

"He partially lost his shit."

I glared at him.

"Okay. So, the thing is, Dad wants to it to work out too. I know he's never around, but he knows that Mom's not doing well. He doesn't want to be gone all the time. So..."

"If he screams at Vincent and Sofia, their dad isn't happy,

and puts the office in Buffalo instead."

"Exactly."

"And that's also why you let her hassle you about the lacrosse team. And hang all over you." As soon as I said it, my hand flew to my mouth. I couldn't believe I'd actually said the words. I was just so happy that suddenly everything made some kind of sense.

"Do you really think she hangs all over me?"

All the relief I'd felt rushed right back out of my body. "Wait a minute. Do you like her?"

"She's fine. Don't you?"

"I...if you like fake, fawning, ridiculous girls, yeah, I guess she's fine."

"What makes you say she's fake? Why wouldn't she want to hang out with me?"

"Are you...oh, my God. That's not what I meant, okay? I'm sorry." Obviously I thought Brendan was cute enough for Sofia to want to hang out with him, and he was definitely popular. But the only real reason Sofia could have for wanting to hang out with the captain of the Mathletes instead of the captain of the lacrosse team was that he was rolling in it.

This was not the time to tell him that, though. Definitely not.

"Look, I never asked her out. We're not together."

"Have you thought of telling her that?"

"What are you talking about? She knows, okay? We're just

good friends."

"You kids ready to order?" I realized the waitress was standing there, and wondered just how long she'd been watching me start to self-destruct.

"Yeah," Brendan said, handing her the menus. "I'll have the country breakfast with scrambled eggs, and she'll have the banana stack."

Hot tears pricked at the corners of my eyes—angry ones. He said he was letting Sofia hang all over him because of his dad's job, but really he liked her. He must have. She was drop-dead gorgeous, and charming, and popular, and grew up exactly how he did—rich. Everything that was the opposite of what I was. She wasn't afraid to be a normal high schooler, because she wasn't afraid of being the next big victim of the popular kids' scorn—she was one of them. If he was with her, he could be normal.

She was everything I wasn't, everything I hated about Williamson, everything that terrified me. And she was trying to take away everything I loved about Mansfield.

And he still wanted to be with her. More than he wanted to be with me.

I stared at the linoleum tabletop instead of at him when I said, "Did you ever think that maybe I wouldn't want the banana pancakes for once? Or maybe even that I could order for myself? I don't need you for everything, you know."

As soon as the words left my mouth, a cloud of flowery

perfume descended on the table. I looked up and right into Sofia's eyes.

"See, B?" She slid into the booth next to Brendan and stroked his arm, but her cool gaze was just for me. "She's not upset about the party. And I knew she wouldn't mind if I tagged along for breakfast. Like she just said—she's just fine without you."

My mouth gaped, and my gut felt like it was tearing itself apart. There were a hundred things I could say right now, but none of the ones that actually wanted to come out of my mouth were appropriate for a public place. So I just said, "I should go."

I slid out of the booth—seriously, if there was ever a less delicate way to dramatically exit a dining situation, I couldn't imagine it—and stalked out the front door, letting it swing shut behind me and rattling the bell that hung over it. I looked back through the window. Sofia had threaded her fingers through Brendan's hair and was kissing him like her life depended on it. He didn't even seem to notice I'd left.

She'd practically crawled into his lap and had both arms draped around him, but Brendan's arms still rested on the back of the booth and the table. Maybe that meant something, maybe it didn't. But right now all I could concentrate on was my trembling body and getting the hell out of there.

CHAPTER TWENTY-ONE

perplexity and agitation every way

Head down, hands shoved in my coat pockets, I fought the frigid wind sweeping off the Allegheny. It chilled me to the bone, but I had to get away from the huge picture windows of Pamela's diner and the scene inside. The last thing I needed was Brendan and Sofia seeing the despair on my face as I tried to figure out what the hell to do with myself. I did a quick calculation—eighteen blocks from the house, just about four miles. Which wouldn't have been too far, with perfect weather, but it wasn't even eight o'clock on a November morning in Pittsburgh and I was already chilled to the bone.

Even though I wanted to just be alone all day long, I knew I had to call Kristin and Bruce. When I pulled out my phone, it was dead—I'd forgotten to charge it when I'd collapsed in bed the night before. The tears started to come back, and I swiped them away. Tear-shaped icicles on my face would not help matters any.

Really, the last thing I needed was to feel like a jerk or a drama queen for crying over banana pancakes and eighteen blocks when Brendan had just told me last night that his mom was an alcoholic and he was just trying to keep his head above water. No matter what he was doing with Sofia in our diner.

Eighteen blocks was nothing.

I stuck my head down and watched my feet flash in front of me, one in front of the other. Before I knew it, I'd be home.

I made it half a block before I heard the unmistakable sound of tires rolling up next to me. The sun glinted off the metal of the car and into my eyes. "Hey," Vincent's smooth tenor came from the window as it rolled down. "Can I give you a ride? It's freezing."

I felt like the wind had been knocked out of me. "You are pretty much the last person I want to see right now." I stuck my head down and started walking again.

The car rolled up next to me again. "Hey. Hey, Ashley. Look, I'm sorry, okay? Last night was completely screwed up. You've gotta know, I didn't mean for any of that to happen. I just wanted a fun night with some good people and a great band. And your favorite cake."

I stopped and looked into the car window. "My favorite cake?"

"Almond with coconut butter cream. Yeah. I have my ways of finding these things out."

I glared at him. "I didn't even get a slice." The wind blew against me and started a shiver that wracked my whole body. My arms wrapped themselves around my body even tighter. "You'll take me straight home?"

A hint of that same old patient Vincent smile showed.

"Anything you want."

I slid into the car's dark leather seat, and immediately warmed up—heated leather. Of course it was.

We rode in silence for a few blocks. "Seriously, how did everyone hear about that party? And why did people come expecting to drink?"

Vincent sighed and ran a hand through his hair. "Sofia. She...as soon as we moved it to Brendan's house, it's like she went into attack mode. She texted everyone, and told them to text everyone. Told them his parents wouldn't be there. She didn't say 'bring a keg,' but she might as well have."

"Why would she do that?" It was everything I could do not to tack the word 'bitch" on to the end of the sentence.

He shrugged. "Brendan has a huge house. She's trying to make friends. Wanted to show off her boyfriend's digs, I guess. Got carried away."

"Her boyfriend?"

"Yeah, I mean, they are going out, aren't they? Please don't tell me that you haven't noticed they're attached at the hip."

"I've noticed," I muttered under my breath. Brendan could say they weren't together all he wanted, but as long as everyone thought they were, it didn't make a damn bit of difference. I knew that better than anyone.

I blew out a long breath, trying to steady myself, trying to make normal thoughts turn into non-angry words and will them to come out of my mouth.

"Whatever." He shrugged. "But, if it's worth anything, I only did one shot. If I had wanted it to be a drinking party..."

"Yeah, okay. Mr. Thomas didn't freak out or kill anyone, miraculously, and no one died, and no cops came, so I guess we couldn't really hope for a better outcome."

He definitely smiled at that. "My dad called him this morning. They got the insurance worked out. Full restoration of the car, on us, no questions asked."

"Wow."

"Yeah." Vincent laughed. "I mean, it's my Christmas and birthday presents until I turn thirty-five, but it's worth it. You're worth it."

He glanced over at me with that spark in his eyes. The one that was a little playful but mostly watchful. I might even call it adoring. Holy hell, he was gorgeous.

"Okay," I said. "Well, as soon as I see Mr. Thomas again and his face isn't all red with white blotches, you'll be completely forgiven."

"Until then?" Again, with the eyes.

"Mostly forgiven." I couldn't help the smile. Seriously, it completely took over my face, cutting off any chance I had at maintaining a scowl or even a pout.

"Well, then mostly will have to be good enough for now." We hit the curving roads that took us up one of the mountains and let us look over the river at the city. It was really close to my water tower. I could have taken him there. He stepped on the gas.

"Good. Because I need you," he said, breaking my thoughts.

I turned to him and raised my eyebrows, questioning.

"I have a proposition for you,"he said. "Can we be friends again? Just friends. I swear. I need someone to teach me how to use this DSLR I just got. I'm jealous of your camera-wrangling capabilities."

"You're the first person to understand that it's not the camera, but the person shooting it. Um, hey,"I said, taking in the stunning view, "Aren't we taking a bit of a detour?"

"We didn't agree on a route, did we? And if you're going to show me how to shoot this, we're going to need something to take pictures of, right?"We pulled into a parking spot at the edge of the road. The sun had just started to really rise in the sky. It glinted off the wind-rippled surface of the Allegheny and reflected back from the millions of windows in the Pittsburgh skyscrapers. It was stunning, in an industrial-meets-nature kind of way.

"Point taken."

He grinned and pulled a long, flat box wrapped in glossy pink paper from the seat behind him. "Here. Put this on."

"What the..."

"Birthday present. Never got to give it to you before the shit hit the fan last night."

I slid my finger under the edge of the paper and carefully lifted the tape, sliding the box out. Underneath the lid of the box and a layer of tissue paper was the softest, most exquisite camel-colored cashmere scarf I'd ever seen. I immediately lifted it to my cheek. "This is... Oh, Vincent. Whoa. I mean...I love it. Thank you." I carefully arranged the scarf around my neck, like it was made of tissue paper itself.

Vincent grinned. A full-on grin. Maybe the second genuine smile I'd ever seen from him. "Okay. Now that you're warm, let's get out and you can show me how to work this sucker."

He reached back behind my seat, and when his hand brushed against my shoulder, electricity jolted through me. He smelled exactly like you'd expect a guy to smell—like cologne and hair gel. In a space this close, it was heady, real. I could let myself be enveloped in it, if I wanted to. Enveloped in him.

He pulled out a box and sat it on his lap. Emblazoned on it in shining bright colors was the logo and name of the most expensive DSLR in its line.

"You're shitting me," I breathed, grabbing it and pulling it to my own lap. "You mean you haven't even opened it yet?"

He shrugged. "You inspired me. It just arrived a couple of days ago."

I shakily undid the stickers holding the box shut, and only realized I was holding my breath after a few seconds.

Somehow it felt weird to be holding onto such a gorgeous piece of technology that cost so many thousands of dollars, unwrapping it straight from its original packaging. Even my voice shook when I spoke.

"See this red dot? That's where the lens lines up with the notch on the body, okay? So just line those up, and it should click in fine." I realized I was talking more to the camera than Vincent, crooning to it almost, and when I finally looked up at him, he was watching me. Enjoying it.

"Did you...uh...did you want to shoot something outside?"

"Whatever's best," he said, opening his door and climbing out. By the time I'd placed all the plastic wrappers back in the camera's box, he was already on my side of the car, opening the door for me.

He'd driven us all the way to the top of Mount Washington. By then, the sun had reached a high enough angle that it glinted off one flat curve of the bridge and most of the skyscrapers. Sometimes I missed my parents' farmhouse, but I had to admit that most of the time I loved the way Pittsburgh sparkled.

I perched myself on the hood of his car and started tinkering with the settings on the camera. The wind bit at my fingers, but I didn't care. Right in front of me, the metallic Pittsburgh shone against the brilliant autumn leaves of the surrounding mountains, and I was holding the most incredible camera money could buy. No way was I missing the opportunity to be in this moment. Just to be. My own little slice of heaven, no matter who else was here.

"So," I said, peering through the viewfinder, "the most important thing for every shot is exposure. That means how much light you let into the camera. So you control that with ISO and shutter speed. Any time you're outside during the day, you can keep it low, two hundred or four hundred. Control that here."

I held the camera out toward Vincent, and realized he was looking at me instead of the camera, so I just kept talking.

"And, uh...shutter speed. That's really simple to remember. For freezing motion, keep it high. For blurring, keep it low. For most sharp shots, you want at least one sixty, because your hands will shake." I looked at him again. His gaze was still fixed on my face, and I just couldn't help it. I grinned. "Do you want to try?"

He grabbed the camera body, first cradling it in his hands like a baby animal, then awkwardly gripping it in a couple different positions. I laughed. "You've never really held one of these before, huh?"

"No, I told you. You inspired me."

"The least I could do is help you out, then," I said, grabbing the camera back from him. "Here." I leaned into him and held the camera with both my hands in front of him, showing him how to place the heel of his right hand against the back and use his left hand to support the lens. He slipped his hands over mine, laying his fingers against mine to get a feel for where he should place them.

It was just his hands on mine, but for that moment I felt like our skin was touching everywhere. My heart stopped, and I drew my hands back. I took a deep breath and said, "Why don't you try some test shots, okay? Just make sure your light meter is just a little right of center."

He peered through the viewfinder and snapped some shots, then drew back to look at them in the screen. "Hey, that's not bad!"he said, smiling. "This really is a stunning city." He started snapping again, then held the camera out to show me what he'd gotten.

"You know? Those are actually some really good shots."

"Don't sound so surprised," he said, leaning back and setting the camera on the hood behind him.

I bristled, and leaned back to pick it up. "Vincent, don't put that camera down on the dirty hood of the car. It's so—"

His hand covered mine on top of the camera, and didn't move. He looked me right in the eye. If I leaned forward at all, our noses would touch. His breath blew hot against my lips.

"I'm so sorry about your birthday."

"Vincent, I—"

"Not because the party was such a disaster. Because I insisted on having it in the first place. I should have known you better. I should have paid more attention."

"Really, just forget about it."I knew his eyes were still on me, and it became so overwhelming, filling me up with a pressure, an anxiousness I couldn't name. His fingertips brushed my jaw, drawing my gaze back up to his.

"I'm sorry I haven't been paying more attention to you. Who you are. That's why I wanted you to teach me how to use this. I just wanted to get to know you. No other kids at school, no Mathletes, no parties, no bullshit."

I parted my lips slightly, drawing a shuddering breath in through them. I didn't know what to do. Didn't know if I should move, or if I wanted to, or if I did, whether it would be backwards and away, or forward, pressing my mouth into his.

His beautiful face was certainly making it difficult for me to choose the former. Either way, I was frozen. A deer in the headlights.

Finally, after one, two, three breathless waiting seconds, Vincent dropped his fingers from my jaw and let his head fall forward, touching his forehead against mine.

I lifted my chin just enough to brush my lips to his. For an instant, he pressed in, so soft and warm I could have been dreaming it. I finally let myself feel what it was like to kiss a guy who wasn't the one in my daydreams.

It wasn't bad. Not bad at all.

I made sure to take steady, regular breaths. I had kissed Vincent, and it was okay. Until he parted his lips against mine, and I felt his tongue flick against my lower lip.

All at once, I knew I didn't want this, and that I had to

find a way to break off the kiss without embarrassing him.

Another car's tires crunching over the gravel gave me just that. Startled, I whipped my head toward the noise.

There was Brendan, staring at us from the rolled-down window of his tan-gold sedan. His eyes were wide and his mouth hung open. How much had he seen? And, more importantly, why wasn't Sofia with him?

I shouldn't have felt guilty, or afraid, or angry, or worried. But I felt all those things. I knew that this was not usually the route Brendan liked to take home. He only drove this way if he was frustrated or upset about something.

My heart thudded so loudly in my chest I was surprised no one looked up to see where the helicopter was.

Finally, Brendan managed, "I...uh...you forgot..." he swallowed.

Oh, shit. I'd forgotten my camera. I'd been so pissed at Brendan that I'd left behind one of the only objects I'd cared about. It made everything worse that I loved it because he'd given it to me, and I'd left it in our freaking diner. I wished I could take it all back.

Now I wished I could take back kissing Vincent, too. Or maybe just Brendan seeing me kiss Vincent. I hated that I didn't know which.

I lifted both hands off the hood and pressed my palms to my temples.

"Look, Brendan, I..."

"No, no. It's cool. I can see I interrupted you, and I...I'll just drop this off at home, okay Ash? I'll see ya."

And just like that, his window rolled back up and he revved the engine on that poor little car harder than I would've imagined it could go. He sped off toward home, taking my camera with him.

Well, his camera that he'd basically given me.

I felt sick, all of a sudden. The world spun around me, the beginnings of an epic panic attack. I let myself slide down off the hood of Vincent's car, brushing dirt I wasn't sure was there off the backs of my jeans.

"Hey, you okay?"

I was definitely not okay. "Yeah, I'm fine." I pressed my palms to my temples again, because that seemed like it was probably something someone with a headache would do. "Yeah, just a headache."

Vincent's eyebrows tented in what could only be very serious concern. He rubbed his hand up and down my back, once, twice, between my shoulder blades. Yep. One hundred percent, seriously concerned.

"Let's get you home. Okay?"

I nodded and ducked into the car when he opened my door. "My house or yours?"

I laughed once, short and soft. "Mine's fine. I want my own bed."

"Yeah, of course. Mount Washington isn't going

anywhere. We can totally do this any other morning."

We rode home in silence, me resting my head back on the seat and closing my eyes. I tried to focus on the rumbling in my belly, or the awesomeness of the camera Vincent had just swiped off the car's hood and tossed into the backseat. Tried to feel the warmth of the sun on my face. But as soon as I thought of that, I remembered the warmth of Vincent's lips on mine, however briefly, and I suddenly felt very warm all over. Then I felt dizzy again.

"Are you sure you're okay? Your cheeks look so red all of a sudden."

My eyes snapped open and I sat up.

"Yeah, I should just probably lie down. You know." I pressed the backs of my hands to my cheeks.

This was getting ridiculous. My mind scrambled for something, anything else we could talk about while I was basically losing my shit in the front seat of Vincent's beautiful car. I remembered how, just moments ago, Vincent's fingers hadn't been half bad at clicking the buttons on the camera in the correct order and quick succession. Even though I was helping him, he seemed really comfortable for someone who had been picking up a DSLR for the first time.

"So that was really your first time with a DSLR?" God, that sounded bitchy. But it was true. I really did feel that way, sometimes. All the time, maybe. Like I couldn't trust Vincent with a single word he said.

He laughed. "Yeah. Really really. Why? Am I so awesome that that's hard for you to believe? Am I a prodigy? Please say I'm a prodigy."

My face fell a little then, and he must have recognized my patented Disappointed Stare, because he backed down. "Whoa, whoa. Kidding. Okay?"

"No, you did get some good shots, for sure. You're good with electronics. Not so much Austen." I smiled at him, but then remembered. His freakishly good grade on the Mansfield Park test without even cracking the book. The way I'd asked him which sibling pair he and Sofia were most like, and he had no idea what I was talking about.

I decided to recheck. Just to be sure.

"I was talking to my Aunt Kristin, and she was all upset about how Mrs. Crawford totally ignored the most important social theme of the book when she was teaching us Mansfield Park. What do you think?" I turned my full attention to him, just waiting for his response.

"I...you know, you really are amazing with a camera. Who taught you?"

"You never read it, did you?"

He ran a hand through his hair and blew out a laughing breath. "Okay, yeah. You got me. Okay? I...uh...I got overwhelmed with new stuff, and I had one of Sofia's friends dig up her answers from the year before. Everyone knows Crawford uses the same tests every year, so it's really her fault, right?"

I just stared at him, my mouth hanging partly open. When I finally reminded myself to close it, I said, "Are you seriously telling me you just cheated on a test at Mansfield Prep?"

He laughed again. "Yeah, I guess. But I mean, it's just a quiz. Doesn't everyone cheat? It's a prep school, Ashley. Everyone's trying to get ahead. Don't tell me this is the first time someone's done it."

It wasn't. I'd heard that all the other kids did it to get ahead. But I was always so crazy about studying, and never really had much else to do. Plus, I was just morally opposed to it in general. And there was no way I could afford to go to an Ivy League anyway, so I just never stressed as much as the other kids seemed to.

And I knew Brendan never cheated. Never would.

As Vincent drove, he flashed his gaze back to me, every few seconds. "Ashley. Ash."

I bristled when he called me "Ash." Even if I had kissed him. Only Brendan called me that.

"The cheating really bugs you, doesn't it?

"Yeah, it does."

"Look, where I come from, it's pretty normal. A lot of kids do it for every test. I only do it when I get really stressed. Okay? I swear. The adjustment to school was rough, and I just remembered we had the test that day. And I haven't done it since then."

"Did you even read the book?"

"That, I wasn't lying about. I really did. Last year. I just...we read so many, I have trouble remembering it. I'm not the best reader."

By then, thank God, we had pulled up to the house. "I just...God, it weirds me out, you know?"

"If it weirds you out, I won't do it. Not anymore. I swear. Look, Ashley." He threw the car into park and brushed his fingertips against the back of my hand. Cautious. Respectful. The same way he'd kissed me.

Or, rather, let me kiss him.

My heart started hammering. Even from that single soft kiss, I could tell he was a seriously good kisser. And he smelled delicious.

"Look. I'm just gonna say this and hope I don't sound like too big of an idiot. I noticed you from the first day I was at Mansfield, okay? You are gorgeous, and awesome, and smart, and not like the other girls. You care about things that other girls don't care about, and that makes me want to spend more time with you. So...I know you know this, but I like you. Really like you. And I get that maybe you don't feel quite the same way, but if we could hang out, that would make me really happy."

I had no idea if he was saying "hang out" in the "let's get together on Saturday mornings to make out" sense or the "no pressure but can I spend time with you" sense. And that morning, between arguing with Brendan, kissing Vincent, Brendan seeing me kiss Vincent, and finding out for sure and certain that Vincent was not same guy I thought he was, I was too overwhelmed to really ask the question.

"Look, I...I'm still not feeling well. I really should go," I said, pressing the back of my hand to my cheek again.

Vincent's face fell. "Yeah, for sure. Can I walk you to your door?"

"I think I'll be okay," I said. "We can shoot again this week, okay? This time I'll bring my camera, too." In that moment, I did feel a rush to my head. Remembering our hands together on that camera. Remembering the warmth of his skin against mine, the tingle that his mouth on mine sent through my whole body.

On came Vincent's standard soft, patient smile. The fake one. "Okay. I'll hold you to that."

"And I'll see you Monday."

$$\Omega$$

I trudged toward the front door, struggling to put one foot in front of the other in smooth motion as I listened to Vincent's car glide down the driveway. I dropped my bag inside the front door, and my keys along with it. They clattered against the newly polished wood, and I winced.

"Breakfast with Brendan?" called Bruce from the kitchen,

where he and Kristin were doing their Sunday morning newspaper-and-breakfast thing at the little round black table in there. Kristin had her feet propped up on Bruce's knees, and he read the paper with his left hand while covering them with the right. She worked a crossword, occasionally pulling a pencil from her tufted bun of hair, and drank coffee. Every lazy weekend morning, exactly the same.

Just like Brendan and I used to be.

"Yeah." I didn't want to elaborate on what else, even though I knew I'd be welcome to butt in if I really wanted to. My heart still tripped a little, and I still felt a little flushed, and the room really spun now. "I'm just going to my room. Read a little bit."

I flopped down on my bed and stared up at Brendan's window, just like last night, and every other night before. Brendan sat at his desk, staring at the computer. I dug my cell out of my pocket and punched in "2" on the speed dial. "Come on, pick up," I muttered.

He reached for his phone, looked at the number, and craned his neck to look out his window. Right at me. Then he reached up and pulled down the blinds.

And a big, gaping hole formed in my chest.

CHAPTER TWENTY-TWO

the height of her ambition

I spent the rest of Sunday holed up in my room. I said I was doing homework, and watching TV. Sunday was rainy, so it probably didn't actually seem all that weird. By the time I emerged on Monday morning, ready for school, I couldn't ignore the look of relief on Kristin's face.

"You feeling okay, honey? You seemed under the weather. And we didn't see Brendan all weekend."

Like I needed the reminder. "Yeah, I'm fine. And he just had other stuff going on." It wasn't a total lie. If "other stuff" was code for "avoiding Ashley." Not like I was trying hard to get in touch with him, although I was doing plenty of staring at my phone and willing it to ring. Unfortunately, I still hadn't really decided who I hoped it would be.

Brendan was obviously angry. But if he was going to claim he didn't like Sofia and then make out with her in the middle of our weekly breakfast date, then he really had no right to be pissed if I wanted to sit on the hood of Vincent's car and teach him to use his damn expensive camera. And maybe kiss him if I wanted to.

All I knew about that was that actually kissing Vincent made me want to do it again. At the same time, remembering the conversation I'd had with Vincent about cheating made me not really want to hang out with him again. Even though he said he would stop.

I was still trying to figure out if I believed him.

All of that was why riding to school with Brendan would not be a good idea today. I'd either scream at him or dissolve into a blubbering heap of tears. Or try to kiss him and see if I liked it better than kissing Vincent. Neither of those things would be good.

"Aunt Kristin. Care if I hitch a ride to school with you today?" A look of confusion swept Kristin's face, but she must have seen the bummed-out look on mine, because she quickly said, "Sure, honey. It'll be nice to get the time together."

Aunt Kristin, at least, knew exactly what I needed to hear.

Ω

Everyone at school was talking about my birthday party, but not about how epic the band or the kegs or the swimming pool car crash was—they were talking about what a miracle it was that no one had gotten in trouble, not a single kid had been arrested for underage drinking. My seventeenth birthday party would go down in Mansfield Prep history as the one with the most alcohol, the most vomit, and least amount of planning, with no—absolutely zero—kids getting busted.

I was hoping to be that lucky avoiding all the people I had no desire to deal with. I ducked into the girl's bathroom between classes until the last possible moment of hallway transit, just to avoid seeing either Brendan or Vincent. It was chicken shit of me, but surprisingly, all the sleeping, stressing, ice-cream eating and stupid show watching hadn't really solved the problem of which guy to talk to in which way.

The only problem with the girls' room was that other girls could go in there. And did, apparently, because on my way out of the stall between sixth and seventh periods, Sofia stood there, leaning into the mirror, daubing something on her already naturally perfect face. And slung around her shoulder and resting on her hip was my camera bag.

I froze. I could barely comprehend what I was seeing. My gray canvas camera bag, with navy padded inserts, holding my camera.

Except, it wasn't mine. Not really. It was Brendan's. He'd gotten it for his birthday, and had absolutely no interest in it. I'd picked it up in his room one day, taken some test shots. Borrowed it one weekend and I was hooked. He'd taken one look at the shots I uploaded from the card onto the school's editing program in the computer lab, squeezed my shoulders, and said, "Well, guess that camera's yours, huh?"

I hadn't been able to stop smiling for a week.

And now this bitch had it resting against her hip, wearing it like it was hers. Like she even knew how to use it.

Oh, God. Did she know how to use it? Was she good at this too? Suddenly, I fought for every breath.

I must have been staring at that damn bag, because she grasped the strap and said, "I know, the bag's totally scuzzy. I ordered a new one this morning. Brendan lent me his camera since I just joined yearbook, wasn't that sweet? And now that I have such a nice camera I'll be able to take the best pictures, so they said I can be in charge."

My heart wept for the idiots at this stupid rich school who didn't' realize that you'd get better pictures from me using my cell phone than Sofia, who knew nothing about camera work, using Brendan's eight-hundred-dollar camera.

The camera that, considering Vincent's three-thousand-dollar one, she definitely could have bought herself.

She leaned over to me from the sink, making a big deal out of looking in all the other stalls, presumably to make sure no one was there. "I think he really likes me. Like, really a lot. He looked kind of emotional when he handed the camera over." She stood back up and kept applying more goop to her lips. "And I know he's not the coolest guy in the school or anything, but he's so smart, and he's so...well, I would definitely be going on the nicest dates and get the sweetest birthday presents. You know?"

I didn't know. Mostly because I'd never really wanted to do anything with Brendan besides eat pancakes and watch movies in his living room. But I did understand what she meant. Everyone knew Brendan had cash. In fact, I'm sure she'd noticed that from the first day she was here. She was definitely the kind of girl to scope out who was driving the nicest cars.

"Anyway. We only kissed a couple times, but—"

"A couple times?" My words came out harder and faster than I wanted them to. I tried to keep my bitch face in check.

"Well, I kissed him. A little. At the diner, and then last night, when he brought me the camera. And he let me. He's...shy, I think."

The idea of Brendan volunteering to bring my camera to Sofia was almost as horrific as the idea of him kissing her.

Sofia snapped her makeup bag shut and crammed it into her backpack. I couldn't see what else was in that thing, but it wasn't too stuffed, and it definitely didn't look like books. "Well," she chirped, "Thanks for listening to all my love life news. It might look like I have a ton of friends, but I don't trust them as far as I can throw them."

She may not have considered them real friends, but I had seen enough of their behavior—hovering near her at lunch, staying away from any guy she got within a ten-foot radius of—that I knew they were her crew. Afraid of her. Would mess with me if she told them to. Maybe she couldn't confide in them, but that was a whole hell of a lot more than I had.

"You're different," she continued. "Quiet. You don't have that many friends, so you don't gossip." She sighed, and I wanted to slap her. "Except Brendan. He really is so cute. And you're his best friend, and I care what you think."

What I thought was that I wanted to slam her head into the mirror. "I think...I want him to be happy. You know?"

"Good." She smiled at me, but there was a challenge in her eyes. "See you at Mathletes."

Ω

My stomach churned all of seventh period. I couldn't get the image of Sofia's gloating face out of my mind.

Did he know I considered that camera mine? Did he even care?

My feet dragged like lead the whole way to Mathletes. One in front of the other, each step laborious. Today we were in a classroom, so we could take the paper tests to see who qualified for State. I knew I'd get one of the best scores, but still, the sooner these tests were over, the sooner I'd be on the team, and the closer I'd be to getting the Mathletes on my resume and competition season behind me. And seeing Brendan much less. Especially Brendan with Sofia.

I knew I was getting there earliest. My plan was to get there, sit in a desk, keep my eyes forward, kick butt at the test, dominate at the board problems, get formally picked for the team, call Kristin to pick me up, and spend the night in my room mourning my camera. Brendan's camera.

Instead, I walked into the classroom, and the first thing I saw was Brendan standing against a wall, and Sofia leaning into him with one palm on the wall, the fingers of her other hand hooked in his belt loop. One of his hands resting in the small of her back. Her mouth firm on his. Their tongues moving together.

I really had to throw up now. Heat flooded my chest, then my face, and I felt so dizzy I had to sit down in the same front row desk I originally meant to. Maybe this wouldn't look like it bugged me that much after all.

All I knew was that, as I plunked down in the chair, I made a strange swallow-choking sound without meaning to. Somehow, I managed, "I'm sorry, I—" before Sofia's head whipped around and, registering my presence there, she rubbed her lips together and gave the slightest smirk before acting surprised. "Oh, my God. Ashley."

Brendan didn't meet my gaze. Instead of trying to look at me, or saying anything, he crossed over to the teacher's desk that he always commandeered for these sessions, and shuffled some papers around. Ten seconds later, the rest of the kids trying for the team trickled in. Two of Ashley's friends, and four regulars, two under class and two upper class.

Vincent's head popped into the classroom, and he smiled at me. The lazy, complacent, gorgeous one that I definitely didn't have time for. He'd pulled out of the running for the State team after his scores on the regional tests, which we'd taken weeks ago, were in the lower half. "Hey, Ashley." After about two solid seconds of that smile, he called, "Hey, Sof. Coach canceled practice today. Want me to wait around? You'll be done soon, right?"

"Twenty minutes, tops," she said, and Brendan looked up at her, cocking his head. Vincent nodded his assent and ducked back out of the classroom, giving me one less distraction for taking these qualifying tests. Thank God.

"Twenty minutes?" Brendan said. "No way that'll be enough time to do boards and paper..."

"Well, I was thinking," Sofia said. The other six people in the room stared at her with either the drama of anticipation or complete and total boredom. "I don't' think we need boards at all."

Both Brendan and I stared at her like she was on crack.

"The scores mostly come from the exams anyway, right? We've worked really hard on getting correct answers on our own in the time limit, but not so much on showing our work in front of everyone. Not so much on competing against each other."

"We definitely need to work on that..."

"But," Sofia interrupted, "it's not going to be the best

indicator. Let's get the fastest, best scoring individuals on the team first, and then worry about training for boards later. Besides, isn't the paper test the one that State gives you to qualify for the competition in the first place? Everyone in the country takes the exact same test, right? It would be the most fair way."

Brendan froze in his shuffling of the stacks of paper. I could practically see the gears turning in his head. "You're right. It would be fair. The board work is more about training and practice."

"I'm good at the boards," Sofia said.

She wasn't. I'd seen her get frustrated at board exercises when Brendan wasn't watching. She might have started out with showing the right work, but always ended up taking shortcuts and arriving at the wrong answer. Or no answer.

Brendan nodded. "Okay."

"Like I said, I'm just thinking about what's most fair for everyone." She shot me a pointed look.

She may have been really bad at boards and really great at written problems, but she was still taking a real gamble by betting that she'd beat me at those.

Sofia continued, "Everyone knows we have the best students and smartest captain in the state. I just think we owe it to you to develop the strongest team to represent him."

Brendan sat up the slightest bit, and I could swear I saw his chest puff out. Sofia leaned in and whispered something in his ear, and he sat back and laughed, then looked at her with the damn mooniest eyes I'd ever seen on him. I felt short of breath, then wanted to vomit. Skittishness rumbled down my limbs and I just wanted to get out of there, be anywhere but there. This stupid, beautiful, math-smart girl had sauntered into Mansfield Prep and invaded the only safe place I had on earth with the same bullshit I'd run away from.

"Okay, Sofia makes a good point. Let's try this method of choosing. It's one hundred percent fair and equal. I heard that's how Northanger does it, anyway, and their team is...formidable. And I know some of you totally kick ass at boards, so if the results are at all close, we'll go to that. Okay?"

Sofia raised her hand and started talking before Brendan even acknowledged her. "Just answers, right? Because that's how it is at the competition? They never ask for shown work."

"Are you kidding me? We should totally show work," I said.

"But the thing is, Ash, Sofia's right. They don't have you show work at the competition," Brendan said, starting to hand out the papers. "There are hundreds of us. No way can they check work."

I spent about half a second realizing that these two unfortunately, abysmally had a point.

"Okay," I said, clicking new lead out of my pencil and poising it over the paper Brendan handed out. "What are we doing for time limit?

"Ten minutes for twenty questions, just like they do at the competition."

I nodded. That much, I knew I could do.

Sofia held up her cell phone, which showed her stopwatch app. "I'm keeping time." She looked around at Ryan and Britt, her friends who were also trying for the team, and who I'd heard seriously kicked ass in their AP Calc class, and the crew of sophomore boys who were trying to skate on this year who looked like they'd been training for this since preschool.

"Okay," she sang, "Ready...set...go."

The sounds of frantic pencil scratching filled the room. I glanced over at that damn sophomore crew and noticed them filling pieces of scrap paper faster than should be human. Meanwhile, Sofia sat perched in her seat, looking calm and perfect, the bitch.

I stuck my head down and got to work. It was a pretty solid mix of calculus problems, graphs, and word problems. I actually didn't need scrap for most of it, even though I did feel steadier showing my work. By the time I'd reached problem 19, which was a pretty complicated calculus proof, I was proud that my brain could still work through it so quickly at the same time I knew that time had to be almost up. Problem 20 was an easy algebra equation, and my brain practically sighed with relief.

Sofia's alarm went off, a ridiculous bell-like tinkling

sound that made me feel suddenly murderous toward fairies and woodland sprites. She held it up and trilled, "Time's up!" Brendan looked up from his desk, where he'd finished the questions minutes ahead of time. He grinned at all of us. "Did you all finish?" Everyone nodded. Some of those damn sophomores finished before me, too, and one looked especially smug.

"Okay, we're swapping papers for grading," Brendan announced.

Britt raised her hand and sputtered, "But—"

"Of course I'll check them after and make sure," he said. "But I just want us all to be able to leave this session with some idea of the team and the alternates. Okay? Let's just pass 'em to the person behind us."

Sofia stretched her prefect tanned arm behind her to hand me the paper. "Have fun," she said, smiling. Something in her expression told me that she understood exactly how little fun I'd be having looking at her damn stupid paper, that was probably half wrong for how little work she did on that scrap paper in front of her. Bitch face back on, decorated with a slight smile.

I passed my paper back and accepted the copy of the answer key Brendan handed me. I lined it up with Sofia's, checking number for number. The first three were correct. The fourth and fifth. All of them. Even the sixteenth, out to the seventh decimal point.

"Impossible," I muttered, glaring down at the paper, scanning the answers I'd already checked for some mistake. Some eraser mark and rewrite, even. None. This couldn't be right. Could not.

After a minute or two, and three obsessive rechecks from me, I whispered, "Impossible."

Sofia whipped her head around and hissed, "Is there a problem?"

I stared at her. "How did you get a perfect score? You barely showed your work, you—"

"Shut up," she said. "It's hard work. I've worked my ass off for this."

I glared at my camera bag at her feet. She sure had, but not by studying math.

Brendan lifted his head from his desk. "We all finished? Pass 'em up here."

There was a lot of shuffling of papers, and alternately stuffing things into bags and staring up at Brendan. I tried to read Ryan's face, since he'd graded mine, but he didn't even look at me. He was way more interested in something on his phone. He was pretending to be cool about this, but we all knew that being members of a state-renowned Mathletes team would be one thing that could separate us from the pack on college and scholarship applications. This was a big deal.

Brendan shuffled through the papers, laying them out in front of him. "Okay. So it looks like...one sixteen, one eighteen, one nineteen, and one—whoa—one perfect score." He smiled up at Sofia, nodding. "Nice work. Sofia's the first spot...then Britt, Daniel, and Mohinder."

He glanced up at me, then stared at the papers again. "Nice work, everyone who made it. Great try, to the rest of you. And next year..." He looked up at me, but I'd already stood up and practically run out of the classroom.

CHAPTER TWENTY-THREE

her mind was all disorder

I made it all the day down a hallway and around a corner, out of sight of anyone who would be wandering the halls after school, before I just had to stop. I leaned against a wall full of lockers and realized I was gasping for breath, even though I hadn't been walking that fast. Then, the tears started to pour down my cheeks.

I was a junior, and if I wanted Mathletes to have any impact at all on my college admissions, making the state team this year was my best shot. And I hadn't. Now I'd probably be going to that ridiculous community college down the lonely, twisting road from my parents' house, spending the next four years living in my old bedroom and dodging the triplets. Trying to avoid all the assholes who had tormented me and, instead of going to the community college, would be staying to work in town, or worse, going to decent colleges and coming home on vacations to smirk at me and ask me why I wasn't doing the same.

But no matter how obvious all those things were to me, I couldn't get rid of the image of Sofia leaning into Brendan, transposed with that stupid freaking perfect score I marked in red pen at the top of her nearly pristine test. And my camera bag resting comfortably next to her designer shoes.

If I couldn't make Mathletes by working my ass off, and if I couldn't get Brendan to be interested in me by being his best friend, what could I do? This combined with the entire previous year meant I was pretty much a failure at life. Things absolutely couldn't get any worse.

Until they did.

Brendan came walking around the corner.

I pushed myself away from the wall and swiped my fingers under my eyes. "What do you want?" I didn't even look at him, but his scent felt like it filled the entire hallway. I wanted to touch him and run away, drown in his presence and get as far away from it as possible, all at the same time. So I just froze, caught in the middle. Like I'd probably be forever.

"I could hear you crying all the way down the hall. You're my best friend, you know? I want to make sure you're okay."

"You know what, Brendan? Saying you're my best friend doesn't mean a whole hell of a lot if you don't act like it."

"Ashley, that's not fair. Tell me one thing I've done wrong as your best friend this year."

I mentally ran through every single thing Brendan had done that had pissed me off, but since each one was some form of "let Sofia touch you," "let Sofia kiss you," "look at Sofia like I wish you would look at me," and "give Sofia my stuff," there was no way I could tell him without revealing how I really felt, and making this whole thing worse. "I—It's nothing." I tried to take breaths to tamp down the angry burning in my chest.

"Seriously. What's this about?"

"To my best friend," I spat, "It should be obvious. I really wanted to be on the team, and I can't believe she made it. That she got a perfect score."

"Sofia?"

I nodded.

"She's smart."

"She's not smart," I sniffled, not looking at him.

"What the hell are you talking about? Have you seen her scores?"

"Of course I've seen them, Brendan. I graded them. But I don't believe them."

He quirked an eyebrow, and took a decidedly defensive stance. "I don't even know what to say to that. Everything was fair. You know that I am always fair about everything."

A lump rose in my throat. "I just...whatever." I ground my teeth. I knew what I wanted to say, that there must be some explanation for how she had gotten such crazy scores, but even I couldn't come up with one. Those papers had been with Brendan the whole time.

Was I going crazy? Obviously I was, because when Brendan whispered, "I'm sorry, Ash," and turned to go, I blurted out, "What do you see in her, anyway? She's so freaking fake. And now you're fake too."

He turned on his heel and stood there, staring at me. "Okay, I know you're upset. And that's fine. But goddamn, Ashley. Could you just give Sofia a break? She's nice, okay?"

"You mean, she's hot." I knew that was a low blow. I knew it. But the anger had nowhere else to go. And there was no way I was going to punch Brendan's sweet face, no matter how pissed off I was.

"Well, yeah. Anyone with eyes can see that she's hot. But do you really want to know why? She's interested in me, Ashley. She's the first girl who's ever been interested in me."

My mouth dropped open. "Do you seriously—"

"Name one other girl at this school who has ever looked at me as more than a friend."

I still stood there, staring at him dumbly. Never in a million years would I have thought he really, honestly, had no clue about how I felt.

"That's what I thought. So before you go yelling about how a girl is fake, and how I only like her because she's pretty, stop and think about how I feel for a second. I'm a senior, and I've never had a girlfriend, and now a girl is interested in me. So, yeah. I'm gonna kiss her."

For a split second, I thought about telling Brendan. Laying it all out there, throwing my arms around his neck and showing him exactly how I felt. Until his face turned angry, and he said, "Just—whatever. You wouldn't get it. You're just fine. You have Vincent all over you."

"Okay, that is—" I fumbled for an answer. He was absolutely right.

Brendan shrugged, but I could still see his anger in the set of his jaw. "You know what? I'm glad you're with a decent guy. I want you to be happy. But then you can't blame me for wanting to be happy too."

He definitely had a funny way of showing it, giving my camera away, shutting me out of his life. And the thing is, I absolutely wanted Brendan to be happy. Just with me, not Sofia. And now I had no clue how to tell him how very wrong he was.

"Do you even like her?" I whispered, squeezing the lump in my throat to the side to get the words out.

"At first? I didn't. Not really. But Dad wanted me to be nice to her. Give her whatever she wanted, you know? And I did it, because I can't handle taking care of Mom all the time anymore. I can't handle managing the house, and all of Julia's stuff, when she's supposed to be doing it. I really can't." His voice broke.

"So, yeah. I was nice to her. And I saw she was a little fake, and a little bitchy, yeah. But I wanted her to want to stay, so we hung out. You were with Vincent, and...then we started to talk. And she's nice. Really."

I rolled my eyes. "Nice enough to give my camera to? To take away the only thing at this whole school that gave me an escape, that made me happy? What the hell were you thinking?"

"What were you thinking, leaving it behind in Pamela's? And after Vincent gave you that shiny new one? Why not?" Now his words were the ones that had a bite to them.

I crossed my arms over my chest. How could he be so freaking blind? Didn't he know me at all? Any thought I'd had about telling him the truth about how I felt died a quick death. Because that wasn't even the point anymore.

And then it hit me. Fine. He thought he was off the hook? Well I didn't need him to take care of me anymore, whether that meant giving me a camera or anything else. I was strong enough to take care of myself.

"Gave it to me? Brendan, I was trying to teach him how to use it. It's his. That's why—"

"Why you were making out with him out on Mount Washington on Sunday? Yeah. Did you forget? I saw that."

"Well, then, I guess it's a good thing you have Sofia, so you don't have to give a shit who I make out with."

I walked five steps away from him, and then stopped dead in my tracks. Not looking at him, I said to the empty hallway, "That's what you notice? Of all things about me, that's the one thing you actually see?"

With that, I stalked all the way down the hall and out the school's double doors, swiping whatever tears had rolled down my cheeks minutes ago away. I was surprised the heat rolling off my skin didn't burn them off.

I raised my head and saw Vincent leaning against his car, head back, eyes closed, basking in the near-winter sun. But, for some weird reason, the only thing I wanted to was to get home, and not in the passenger seat of his car.

I ducked around the corner of the building and dialed Aunt Kristin on my cell, muttering "please pick up" into the speaker. When she finally answered, it was all I could do to ask her to come get me, and sink to sitting against the side of the building until she texted me that she was about to pull up.

CHAPTER TWENTY-FOUR

to feel affection without fear or restraint

I loved Kristin so much. She drove me home, saw that I'd been crying, and didn't say a word. She carried my bag into the house for me, and when we walked into the foyer, cocked her head toward the kitchen and asked, "Ice cream?" I nodded and followed her. We spent the next hour at the kitchen island, me sobbing into a half-gallon of mint chocolate chip and her rubbing my arm and listening. I told her all about Mathletes, and Brendan, and Vincent, and Brendan and Sofia.

Turned out she always knew I was in love with Brendan. Probably, everyone did.

"The thing is, honey," she said, squeezing my hand, "boys are stupid. Especially high school boys."

"You mean, it doesn't end in high school?" I said.

She laughed. "Afraid not. Have you ever seen Uncle Bruce take out the trash unless I look him in the eye and ask him to do it? Even if there are three bags waiting by the door?"

"I guess not," I laughed.

"So, the boys are stupid, which means you have to tell them exactly what you want. Exactly what you feel. It doesn't mean we love them any less, unfortunately."

"No, it doesn't," I said, moving my spoon to dig into the ice cream again.

"What about Vincent?" she asked.

"He is...very cute. And he really likes me. Like, a lot."

"I can tell. I think probably anyone could. Do you like him?"

I knew I should like him. I knew everything about him was right. And I knew that when I closed my eyes and imagined kissing someone, no matter how much I wanted it to be, it still wasn't Vincent. It was Brendan. Even after our fight in the hallway, he was still the guy I'd fallen in love with last year. It didn't make sense, but even I couldn't rationalize my daydreams.

Then I looked out the kitchen window to see Brendan pull up in his driveway, walk around to the passenger side, and open the door. He took Sofia's hand and helped her out, slinging his arm around her shoulders as hers snaked around his waist. They walked through the front door like that and I felt like crying and throwing up in equal parts.

"I...I don't know. You know what? I just don't know. I think I need to get out of here for a little bit. Away from him."

"Well, Thanksgiving is next week." She shifted in her chair. "I know we're supposed to host here, but I'm happy to drive up to Williamson for the week. Stay in a hotel, come in and help your mom with the cooking. She's been missing you,

I think. And since I'd be there, things wouldn't be hectic for her. I could give her a call."

I thought about that for a minute. Normally, going back to Williamson would fill me with dread. Thinking about running into Kaylie Mitchell, that bitch who initiated all the torture, at the grocery store, or even at the playground with the boys. At the worst of Project Bully Ashley, they were throwing eggs at my car as it passed, and knocking my grocery basket out of my hand. But it was Thanksgiving. And if I really wanted to, I could hole up in my room for the whole week. Read a book. Not talk to anyone. Not look at Brendan's stupid smug house and watch him making out God knows where with my least favorite person in the universe. Not think about Mathletes. Get away from everything.

"Yeah, okay. I think that'd be good."

"Okay. Want me to call her?"

Mom hadn't done that much about the bullying, besides arrange for me to go to Aunt Kristin's. I could tell it was just one more overwhelming thing on her already exhausted plate. Not that I blamed her, but we hadn't been very close since then. I was in no emotional state to start calling her now.

"Yeah. Yeah, that'd be awesome. And...can I just stay home from school Monday and Tuesday?"

Ω

My phone rang about seven times on Saturday morning,

all from Brendan. I didn't care. Didn't pick up, didn't answer one of his million texts. I did talk to Vincent, but only for a few minutes and to tell him I was going home for Thanksgiving. He was predictably sweet, funny, and awesome.

God, why didn't I like this kid more?

Aunt Kristin and Uncle Bruce were the most awesome people to go on a road trip with that you could imagine. Uncle Bruce liked a quiet drive because he said any noise distracted him, or something. Aunt Kristin liked to listen to old political speeches for work reference on her headphones, so I was free to do what I wanted. I spent the entire three and a half hour drive drowning in classical cello. Deep and mournful and beautiful, it was absolutely perfect for the waning autumn scenery flashing by my window.

Thank God, I didn't see a soul as we drove through town. I don't know what I was expecting, really. It was mostly farmland. But I had imagined a gauntlet of all the assholes from school lining the streets with insults to hurl at me as I passed through.

I was totally accosted by the triplets—Luke, Teddy, and Tess—when I walked in the house. And, for that moment, I totally loved it. Tess alternately clung to me and stared at me like I was a starlet. The boys jumped on me and screamed, "Love pile!" and I really didn't mind all that much that they wrestled me to the ground and messed up my hair. At the same time, I made a mental note to call them more often, and to further appreciate that my mom was plenty busy, even without all the stress my bullying brought into the mix. As much as I loved that fresh-baked bread smell that seemed to cling to every surface of the house even when it wasn't baking day, and missed the view of sunrise, misty orange and blue against a tree line that stretched to eternity pretty much every morning, I knew that it was best for me to be in Squirrel Hill.

Ω

The second morning I was home, I sat with my mom at the breakfast table, before any of the triplets had really stirred from their rooms. For the first time in a long time, I felt profoundly glad that I was a morning person. I wondered if this was why my mom was one—a skill she had cultivated to spend some time with just her coffee and the misty farm sunrise. I totally understood.

We chatted about everything, Brendan and Vincent and Sofia. Photography, school. What I liked best about Pittsburgh. What I was thinking for college. Mom said she'd take me on a college visit. I smiled.

I heard the kids start stirring in the back of the house, and one by one they trickled in to the kitchen. "We miss you, you know," she said, mussing Tess's hair.

"I know."

"And I think it's best for you to be with Kristin and Bruce."

"I know that too."

"I didn't know what else to do," Mom said, with a heavy sigh, wiping one of the boys' noses. "You were so..."

"Depressed?" I offered.

"Yes, though I hate to say that. It sounds like it was all about you. But it was this school, and this small town..."

"And the things asshole kids will do at a small school in a small town. I know. But...here's the thing. All I learned was how to run away from my problems. How to duck and hide instead of fighting back."

"Oh, honey. There wasn't much fighting you could do."

"I could have stuck it out," I muttered, twisting my hands together. "I could have..."

"What? Gotten revenge?" Mom covered my hands with one of hers.

I knew she was right. Facing the thing that was keeping me down would have been a recipe for disaster at Williamson, where the bullying had started to approach violence.

"Sometimes I just wish I was the kind of person who knew how to stand up for herself." I swallowed a lump back.

Mom squeezed my hands. "Well, then it's up to you to learn when to back down and when to stand up for what you know is right. Moving was the right thing for you. School at WHS would have been horrible for you no matter what you did."

I swallowed again. "I know. You're right. Now I just need

to learn not to run away from everything else that's hard." I sighed and looked around me. The kitchen window's edges still had spray paint from where someone had scrawled "whore" across the front of my house. Even though the school district had paid for the repainting and the professional window cleaner, and suspended Kaylie, you could never completely get rid of the traces.

"But, you're doing better, right? You're here because you just wanted to come home. Right?"

I looked around the house. It was a disaster, and Mom sat there with bags under her eyes, her hands dry and cracked from doing so many dishes and laundry. She was probably counting down the years until the triplets started school. Until she could get a moment of peace and quiet to herself.

"Yeah. I just wanted to come home. Missed your cooking. Kristin's always ordering out." I smiled, covering her hand with mine. It wasn't true. Kristin was a great cook. But even though this house was messy and chaotic, and it was way harder to relax here, it would still always be home. Mom would always be my mom.

She smiled. "You always wanted there to be more takeout places here."

"Yeah, well, greasy pizza and bad Chinese is still greasy pizza and bad Chinese. But it's nice to eat something that doesn't come out of a carton every once in a while. They're taking great care of me, but I miss you."

Mom gave me a smile that looked grateful, and it was a really nice moment, until I heard a crash from the other room. Her head whipped around.

"Better take care of that," I said, smiling.

CHAPTER TWENTY-FIVE

a foolish precipitation

It was the Friday after Thanksgiving. The triplets had been out of school for three days in a row, and Mom and Kristin had cooked up a storm in the kitchen for hours. (This made Mom question to a small extent my insistence that Kristin didn't cook, since she whipped up a mean cauliflower gratin from stuff she found hiding in the corners of the freezer, pantry, and fridge.)

The house was a total disaster. I was a complete disaster, too, and it felt wonderful. I'd rolled out of bed and pulled on yoga pants and an oversized turtleneck, piled my hair in a bun on top of my head, and swiped on some lip gloss to combat the dry air. It was four o'clock in the afternoon, and Tess and I were recovering from a late lunch of pecan pie and mashed potatoes by snuggling on the couch and watching How to Train Your Dragon while the boys did the same by playing the ten thousandth game of football on our front lawn.

We were just making the requisite swooning noises over the scene where the two kids fly on the dragon for the first time when my phone buzzed against my hip. I pulled it out to see a text message from an area code I didn't recognize.

First·

HAPPY THANKSGIVING. WHATCHA DOING?

Then, two seconds later,

(THIS IS VINCENT.)

Despite myself, I smiled. There was something about the familiarity of being home while texting with Vincent, or maybe being far away from Brendan, or maybe just living in a completely suspended reality, that made me one hundred percent comfortable.

I texted back·

NOTHING. BUMMING AROUND WITH BABY SIS.

Almost immediately, he replied·

GOOD. OKAY IF I STOP BY?

I made a strange choking-gasping sound and basically launched poor Tess off my lap when I jumped off the couch.

"Ow!"she whined. "Why'd you do that?"

"I'm sorry, sweetie. It's just....oh my God." My hand flew up to my face and felt how greasy it was. "He's coming? Over here? How is he here?"I texted the question to him and got no answer.

I buzzed with a weird nervous energy as I dashed up the stairs to pull on some jeans, splash some water on my face and swipe mascara on my lashes. I stood back from the mirror. I touched my fingertips to my lips and remembered that morning, just a week ago, on Mount Washington. I hadn't been crazy about Vincent by a long shot, but his lips had felt so good on mine.

And my first thought when I got that text wasn't how to get out of seeing Vincent, but how to look nice when I did.

I stood in front of the mirror, tugged the elastic tie out of my hair, then winced at how frizzy and misshapen my hair looked. I normally ironed it before school, and this was a disaster. I tied it back up again.

I checked my phone. Nothing from Vincent.

Then, a knock on the front door. Holy shit.

Holy. Shit.

I half skipped, half tumbled down the stairs to see Mom answering the door and Vincent's dark honey-colored mop peering in. "Good evening, ma'am," Vincent's smooth voice said, "Is Ashley home?"

"You can call me Linda." I heard the smile in Mom's voice. Even she was charmed by Vincent. She turned around and called "Ashley!"but I was already standing at the door.

"Hey," I said, surprised at the breathiness in my own voice.

"Hey."He smiled. "Doing anything for dinner?"

"Not that I know of," Mom chimed in. I turned around and she was grinning too. "Introduce me, maybe, Ashley?"

"Uh, yeah. This is Vincent."

"Right. The Vincent you told me about."

A triumphant smile spread across Vincent's face, and he bounced a little. If I hadn't known better, I'd say he was barely restraining himself from doing a victory dance.

"So, can I take you out? I promise I'll have you back before ten."

"Yeah. Yeah. Let me just get my purse." I ran upstairs, checked the mirror one more time, decided my ridiculously flushed cheeks did not need any blush, and sprayed on some perfume for good measure.

Ω

I climbed into the giant pickup truck Vincent was apparently driving around my hometown. "Nice ride," I said.

He shrugged. "Just a rental."

"Are you...I mean...how long are you here?" And what are you doing here?

"I was bored. Day after Thanksgiving and all. I was going to call you and see if you could hang out when Brendan told me you were here."

"I don't remember telling him that."

"You didn't, but you did tell Julia, and she told him."

"And he told you."

He nodded. "He was over this morning."

Oh. He was over at the Cole house. The morning after Thanksgiving. Yeah, he and Sofia were definitely a Thing.

"Anyway, I missed you. So Brendan gave me your address and here I am. So...can we hang out?"

"Yeah, but won't you be back kind of late?"

He shrugged again, like a three-hour trip to see a girl he wasn't even officially dating was no big deal. "Got a hotel. I'm yours all night."

"Vincent, I..."

"Oh, God. No. No, I didn't mean it like that. I swear. I swear, Ashley. I just meant I don't have to drive back at any particular time."

I laughed. "Okay, I got it. Don't freak out."

"Okay. But you don't freak out. Because I've got something I think you'll like."

He had hit cruising speed along the narrow winding country roads, and the cold gray sky against the last orange leaves holding out on the trees looked eerie and beautiful all at once. "Where are we going?"

He tapped the GPS on the dashboard. "Tioga National Forest? The one you told me about? I called their park ranger's office and they said they still have a couple areas with foliage. There isn't much in Pittsburgh, and I'd never seen it growing up. California has, like, one season. So I thought you could show me."

Ω

We talked about Thanksgiving the whole ride out. I told

him about the boys and their jumping on me at two in the morning for fun, and my mom's sweet potato casserole I loved so much, marshmallows melted and browned over the top. I learned his favorite type of pie and how he took his coffee—black, like me. The only way I respected it, really.

By the time we got to the forest, the sky was beginning to turn a deep blue. Soon we'd be watching a classic Northern Pennsylvania autumn sunset, the colors somehow deeper and richer and truer against the gray-blue backdrop than the bright pastels of summer.

He parked the car on a lookout, not unlike Mount Washington. Again, instead of feeling apprehensive, I felt okay. Warm. Happy for his company. He looked over at me and flashed a grin. "Wait here. Okay?"

"Okay. Are you getting your camera?"

"Just wait here." He grinned, climbing out of the truck cab and slamming the door behind him.

A couple minutes later, he pulled open my door and held out a hand to help me down. I put one hand in his. When he grasped my waist to help me hop out of the cab with his other hand, a thrill ran through me.

He walked me around to the back of the pickup, where the walls of the bed were lined with pillows and the floor piled with at least four fluffy blankets. In the middle sat a large picnic basket.

"What...? Wow."

"I have brownies, M&Ms, and hot chocolate. So, basically, chocolate in all forms, along with apples and caramel dip," he said, smiling at the ground and pushing his fingers back through his hair.

That hair. How had I missed how tempting it was to reach up and touch it?

"Wanna have a seat?"

All I could do was nod. I was smiling too hard to do anything else.

$$\Omega$$

Once we were settled, our backs to the giant pillows he'd propped there, he pulled out two mugs and a thermos. When he turned the lid, I heard the air whoosh out as the suction broke. Steam floated through the air, carrying the scent of chocolate with it.

I raised my eyebrows. "Hot chocolate?"

"Mmhm," he said, nodding. Something about the way one corner of his mouth pulled up more than the other tugged at my heart.

"What's in it?" I asked, leaning in to catch a better whiff.

"I made it myself," he said, his smile growing wider. "Scalded milk, and Belgian chocolate."

"And?"

"And that's it. I promised—no more messing around. And I meant it. I didn't spike it or anything. Didn't even think about it."

I finally smiled back. I leaned against one of what must have been three dozen pillows padding the back of this thing and accepted the mug he passed me. "I can't believe you drove all the way out here just to hang out with me."

"I didn't come out here to see you." He reached into his bag, pulled out his camera body, and fished around for a lens. "Joining that art class late means I have to get this photography project done over break. No place more beautiful than Tioga."

My cheeks blazed red. Of course he didn't come here to see me. "Oh...right. Yeah, of course."

"Ash. Come on. I'm kidding." He stretched his arm over my shoulders and pulled me in to him.

God, I was an idiot. I laughed, half with embarrassment, half with relief. "Still, three hours? That's a drive."

"It's boring in Pittsburgh. There's nothing to do," he said, leaning back too, letting his shoulder just barely touch mine.

I laughed. "Um, I think it's here that there's nothing to do."

"Well, I guess what I meant is...everyone there is boring. The only person I really want to hang out with is you."

I drew my eyebrows in and looked at him doubtfully.

"It's true!" he protested, catching the look. "And the leaves are gorgeous. Not as gorgeous as you, but..." He looked at me. Patient, gentle smile. His eyes boring into me. Then practically whispered, "Ever since happiness heard your name, it has been running through the streets trying to find you."

"Very nice words," I giggled. Vincent always sounded very smooth, but this was not like him at all. Still, the way he looked at me right now made me think he was very, very serious.

"So. You're into photography. I never tell anyone this, but want to hear my other extracurricular obsession?"

Something in me sensed that this was serious. However many times Vincent was putting on a show, this wasn't one of them.

My voice softened. "Sure."

He leaned in and whispered at my ear, "Poetry." His breath tickled my neck, blowing away the wisps of hair there. I gasped a little.

He leaned back and looked at me. "What? Are you surprised? Didn't think I was smart enough for poetry?"

"No, just never seen you interested in it at school."

"Have you ever seen me interested in anything at school?"

Now that he said it, he had a point. I hadn't.

"No, seriously. That doesn't get me many AP points, and imagine me sitting in class freaking out about how badassed a Neruda poem is. But…it is."

"Neruda," I said. I knew one line from a Neruda poem. "I love you without knowing how, or where, or when…"

"I love you straightforwardly, without complexities or

SOLVING FOR EX

pride. Because I know no other way,"Vincent finished.

Whoa.

I had been looking out at the foggy sunset when I was saying that line, daydreaming. But, I now realized, Vincent was looking right at me. He leaned in, brushed his nose with mine, and kissed me lightly. I let my eyes drift shut, lingered there for a moment, and felt my shoulders relax. Then I drew back, and with my eyes still closed, leaned against the pillows, tilting my head toward the sky. I opened my eyes, and a thousand stars filled my vision. So many points of light in such a huge sky.

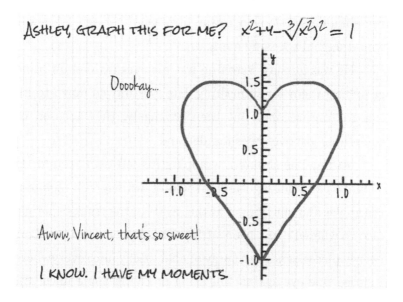

CHAPTER TWENTY-SIX

what had used to be essential points

We sat there for a long time, watching the stars emerge through the trees on the horizon, taking the crisp air into our lungs and blowing it back out in billowing white clouds.

The chill in the air became so intense, so quickly, that it felt like it had reached through my skin and wrapped around my bones. Vincent must have seen me shiver, because he shrugged out of his heavy canvas jacket and draped it across my shoulders. I looked up at him, even though I knew it would start him kissing me again.

He was already watching me, his eyes trained on mine. Searching them for something. His eyes moved down to my lips for one second. But then, strangely, they focused on something just over my shoulder, and...

"Ashley!" he shouted, wrapping his left arm around my shoulders and pulling me tight to him, while grabbing one of the apples and chucking it at the inside of the truck bed, right next to where I'd just been sitting. The apple broke into about twenty pieces, sending a spray of cold, sticky juice everywhere. I closed one eye against the sting of flying apple juice, and swiped at the cheek beneath it.

"What the hell, Vincent?"

"There was a spider. Definitely a spider. Probably a black widow. Maybe."

His fingers still wrapped around my shoulder. He held on so tight that I could feel them digging into the skin, even through my coat. And that's when I realized that he was shaking. His arm across my back was trembling, and so was his whole body. Just the slightest bit. I would have never noticed it if I wasn't pressed up against him, so close that his breath, smelling of rich chocolate, steamed against my cheek.

"You're afraid of spiders?"A smile teased at corners of my mouth. He still held me tight to him, and I fought the urge to relax against his arm, to lay my head on his shoulder.

He flushed, though he didn't look away. "Some of them can kill you. I didn't want..."He reached up into my hair and plucked something out.

"Oh, God. I'm so sorry."

"What? What is it?"I prayed there was not a damn dead spider in my hair.

"It's...when the apple broke..." He held up a tiny, white piece of apple, then dropped it and went back in for some more. Only with one hand, though—the other one wrapped firmly around my shoulder, still.

I giggled, at first nervously, then at the flush that continued to creep up his cheeks as he fished bits of apple out of my hair. "It's okay,"I said.

Did that come out quieter than I meant it to? I didn't know. Couldn't be bothered with the thought, actually, because then, all I could pay attention to was his strong jaw, and the smooth fullness of his lips. The ones that were just an inch from mine.

"Yes. Now you know," he murmured, tucking a strand of hair behind my ear, "I'm afraid of spiders. But, Ashley Price," he moved even closer to me, so that his breath tickled my lips when he spoke, "I am not afraid of you."

He tilted my chin up and brushed his lips against mine, feather light, soft, and delicious.

My whole body trembled. It knew, maybe more than I did, that this was the time to make the choice. Break it to Vincent that Brendan would always be the only one for me, or break it to myself that maybe, just maybe, that wasn't true.

I was so tired of the struggle of wanting-and-not-having. I deserved this. I deserved to be wanted and adored, and to be really, truly happy about it. Vincent liked me, and there was no reason for me not to like him too.

So I fell into him. He was waiting for me, I knew, because I felt his body relax too, and a little puff of air blew against my upper lip when he pressed in, molding his lips to mine. His fingers, having stopped clutching my shoulder, played along my hairline and under my jaw. He held me firmly and gently at the same time, like something he was afraid to lose. Like a treasure.

My heart didn't thrum wildly in my chest, and I wasn't overwhelmed with love for Vincent. But I did love the way I felt now—like I was sweet, and desirable, like I existed as something powerful all on my own. Like people should want me.

I really loved it.

Which is probably why, instead of just letting him kiss me, I reached up and threaded my fingers through Vincent's gorgeous curls, and opened my lips, letting his breath mingle with mine. And when he pulled away, grazing my bottom lip with his teeth gently enough to make me want more, I went after it, clutching at his shirt, pressing my chest against his, and letting the quietest moaning sigh tell Vincent that I was definitely not afraid of him either.

He pulled away, leaning his forehead against mine. When he spoke, his breath brushed my face again, and I shivered when a little tingle ran down my spine. "We are in a truck bed. So I think it's probably a good idea for us to stop this right now, and get you home by ten. Like I promised."

I swallowed and said, "Yeah, you're probably right."

Grinning, we climbed out of the truck bed, picked everything up, and climbed into the cab. Vincent looked at me, studying me for a moment. "It was nothing."

My heart burned, then dropped. "What? What do you—"

"The drive. Three hours. It was so worth it. Even if it was just for that last kiss."

I had to look down. I knew my expression was a mixture of giddiness and confusion and embarrassment.

We pulled up to my house. I looked up to the second floor. My light was still on.

Vincent cupped my face in his hand again, and swiped at my cheek with his thumb. His gaze was steady, pressing into me in a way that was not unpleasant. At all. "I think you still had some apple guts there,"he said.

CHAPTER TWENTY-SEVEN

confusion of discontent

I couldn't believe I finally let Vincent Cole kiss me. Hell, I more than let him—I kissed him back. I even let him French kiss me. I definitely enjoyed it.

And I definitely had swollen, tingling lips by the time it got so cold that he took off his jacket, wrapped it around my shoulders and helped me down from the truck bed like a perfect gentleman. When he drove me home, walked me to the door, and said goodnight without trying to get his hands up my shirt or down my pants, I was actually floored. Right before he left, he took my hand, kissed it, and looked into my eyes. "Every night you turned me down was worth it, if all I ever get is just this one."

I just stood there, with my stomach sinking, feeling like I should be smiling bigger, like my heart should be doing jumping jacks inside my chest. Like I should be a little more excited about this. I didn't know what to say, but of course, he did.

"Tell me it's not just this one, though," he said, cupping his hand around my jaw. He leaned in and planted the most gentle kiss I could imagine on the corner of my mouth. "I do feel bad about what happened at Brendan's. We shouldn't have trashed everything like that." I suddenly wanted, very badly, for him to kiss me again. Hard. A lot.

"Can I see you? Tomorrow?" he asked, his eyes glinting in the light from the front porch.

"I...." How could I say no? I looked at him, how beautiful he was, how nicely he was dressed, how good he smelled. Why would I want to say no? Maybe he really meant it. Maybe I was overreacting about that one time he cheated on that one little test.

"Yeah. Tomorrow's great."

"Thank you," he said. It sounded almost like a prayer. I smiled and ducked inside.

Ω

That night, I lay in bed, waiting for the warm fuzzies to come. I had a boyfriend. Someone who drove halfway across the state to see me over Thanksgiving break, who decked out his rented truck bed and put together a picnic just for me, who begged to see me again tomorrow.

But instead of feeling the creeping warmth that would push my face into an unshakable grin and keep me up imagining picnic dates as far as my calendar could see, all I felt was tired. I fell into a black, dreamless sleep.

Ω

The next morning, I forced myself out of bed and into the shower. I had been so exhausted last night, and maybe so eager to crawl into bed and try to get excited that Vincent was my boyfriend, that I'd fallen asleep in the same clothes I'd worn the day before. I had brought some cute sweaters back with me, and I should have worn one of those and bothered to do my hair. Instead I threw on a hoodie that was fraying at the cuffs, and my most broken-in jeans. I tied my hair in a hasty ponytail and sighed deeply on my way out the door.

I knew something was wrong. I knew it. But I didn't want to know it.

Ω

I didn't even hear half the things he said in the truck on the way to the diner. Some stuff about lacrosse, and another party he was going to when he got back to Pittsburgh—designated driver, he assured me. Everything punctuated by an occasional wave of his cologne in front of my face.

"What'll you have, honey?" the waitress asked.

"Just the banana pancakes, please."

"No bananas today, hon."

"What?" I looked at her like she'd said they only served worms and pigs' feet.

"No bananas," she said, slowly and loudly, like I was mentally impaired.

"Regular pancakes sounds great," Vincent said, grabbing

my menu from me to hand back to the waitress, and flashing his white-toothed grin. "I'll have that too." I swear she looked like she'd melt on the spot.

I tried to ignore the vaguely sick feeling in my stomach.

Maybe it was the diner. Maybe it was the way the waitress couldn't do my regular order, or that it had tables and chairs instead of booths. Maybe it was that Vincent held the door for me, and pulled the chair out before I sat down.

The metal chair legs squealed as Vincent scooted up to the table. A shiver ran down my spine.

"So?" Vincent reached out and covered my hand with his, flashing that killer dimple at the same time. I wanted to pull my hand away, but instead I just sat there, fighting it. Willing this to feel all right. "How did you sleep?"

"Um," I said, using a swig of coffee to buy myself a couple more seconds. "Okay. You?"

"I dreamed about you," he said, ducking his head a little and trying to look me in the eye. Damn, there was no question that those eyes were swoon-worthy. Deep melty brown and just like the hot chocolate we'd shared last night.

I raised my eyebrows at him, against my hormones' better judgment.

"I did!" He laughed. "I dreamed that we were taking a walk through those woods. And for the first time, I didn't have to dream about what it would be like to kiss you."

My stomach twisted. Oh, God. This wasn't good. My

heart should have been fluttering like a damn butterfly, and I should have wanted to drag him out of the diner by his belt loops, throw him into the cab of that truck, and jump him.

Instead, I fidgeted, glanced around, and found I couldn't get comfortable in my chair. The waitress brought our pancakes and a whole pitcher of warm syrup. My stomach turned.

"Vincent, I..."

"Yeah?" He leaned forward, hanging on my every word, stroking the back of my hand with his thumb.

And then, I knew. When I looked at this guy, who basically thought the world revolved around me, and who was confirmed by every other girl there to be the cutest guy in the whole school, and all I felt was the sensation of my skin crawling, I knew. As nice as it was to be kissed and held and flattered and admired by Vincent, I didn't love him. Didn't even really like him that much, if I was being honest. His attitude was too perfect. So were his pretty words about his dreams. There was just something I didn't trust.

It could have been a lot of things. It could have been that I didn't get dressed nicely that day. It could have been sleeping in my old bed last night. Hell, it could have been that the pancakes were plain instead of banana.

But I knew it wasn't. I knew it was him.

So when he leaned in to kiss me over the table, and I tried to let the soft, warm sweetness of his lips wash over me, all I felt was the weird stickiness of pancake syrup holding us together for an unnatural extra fraction of a second.

"This is all wrong."

His eyebrows scrunched together. "What's wrong? Is your breakfast okay?"

"It's...actually, no, it's...it's not at all." His eyebrows scrunched together. "I can't do this, Vincent."

"Okay, well, we'll get you something else," he said, waving for the waitress to come over.

"No." I pulled my hands away from his. "I can't do us."

"Like...you can't be with me? I don't get it, Ashley." Now he sounded angry. "I set up that whole thing for you last night. And when you kissed me, I could swear...I mean, you liked it, right?"

"Vincent. You're very sweet, okay? And the picnic was really nice. Really. It's just...I don't know. Isn't this kind of fast?"

"Jesus, Ashley." He sat back and raked the hand that had been holding mine through his hair. "I told you I changed. I drove all the way out here just to see you. What else do you want?"

"I don't know...nothing, I guess. Maybe take things slower? I'm sorry, okay?"

"Do you have any idea how many girls at school would kill to date me?"

"Yeah, I do. Maybe that's part of the problem."

"What the hell, Ashley? I did all this to show you I want you."

"It's not right, Vincent. It hasn't been. I just didn't know for sure until now."

I wanted to tell him to treat me like me instead of treating me like he thought girls wanted to be treated. I wanted to tell him I wasn't impressed by his cologne or his nice clothes. I wanted to tell him that I didn't really care about parties, or cars, or fancy restaurants.

We made the drive back to Mom's in silence. When we pulled up to the house, he stared forward through the windshield, his jaw hard.

"Have you ever heard of Hafiz? Persian poet?"

"Vincent, I..."

"He wrote, 'Sometimes love wants to do us a great favor—hold us upside down and shake all the nonsense out."

My heart wrenched. I knew what he was saying. And I didn't care. "I'm sorry," I whispered. "I am."

"I can't believe I ever liked you. You play hard to get, drag a guy along for weeks, then ditch him? My sister might throw herself at guys, but at least she's not a frigid bitch." His words had a snap to them far colder than the winter chill.

My eyes, now set in a cold, hard stare, shot over to him. He wasn't wrong. I'd gone out with him, I'd even kissed him. But that didn't change what my gut was telling me right now. Something about this wasn't okay.

And nothing I'd done made it okay for him to talk to me like a piece of trash.

I swallowed hard. "You're the one who was after me. You chased me. And, yeah, I was interested. I'd be stupid not to be. But the dance and the birthday party and the camera, that was you. Pursuing me."

"Yeah, so can you blame me for expecting anything in exchange here? I'm just glad I found this out now. I mean, Jesus Christ, Ashley. How many guys did you lead on like this only to fucking blue ball them? You know what?" He leaned in so that his breath blew in my face. The sharp scent of coffee there made me nauseous. "I'll bet that rumor about the lacrosse captain was one hundred percent true. Except you probably got off on almost screwing him, and then bringing out your 'I'm sorry, I can't' act."

"Excuse me?" I knew he was pissed, but this was a lower blow than I would have imagined was possible. "It's not an act, you asshole."

He looked me up and down, a storm in his eyes. "Wasted a shit ton of time when I could have been with girls who were actually interested in me. But all that energy I put into going after you? For nothing? Didn't get laid, didn't get anything. Shit, you're not even pretty."

"This isn't even about you," I snarled. "Or it wasn't until about sixty seconds ago."

"Oh, that's right. It's always about Brendan. He doesn't want you, you know that? He never wanted you. And now it finally makes sense to me why he didn't."

"Shut up," I said, staring at the seam where the truck door fit to the floor. My voice was a strangled whisper, and the acid churning in my stomach intensified, making my head spin.

But then, I took a deep breath. If there was any time to get a hold of myself, this was it. Vincent had lavished a ton of attention on me, and he definitely liked me. Or, at least, he seemed to until about three minutes ago, when he made it glaringly obvious that becoming my boyfriend was some weird challenge to him, and getting laid was the grand prize. But no matter how sweet he had been to me, one thing I knew for sure was that I had a right to say no to him.

"Shut up," I said again, much stronger this time. "You have no right to talk to me like that. Fancy parties and truck bed picnics are not an automatic ticket into my pants."

Vincent reached across me to pop open my door, pushing it so it swung wide open. A shock of cold air swirled around my ankles, and my skin crawled at his closeness. "I don't know why I even bothered to waste a goddamn fucking second on you. If I were you, I wouldn't expect Brendan to either." He lifted his head and looked at me with an expression of enraged disgust. "Get the fuck out of my car. I have things to do back home."

If I was in doubt before, this sealed the deal. I wasn't in love with him, but he sure knew how to gut punch me anyway. Last night, I'd been on top of the world. Now, all I wanted was to shrivel up into a ball, like one of those potato bugs that curls at the slightest touch, and wait right there in the driveway for someone to step on me.

I hoisted myself out of the cab and threw a sharp "Fuck you," over my shoulder before slamming the door behind me.

What part of

$$i h \frac{\partial}{\partial x} \Psi(\vec{r}, t) = \left(-\frac{h^2}{2m} \nabla^2 + V(\vec{r}, t)\right) \Psi(\vec{r}, t)$$

don't you understand???

CHAPTER TWENTY-EIGHT

yet a keener solicitude

I hadn't been back in my Mom's house for longer than ten minutes before my phone rang. I pulled it out of my pocket just in time to see Brendan's picture, that stupid one he'd made me take with his face pressed up against the window so it'd look like he was trapped in my phone. I wanted to roll my eyes, laugh, and cry all at the same time.

"Hey," I said right when I picked up. I tried to keep my voice sarcastic, vaguely friendly, and measured all at the same time. To match the eye rolling, laughing, and crying.

I had forgotten how awesome living next door to someone was for ease of communication. When you could just go next door to talk to someone, you could use things like facial expressions. That was lost to Brendan and me, at least for today.

"Hey," Brendan said on the other end. "How was your Thanksgiving? How's your mom?"

"They're...uh...fine. What's up? Aren't you busy?" I left off the part I was really thinking— With Sofia? Possibly making out with Sofia in your room? I shook my head. I couldn't think of that now.

"Actually, yeah. Getting ready for State. I...things aren't going well. I need you."

"I need you" was in the list of top five things I would have killed to hear Brendan say to me. Just not in the context of Mathletes. But whatever.

"I'm not even on the team anymore, in case you forgot." That one stung, I knew it. But it stung me too.

Brendan sighed heavily. "I know. And that sucks, and you're pissed off, and I get that. I really am sorry it turned out like that, Ash. You have to believe me. But right now...I really think you're the only one in the whole damn school who can help us."

Now I was listening. Damn Brendan for knowing that Mathletics-related flattery could get anyone pretty far with me. I sighed, too. "Okay. What's going on?"

"I tried running some board problems with Sofia. You know, for fun."

I rolled my eyes. Only Brendan would think that running Mathletes competition questions on opposing whiteboards would count as fun with one's girlfriend. Only Brendan would actually have two giant whiteboards set up in his room for that purpose. And only I would have been totally on board with that as a recreational activity.

"And? She kicked your ass? What does this have to do with me?"

"No, Ash. She was...slow. Actually," he blew out a long

breath, "I'm not really sure she knew how to do them at all."

"Well, that's...."

"Impossible, I know."

I was going to say that it actually made a lot of sense. But I bit my tongue.

"That's why I'm calling," he continued. "I want to run a crash course. Tomorrow. And I need you to help me."

"Are you seriously asking me to come home early from Thanksgiving break to help you and your girlfriend train for a Mathletes competition that I so desperately wanted to go to?" There was a long pause.

"I....well, yeah. I guess I am. I'm sorry, Ashley. About the team. You know. But it doesn't mean that you're not awesome at this, and that we still couldn't use your help. And it'll make you an awesome captain next year.

"I'm going to need you at the competition, too. Will you come? Please? Be an honorary team member. I need you, okay?"

"Okay, okay." As much as I would have loved an extra day to emotionally deal with the fact that I had just rejected the most beautiful guy at school, I'd go home early, and I'd help him.

"Let me round up Kristin and Bruce."

Ω

I'd barely dropped my duffel bag back in my room at

Kristin and Bruce's before I went over to Brendan's for the practice session he'd called.

"I'm just going next door," I called. "Practicing board problems, everyone's at Brendan's."

"A little late for that, don't you think?" said Aunt Kristin.

The only time everyone could get together was eight, since everyone was getting back from traveling over the holiday. On a Saturday night. I guessed most kids would have been bummed about practicing instead of partying, but on a night as frigid as this, I wasn't even willing to sit in the car long enough for the heat to take the chill off the air. The only thing that definitely royally sucked about Mathletes practice being held on this Saturday night was that Sofia would be there to hang all over Brendan and pout about having to practice.

I didn't bother to put a coat on as I bounded out the door wearing my slippers instead of real shoes—I knew it would take me exactly eighteen long strides to reach Brendan's front door.

I stood on his porch, my breath making clouds that puffed all around my head. I'd barely knocked once when he opened the door. "Oh, hey, Ash."

I stepped in, stamping the snow off my feet, then stepped out of my slippers. I looked down at my feet and realized that I hadn't changed out of my pink, purple, and green striped fuzzy socks. I rolled my eyes at myself. Very mature.

Brendan and I walked up the wide stairwell to his room, and his arm looped around me like old times. "Geez," he said. "You really should have worn a coat. I think the Pittsburgh air froze your sweatshirt." He rubbed the length of my arm, and it was all I could do not to turn into him right there and let my body fall into his.

Instead of the whimper that wanted to break free from my throat, I forced words. "You got the boards set up?"

"Yeah. Even made popcorn." Brendan led me up the stairs to his room. When I'd first moved here, I'd spent plenty of depressed hours stretched out on his floor watching funny movies in Brendan's attempt to cheer me up. Now I'd have to sit there watching Sofia arrange herself suggestively on his bed, probably, while I'd teeter on the edge of needing to be cheered up from scratch.

Sometimes I wanted nothing more than for us to be able to go back to last year, when we were just best friends, always one hundred percent comfortable around each other. And I guessed my goddamn socks illustrated that.

"Have a seat, and I'll go get some pop," Brendan called on his way back toward the kitchen.

I settled into the same spot where I always sat on his perfectly made-up bed. Brendan returned with a galvanized tin bucket full of ice and pop cans. He cracked open a Dr. Pepper and handed it to me.

"Thanks," I said. If I couldn't count on him for anything

else, at least Brendan would always know what kind of pop I wanted.

"Even kicked my parents out so we could practice in peace." He grinned.

"You sent them to Guiseppe's, didn't you? The words 'portobello ravioli' get your mom every time."

"Of course." He smiled a small smile. "Except now I think it's more like the words, 'Extra dry martini.'"

"Shit. I'm sorry, Brendan."

Just as I was enjoying the most unbroken eye contact I'd had with Brendan in months, however sad, his phone rang. He scrambled to dig it out of his pocket and checked the display. His voice dropped the slightest bit when he answered, "Hey, Sof."

It was all I could do not to cringe.

But then his eyes narrowed and he scratched the back of his neck. "Well, yeah—I know they have that party tonight but we—I mean, I guess I could, but you know I don't have a car tonight..."

My heart stopped. Brendan's car had been in the shop getting a fancy tune-up over the holiday weekend. But I had a car. I definitely had a car.

I was definitely not going to say anything about it.

"Okay. Yeah. No, Ashley's here. Okay. Goodnight." He didn't sound psyched about me being there, but he didn't sound too upset either. My heart started beating again.

Brendan cleared his throat. "So, they're not coming. Guess there's no point in practicing."

"Are you kidding me? There's always a point to practicing math." Not that it was the number-one thing I wanted to do with Brendan, but right now, it felt like the easiest.

"Come on. Let's start with something easy." I picked up a marker. "Find the integral." I jotted $\int 2/x\, e^\wedge 3\, dx$ on the board.

Brendan rolled his eyes and started attacking his board with the marker. Two seconds later, I saw his mistake. I lunged forward and grabbed his marker.

"No, no, no. You're adding one to the existing power and then putting the new power in the denominator. But what you want to think of is, what are you taking the integral with respect to? It's not about the x. You're trying to solve for x, even though you can't."

"Oh, shit, Ash. I was trying to use the Simpson rule, but that's obviously wrong. Shit. That would have bitten me in the ass when it came to a differential equation."

"Well, at least you caught your mistake at the beginning." I smiled.

"You caught it. I'm always messing that up. So glad you're here." Then his face changed from smiling to dead serious, but he didn't break eye contact with me for a second. He spoke, his voice a pitch lower than it had been a second before. "Sometimes we have an inclination for something that we just can't shake. You know?"

He was definitely not talking about the damn integral anymore. I swallowed hard and stared at him, afraid to break eye contact. Afraid to interrupt the most intense conversation we'd had in months, even if it did start with a simple equation that got messed up. "Yeah. I know."

We stood so close together at the board that I could have touched his foot with my toe without moving my heel. Then, his eyes traveled down my face, lingering on my lips. He reached out and ran his fingers down the inside of my forearm. Light and testing. I didn't pull away. I waited for him to stop, to look embarrassed, to say he was sorry.

But instead, he raised his eyes to mine, hungry, searching.

He reached up, pushed his fingers through the hair at the back of my neck and pulled my face to his. His lips, soft and warm, moved insistently against mine, and I gasped. His breath rushed into my mouth, and I was full of him, like a fire had taken up residence in my chest and the only way to keep it from spreading was to keep kissing him. The delicious pressure of his lips on my lips, his chest pushing against me, and his fingers raking through my hair, completely consumed me. My head spun and the only help for it was letting myself get closer to him. All that was, all that ever existed in the world, was wrapped up in this kiss, full of excitement and terror and promise.

His hand slipped down to my waist, pulling my body against his. I reached up and cupped the side of his face with my palm, wanting to hold on to the place where our lips met, never wanting to forget how it felt to taste, to touch, to feel. He parted his lips against mine and pressed his fingers into my waist. I arched my back, pushing my chest into him, and parted my lips, too, tracing his bottom one with my tongue. The tangy richness of the Dr. Pepper mingled with the sweet warmth of his breath.

Nothing would ever taste as amazing to me again.

I had no idea how I knew how to do any of this. My lips must have known what they wanted to do to him long before I did. Like my body was instinctively guarding against the inevitable loss of contact, I sucked on his lip for a fraction of a second, letting my teeth graze against it. He clutched at me even tighter as a sound rumbled from his throat, vibrating through me. I wanted to devour him.

His lips moved against mine desperately, like there was no way he could ever get enough of tasting and exploring whatever was so irresistible. God knows I felt the same way. When his tongue slipped into my mouth and his hand slid under my shirt, I moaned. His palm pressed against the bare skin of my back and his fingers splayed out, digging into my side. But in one sudden breath, the heat between us grew so intense that whatever connection had been holding us together strained and snapped. The kiss broke and my hands dropped from his face. I stood there, chest heaving, and looked into his eyes again.

But something was wrong with his face. It had the wrong expression on it. Instead of smiling, grabbing me again, and kissing me until I couldn't see straight, he sat up even straighter, pulled his hand away from my waist, and looked down at it.

Oh, hell. Sofia. My hand flew up to my lips, which still vibrated from the memory of his against them. I wanted to press it away, wanted to forget how he had made me feel. Like we were the only two people in the whole word.

Of course that wasn't true.

Seconds dragged by. I was so afraid of Brendan's response to what I was about to say that I almost didn't want to say it. But I knew I had to. "You're still with Sofia."

"No, let me—"

"Brendan," I said, an edge of warning to my voice. He would know, he had to know, that now was not the time to play games. "She was making out with you—at our café—like a week ago. Don't give me that shit."

"It's complicated, Ash."

"What, and I'm too stupid to understand?"

"We were never really together. I told you that."

"Well, you're not exactly just friends either, are you?"

"Okay, yeah. We made out. So?"

"So, if you're going to grab me and kiss me, you owe me

an explanation."

His face turned red, and his expression twisted. He looked like he was in pain. "You wanna talk about Sofia? Then I guess we can talk about Vincent, too. What do you see in him, anyway?"

Brendan didn't know that I'd told Vincent no. My stomach twisted, but I steeled myself. I didn't really want to talk about that debacle, but there were things I liked about Vincent. And since Brendan was so damn clueless..."I don't know," I said, exhaling heavily. "He pays attention to me. He wants to take me out. He was excited about Sadie. We do things. He takes me places. He...he got a camera." Now that I said these things, they sounded lame. The reasons I always loved Brendan had nothing to do with any of that, but at least they were real. Tangible things I could touch.

"You never used to care about any of that stuff," Brendan said.

"Well, now maybe I do."

Brendan's unbreaking gaze made me feel jumpy. I couldn't let the silence continue, and the fact that Brendan was even allowing the silence made it that much more infuriating.

"Besides, he drove to Williamson to see me, which is more than you did. You didn't even call. I mean, God, Brendan. I know you have Sofia, but we're best friends. We were."

"I have..." He stared off into the distance, clenching and unclenching his jaw.

"I know I told you that I thought you should go out with Vincent," he said, his voice suddenly louder. Assertive. "But now..."

I glared at him. If my eyes were daggers he would have been dead five times by now.

"Now, what?

"Now, I don't know."

I continued glaring at him while my brain tried to work out what the hell was going on. Why he suddenly cared what I did with my love life after too many months of not realizing that I even wanted one with him.

"Listen, Brendan. You..." I swallowed hard while I tried for a split second to figure out if I actually had the guts to say what I was about to say. You missed your chance. Instead, I choked out, "You never cared if I was going out with someone before."

"It's not that I care if you're going out with someone, Ash."

A lump formed in my throat that kept my words from coming out louder than a whisper. "Well then, what is it?"

"It's...I have a weird feeling about him."

"Does the weird feeling have anything to do with the hood of his car and Mount Washington?" Tears burned at my eyes, and I had no idea which of the twenty emotions running through me right now was responsible for them.

"Jesus fucking Christ, Ashley. I'm trying to—I know something about him, and I think you should know."

I stared at him, waiting.

"I had dinner with my mom and dad last night. Dad told me why he and Sofia are really here, at Mansfield Prep."

"Yeah, I know. His dad's looking to open a new office, Mansfield's a snobby college prep school..."

Brendan rolled his eyes. "No, more than that. He was in some trouble at his old school. Cheating, big time. Hacked the AP testing system, sold answers to about twenty kids. They all got expelled, lost their scores."

My chest constricted with a strange mix of horror and relief. Vincent was more than just pissed off that I didn't want to make out with him anymore. He was exactly the kind of person responsible for the worst misery of my life. And I'd known well enough, somehow, to get away from him. "Holy hell."

His foot scraped back and forth against the chipping paint on the bottom stair. "Yeah, and I don't think it's good if you're mixed up in that. I'm just looking out for you, you know."

"Oh my God. You can quit, Brendan, okay? I don't know what your freaking problem is, but we broke up."

"Looks like he hurt a lot of people. Including you." Brendan's eyes studied my face.

"No, I'm okay." I shook my head and looked right back at him, wanting him to hear the depth of what I said. "I mean, we only went out a couple times."

"Still. Considering everything..."

What did Brendan think we'd done? Oh, hell. I had to clear this up. "We didn't...do that. No. Just...no. I wouldn't have...God, Brendan!" I cried out and hoisted myself up. Why did saying things like this to him have to be so damn difficult?

His eyes flared wide, but he stood still as stone. "You guys didn't...?"

"No! We drank hot chocolate, we kissed, I dumped him the next morning at breakfast. Because there were no banana pancakes. If we're gonna pretend that you give a shit at all. Because for some reason, the only person I want to eat banana pancakes with is you."

I wanted to tell him everything. Wanted to blurt out that I'd loved him since the day I'd met him, that him kissing me in his bedroom and pulling my body to his and digging his fingers into my skin was everything I'd dreamed of since then. Wanted to throw myself at him and grab his shirt and slam a kiss on his mouth and never break away from him ever again. But I couldn't do that until all this Sofia shit got straightened out. Of course I wanted Brendan—hadn't ever stopped wanting him, I admitted to myself—but no guy was worth being a girl guys cheated with.

I stood up straight, looked him in the eye, and said, "I don't know how you feel about her. And I don't know how you feel about me."

Brendan opened his mouth and stuttered out a few syllables, but I cut him off. "I don't want to know. Not now. Get your shit together, and when you do, we can talk."

Suddenly, I couldn't get out of there fast enough. Before I even thought about doing it, I'd shoved my stupid neon striped socks into my gross slippers—seriously, how could I have worn these things over here?—run down the stairs and threw the front door open. The wind gusted in, chilling me to the bone.

"Ashley, wait!" Brendan stood at the top of the stairs, his face twisted in an expression I didn't recognize.

I stopped at the door. "Yes, Brendan. I'll still be at the competition. But only because I'm gonna be the captain next year, and we both know it. So I kind of have to see it anyway."

"That's not what I wanted to say." He ran his hand back through his hair, and for a moment, I was seriously lost. What had I been doing, trying to convince myself I wasn't still in love with him? "I...uh...You gonna be okay out there?"

I dropped my gaze. A short laugh barked out of my throat, and I swore that was the only thing keeping my heart inside my body. "It's just next door, Brendan." My voice sounded poisonous. I didn't mean for it to. Tears pricked at my eyes, burning now.

My feet had crunched through the frosty grass once, twice, three times, before Brendan called, "I'm sorry, Ash."

I didn't turn back. Couldn't look at him, even from across the lawn and in the dark.

I got home, fell into bed, and let the floodgates open. Anger and hatred for myself, for what I couldn't say, sent the tears tumbling out of my eyes, dripping off my cheeks and onto my comforter. Sobs wracked my body, and got even worse when I realized that, just two minutes ago, gasping for breath had felt like a really, really good thing.

I stared out my bedroom window up at his. I watched as his light went off, then held my breath, only exhaling when he turned it back on. He did it again—off and on. My signal to do the same. But all I could do was raise my hand, trembling, to my lamp, turn the light out, roll over, and squeeze my eyes shut.

hey Ashley, ask me what I did for Thanksgiving.

um, okay, what did you do for Thanksgiving?

$\sqrt{-1}$ 2^3 $\sum$ π !!!!

...and was it good?.

OMG it was SO GOOD.

I am so rolling my eyes a you right now.

CHAPTER TWENTY-NINE

varnish and gilding hide many stains

The Mathletes State competition was completely packed, with twice as many adults as high school students present. The crush of bodies into classrooms designated for teams, crowded hallways where vendors set up sales counters for everything from cheesy T-shirts to DVDs of their kids doing the board problems, and the actual auditorium, where parents spread jackets and handbags across seats to save them for later. I couldn't even retreat to the classroom assigned to our team, since I'd walked in on Vincent and Britt making out in one of the desk chairs, her perched on his lap and him sticking his tongue down her throat and his hands up her shirt. Whatever was sexy about two handfuls of boob in a public-school classroom, I couldn't begin to understand.

Why had I agreed to come to this hellhole where three out of six people traveling with me were the guy I loved, his girlfriend, and my ex?

Oh, right. Brendan. Even though being around him almost hurt, he and his whole stupid Mathletes team needed me around. At least Brendan had told me that I could put "Mathletes official coach" or some other nonsense on my college scholarship applications, and get his full backing.

We hunkered down in our classroom, and got to work running paper drills. As much as he loved the Mathletes, I thought Brendan hadn't been quite tough enough on these kids.

After a stretch, a walk for some fresh air, and lunch, we were ready for the writtens.

Part of me was dying inside. Even though on the practice tests in that classroom, Sofia had totally dominated, it was seriously freaky how little work she actually had to write down. Less than I did, even.

But the writtens went perfectly. Our team was so fast, with Sofia and Mohinder setting pencils down minutes before time was up. I finally took a deep breath. Brendan sat there too, holding his pencil till the very end, though I knew that it was only because he was double and triple checking his work right until the buzzer sounded.

Everyone gathered out in the hall, waiting for scores to be posted. Only the top ten teams from all of us in the state would go on to the boards round. Brendan pushed his way through the crush of the crowd gathered around the corkboard where they were posting the sheets with scores. A few tense moments passed while we waited for him to catch a glimpse of the results, and then I saw him. Brendan, striding toward us, with fists raised in the air in victory. When he reached the team, he threw his arms around all of us, even me.

Even though when his hand squeezed my shoulder, I stiffened and drew back, I still celebrated with the rest of the team.

We were so close to winning State I could taste it.

$$\Omega$$

The whole team waited outside the auditorium. Even though they weren't the best at boards, they were decent, and, I was willing to bet, better under pressure than most. Brendan had wanted to practice, convinced that that was what had won us after the paper round, but I saw the stress and exhaustion in the rest of the team's eyes. Even Sofia looked a little droopy. I advocated a nap and some relaxation before boards, which would take place in front of an entire audience after dinner. It would even be live broadcast on one of those local programs. This was a big deal.

Half an hour before the boards were to start, the final ten teams assembled in the auditorium. We were only going to hear which team we were up against in the first bracket of boards ten minutes before they started.

These parents were seriously buzzing with energy. It was palpable. They were completely obsessed with math. I knew that even though Brendan was too, it was something his parents didn't understand. They weren't even here, as far as I could tell, even though they said they'd try to make it.

The emcee strolled across the stage with one of those big clear balls they used for lottery tickets. Pretty silly, since there were only ten teams. But the parents seemed to really like this show.

"For the first round," he boomed, "Mansfield Prep versus Central!"

The crowd cheered. Brendan looked half tortured, half relieved. And Sofia quietly slipped out of the auditorium.

With ten minutes till board time. And in the commotion, no one seemed to have noticed.

And if they hadn't noticed her, I knew for sure that no one would notice me slipping out after her.

I followed the click of her prissy high heels all the way through the now-empty hallways back to our classroom. She must have forgotten something. I walked past the door as she was crouched over her backpack, rummaging through. It was only when I saw her pressing on the inside of her ear with her pointer finger that I paused.

Then she started talking to no one.

Ashley, look!

what?

$$\left(\sqrt{(-shit)}\right)^2$$

well that shit just got real.

I know, right?!

CHAPTER THIRTY

cold-hearted ambition

"No, idiot, we're up first. Yes, the first session. Well, is it my fault you didn't pay any attention in math class? No, I don't—well, look up the symbols dictionary again. Well maybe if you had spent more time studying with idiot Ashley instead of flirting with her, you would—oh shut up!"

Then, when she finally shut up herself, I heard a voice, impossibly, coming out of the space she'd pressed inside her ear. Even through the speaker, I recognized the smooth tenor I hadn't heard, had avoided hearing on my own phone, ever since I arrived back from Thanksgiving.

"No, it's broadcasting live. You just have to match the problem to what you see in the system screen and read the solution back to me. Yes, including work. Well then learn the goddamn symbols Vincent, I don't care how, just do it in the next ten minutes! If you want my allowance from the last month, do it and do it right."

Shit. Oh, shit.

This was how she'd done it all—going so quickly through the problems, without showing her work.

She and Vincent got the answers ahead of time, and he

read them to her in her earpiece. And she was perfectly right every single time.

Half of me wanted to duck out of the classroom, go back to the group, and pretend this never happened. The other half of me wanted a confrontation.

The other half of me, somehow, amazingly, won. I stood up tall and stepped into the classroom.

"Hey, Sofia. Sounds like you're doing some last-minute studying."

"Oh, I was just..."

"Listen, save your breath. I heard everything, okay? Including Vincent, your little answer monkey via wireless speaker and freaking local broadcast channel."

"Oh, please. There's nothing you can prove."

"No, but I've been watching you. At the very least, I can provide some damn compelling evidence."

"Listen, you little bitch," Sofia said, approaching me with one perfectly manicured finger outstretched. "Don't you say a word of this to Brendan. Or anyone. Do you hear me? I'm going to the college I want to go to, and I'm going to be Brendan's girlfriend, and if Mathletes is the way do both those things, then yes, I'll steal answers and cheat at anything I want."

"And if I do say something?"

"I will personally make your life a living hell. So help me, you will regret the day you were born. Thanks to Vincent, I've got half a dozen rumors about you in my back pocket, ready to be fired."Then she leaned in and whispered, "You know, this is all your fault. If you hadn't turned Vincent down, there's no way he'd be helping me do this. So don't blame me, Ashley. Blame yourself. And learn your fucking place."

Finally, she backed up, hoisted her bag over her shoulder, and pushed past me out of the room, and back to the auditorium.

I stood there, frozen for half a second. Then, right as she crossed the threshold to the classroom door, a smile swept across my face.

Someone had made my life a living hell before. And that wasn't even for anything important—just a stupid guy wanting to look good. I couldn't stand up for myself back then, but I sure as hell could now.

Ω

I was really only about twenty steps behind Sofia. Just far enough to make her think she'd won her little threat-fest, but close enough for me to still catch her and the team before they went on to do boards.

The team was already gathered at the wings of the stage. I was just grateful they hadn't gone on yet.

They were all huddled, Brendan giving them a last-minute pep talk. Even Sofia was there, not even out of breath. She must have taken gym courses in running in heels to have gotten all the way here in those shoes without breaking a sweat.

I, on the other hand, was so worked up my hair probably looked like Medusa's, and I'm sure I spit when I talked.

"Wait, you guys! Hold it. We can't do this." I knew my voice sounded crazy, uncontrolled. I didn't care. I'd made my decision, and I'd be damned if I didn't go all the way with this.

The whole team stood in the worst possible spot for me to be yelling just this thing—right outside to the door to the stage.

I knew Sofia hadn't practiced. Of course she hadn't. She'd never practiced a damn math problem her whole life. This was only to go on her college applications, so that she could be fake with her fake application and fake a perfectly good college into taking her over some hardworking student. Like me.

Worse, if I let her go onstage and she managed to win, and she was uncovered later, things would be very, very bad for the captain of our team. Brendan.

"Ashley. What's going on? I don't want the judges to hear you, okay? It would be embarrassing."

I snorted. "You know what'll be embarrassing, Brendan? If they find out what's been going on here."

He stared at me blankly, his eyebrows drawing in. Oh, my God. He actually had no clue what I was talking about.

"Are you seriously freaking telling me you have no idea

how we got here?"

Sofia gave me the sort of look that made me surprised she hadn't started sprouting snakes for hair. I actually almost expected to drop dead.

I didn't want to embarrass Brendan. I really, really didn't. But my God, the way Sofia stood there staring at me like she owned the whole freaking state competition when I knew damn well how she'd gotten there made my blood boil.

"She cheated. She's a goddamn cheat, you guys!"

Brendan shook his head, slowly. "But in our paper tests, she totally killed it. She was fast."

"Yeah, you know why?" I asked, seriously trying to keep my spit in check. "She either memorized the answers, or had Vincent reading them to her in her damn headset."

Now I felt ballsy. I reached my hand back into Sofia's ridiculously voluminous hair, which I now realized would be the perfect way to hide even the bulkiest cell phone headset, unhooked her stupid pink one from behind her ear, threw it on the ground, and stomped on it.

She glared at me, fire burning in her eyes "What do you think you're doing, you bitch?"

The right thing. For the first time, I was doing the right thing.

"Showing everyone what a lying, cheating bitch you are."

"I can't believe you would even say that. B. Do you hear how she's talking to mc? There's no way I would ever do that.

Do you think I would ever do that to you?" She was downright simpering now.

"Yeah, okay. Keep trying to tell us that with no way to prove it."

"I would watch my mouth if I were you, Ashley Price. Burn through your popularity here and you have nowhere else to go, do you?"

She definitely knew how to throw a punch straight to my gut. I instinctively looked to Vincent, standing against the wall, and he held his hands up, palms out. I'd never know what it was that he had ever liked about me, but it sure as hell wasn't strong enough to make him defend me against his sister when the time came.

I looked over at Brendan, whose face was screwed up in a look that could only be confused-slash-embarrassed. I rolled my eyes. Great. I was really all on my own here.

Except the other five kids on the team were all watching me. Including Britt, who'd been Sofia's closest friend since she'd arrived at Mansfield.

I blew out a breath, and looked between Sofia and Brendan, who was watching me now, too. Sofia shook her head back and forth, slowly, and glared at me. I stood up a little straighter and squared my shoulders.

"You bitch," Sofia said, so softly I wasn't sure anyone but me could hear it. But Brendan did. He looked up and moved his gaze from me to her and then back again.

"She hacked the system. Got the answers to the writtens and memorized them. She and Vincent had a plan. He was planning to watch the live feed and feed her the answers to those, too, through that earpiece."

The silence then was ridiculous. Brendan stared at Sofia. She threw her hands in the air and cried, "Look, Brendan, you believe what you want, okay? It's your reputation on the line. I just promise you that if I go out on that stage today, we will win."

I was actually a little impressed that she didn't lie. Bitch could bring herself to cheat almost shamelessly, but not to full-on lie to Brendan. He must have heard her confirmation that she was a cheat.

He stared at his feet as he said, "I think you should stay back, Sofia. Until we clear this up."

Brendan looked at me one more time. "Ashley, I don't know what to say." And then he was quiet again.

"Well, you have to say something." The growl was back, but dammit, I couldn't exorcise it now. I was on a roll. I couldn't have stopped the words if I'd tried, now. "You have to say something, for once. For once in your freaking life, Brendan, you have to look at what's staring you in the face and either do something about it or walk away."

His eyes snapped to mine, then to Sofia.

"Sofia," he said in a low voice that I could swear had picked up some of my rumbling, "Add any integer N to the square of 2N to produce integer M. For how many values of N is M prime?"

"I..."

"None, two, or an infinite number?"

Sofia stood there, her mouth hanging open.

"You don't even know how you'd start to solve the problem, do you? Do you? Should I try another one? Just to be sure?" Brendan was yelling now.

"What does a graph of x plus y squared equals x squared plus y squared look like?"

Sofia looked up at him, wide-eyed.

"Please tell me you didn't actually hack the system for the writtens, Sofia," Brendan asked, clearly trying to control his volume.

Like a switch had been flipped, Sofia stood up straight and stared Brendan right in the eyes. "Everyone cheats. We are trying to get into really good schools. Everyone has awesome grades. Everyone needs to find a way to get a little something extra, you know?"

"So you get that," Brendan said, "by studying, joining Mathletes, and competing. Not by stealing the fucking test answers!" His face turned red, and I swore I could see his body trembling even so many yards away.

Vincent cleared his throat, breaking the deafening silence. "Before you embarrass her any more, I had an equal part in this, okay? Yeah, I'm pretty good at hacking computer systems, and ironically, Mathletics State doesn't have the craziest barriers on theirs. This is what we do, man. Steal answer keys, get straight As that make for perfect transcripts, get some dumbass State Mathletes and drama club creds on the college applications..."

"Get expelled, let your dad clean up the mess you made by bribing the principal, move schools, do it all over again. I know. My dad told me. He doesn't seem to think anything is wrong with it either." Brendan's gaze was cold and focused on Sofia instead of Vincent. "I knew about the tests—English, History. But Mathletes? I didn't think even Sofia was capable of royally screwing someone over on such a personal level. Someone she was supposed to like."

Vincent shrugged. "We might as well." Then he turned and stared at me. "It's not like we have anything here to lose."

There was a small squeak from where Britt leaned against the wall a couple feet away from Vincent. She mumbled something about the ladies' room and hurried out.

Brendan stared at his shoes again and swallowed hard. "Well, everyone, pack up your stuff. I'll tell the officials the situation. We're forfeiting."

"Brendan, no," I whispered.

"Obviously I've been the most idiotic team captain in the history of the Mansfield Mathletes. Obviously I've had my mind on too many other things," he closed his eyes and grimaced, "to see what was really going on here."

He was being so careful not to say her name. It must have sucked to have been the goddamn-lucky boyfriend to the perfect girl who was now not so perfect.

And I didn't give a shit. Still, I couldn't bring myself to say anything. At this point, with my bitch face in full force, and my bitch voice already engaged, he was probably doing a much more mature job of it. A job that definitely would not involve grabbing Sofia's hair and screaming and probably getting into a fistfight and tearing down the backdrop curtains on the Mathletes stage.

"And Ashley's the only one who's been able to take her head out of her own ass for long enough to pay any attention."

Brendan raised his eyes to me, and they were so huge and blue and sad that all I wanted to do was stand up, throw myself into his arms, and forget the competition, and this classroom behind the stage, and all the other members of our team existed. My chest felt like it was on fire.

"Brendan." Sofia stood up and brushed her hand at Brendan's shoulder. For such a gentle gesture, it looked forceful. Brendan's shoulders tensed. "We've come this far. We might as well keep competing. Probably no one will even find out, it'll be..."

"The most inappropriate thing we could possibly do?" Brendan finished. He turned his gaze on Sofia, but now it was intense, and not in a good way. If I knew Brendan, he was fighting to keep himself from letting out a stream of curse words in front of the rest of the team.

He was daring her to keep talking. But that stupid bitch wouldn't give up. "I mean, it's not like we didn't prepare at all. And we're good at the problems. We can figure out how to work them. We've just...prepared a little differently than everyone else. That's all."

Her damn eyelashes batted a mile a minute, but Sofia was so used to not paying attention to Brendan, not caring one bit about his mannerisms, the way he stood and held himself and breathed when he was upset versus when he was still trying to decide whether to forgive someone.

He was definitely past forgiveness now.

Brendan's chest rose as he took a deep breath. When he finally spoke, his voice came out low and gravelly. "Get out." He had been looking down at his shoes, but when Sofia didn't make any effort to leave, he raised his eyes to hers. She stood there, staring at him, mouth hanging open. He raised his arm and pointed to the door. "Get. Out." His voice was ever so slightly louder now, but with an edge to it that I had never even heard before.

There was "I can't believe the Pirates lost" anger and then there was this anger. The kind that came from shame, and disappointment, and embarrassment all at once.

Impossibly, Sofia's bottom lip trembled. She shuddered out a heavy sigh, then bent to pick up her backpack. Sofia glanced at Britt, and Britt glared at her, steely-eycd, and shook her head. Sofia's feet echoed across the thin classroom carpet as she stomped out of the room, tugging Vincent by the wrist behind her.

Britt's strangled voice punctured the silence. "Guess you couldn't have waited until after we won to spring this little surprise on us, huh, Ashley?"

Every head in the room turned to me.

Suddenly, triumph at Brendan's trust in me and having done the right thing all washed away with the panic of realization—it was happening all over again.

I had ruined our chances for winning. This was even worse than the last time. Instead of being the subject of an untrue rumor, I was at the actual center of the downfall of the entire Mathletes team, and the seniors' last chances at winning State.

I fought back tears with everything in me. Brendan didn't say anything else. I stood there waiting for him to do something while wondering what I really expected from him in the first place.

Sofia didn't need to make my life miserable at Mansfield Prep. I'd done that all on my own.

In one fluid motion, I grabbed my bags and got the hell out of there.

Ashley...

$$\sqrt{\heartsuit} = ? \quad \cos\heartsuit = ?$$

$$\frac{d}{dx}\heartsuit = ? \quad \begin{bmatrix} 1 & 0 \\ 0 & 1 \end{bmatrix}\heartsuit = ?$$

$$F\{\heartsuit\} = \frac{d}{dx}\int_{-\infty}^{\infty} f(t)e^{it\heartsuit}dt = ?$$

My normal approach is useless here. I'm so sorry.

oh, Brendan...

CHAPTER THIRTY-ONE

as secure as earthly happiness can be

I had to be alone. Really, really alone. After she'd driven all the way out to get me and all the way home in silence, Aunt Kristin would want to know what was wrong. Uncle Bruce would just try to make jokes with me. I needed space. To breathe, and to be. And I needed Brendan.

As always, the one thing I couldn't have.

The only completely empty, close by, covered place was Brendan's porch. I dashed over from ours, and in the eight seconds it took me to reach it, a layer of rain clung to my shirt and hair.

I couldn't get the image of him out of my mind. Shaking his head back and forth, staring at me, staring at Sofia. At least he didn't defend her. That was something.

Sheets of rain sliced through the air, and rivers of it bubbled and ran through the street. The steady hiss of the downpour matched my mood, at least. I leaned my elbows on the porch rail and glared at the white froth it made when it crashed into the concrete, letting the sound wash over me. Until it was interrupted by blinding headlights.

He stepped out of the car, and my heart thudded to a

stop. His Mathletes polo was soaked through, his hair wet and dark.

"What the hell? Don't you have an umbrella?" I shouted over the noise of the storm.

"I was looking for you," he shouted back as he jogged toward the house. "I would have driven you back, but you ran out of there so fast, and I still had to take care of team stuff. One of the other kids said they saw someone pick you up."

"What about Sofia?"

"What about her?"

"Did she get home?"

"I have no clue. And I don't give a shit. Told her as much before the competition." He reached the porch, and swiped at the rain that ran in rivulets down his forehead.

I stared at him. "What are you saying?"

He looked steadily back at me. "I'm saying I told her there was nothing between us. In no uncertain terms."

I had no idea what to say to that, so I just stood there, trying to keep the giddy smile I could feel building from taking over my whole face.

"Where did you go?" I finally asked.

"Where do you think? Where you always go when you think I won't go after you."

"The water tower?"

He nodded, running his hands back through his hair.

"Do you think I'd climb the water tower with a storm

coming in? What, do you think I'm an idiot?"

"No. No, I've never thought you were an idiot. I swear. I may have made a lot of mistakes, but I never made that one." He stood there, cast in the weird yellow of the porch light against the deep gray sky, his expression pleading

"You were right about Sofia, okay?" His voice dropped and softened. "You were always right." He stepped toward me, gingerly, like he was afraid of spooking me, then reached down and took my hand. "But if you're always right, then I feel like shit ever being wrong. And right now, I need to tell you that I was wrong. And I need you to still like me. Or at least not to hate me."

My chest fell, and air rushed out. I squeezed his hand. "Brendan. I could never hate you. And believe me, I wanted to a couple times in the past month or so." His face twisted, like I'd stabbed him or kicked him or something.

Droplets of rain dripped off the tips of his hair and onto his shirt. My eyes drifted down to his chest, where his shirt clung now, sopping wet and heavy. For two solid seconds, we breathed in and out at the same time.

He licked his lips and blurted out, "Vincent is a total tool. I should have seen it, and—he's just a tool."

I caught a breath between my lips, and looked at him through half-narrowed eyes. "Yes..."

"It's just that he hurt you. And I hate that. Ash, I—"

"No. He didn't." I pressed my lips together and shook my

head. "He didn't. I'm just happy I don't have to deal with him anymore."

Brendan's eyes focused on my face in the strangest way, and his voice changed to something lower. Softer.

"When you said that, at the competition. About everything being right there in front of me and me not being able to see it, or refusing to pay attention to it, or whatever...you weren't talking about Mathletes, were you?"

I twisted my hands together. My mouth did this weird thing where it wanted to break into a goofy smile that didn't match my emotions. I forced it from turning upward, forced my whole head down. "I was talking about Mathletes," I said.

Brendan's face fell. Oh, God. Oh, Jesus. He was disappointed. If I was ever going to have a chance at telling him with certainty, without completely embarrassing myself, this was it.

"But that's not the only thing I was talking about." Something about that short sentence knocked the wind out of me. I struggled to fill my lungs.

He didn't say a word. I couldn't stand it anymore. All the anger and all the confusion would gather up in a ball in my chest and propel me toward him. I'd tackle him right there on the front porch.

That's when a deafening crack ripped through the sky right above the house. I must have jumped a foot. And that marked the moment when we couldn't just stand there anymore. I either had to leave, or tell him how I felt. There was nothing I needed more in the world than to be near him right then. Even if I'd wanted to turn around and stalk off across the front lawn, like I had so many other nights, I couldn't.

Then, thank God, he said something. "Can we get out of the rain?"

I nodded dumbly and followed him.

He swung the door open to a dark house. Our steps echoed on the shining marble floor.

"Where are your parents?"

"They're meeting some friends for dinner in the city. I'm sure they'll get so trashed they'll just stay there. Again."

He tossed his bag at the bottom of the steps just like any other afternoon, and I reflexively sidestepped it. He kept going, up to his room. Just like a normal evening.

Except this wasn't. This was so far from normal, even the tips of my hair felt electrified.

But as we moved through his house in the same path as always, a strange calm overtook me as well. We made it to his room, and the perfectly made-up bed that was always my seat invited my beaten, exhausted body to sit down. But I didn't. Couldn't. I was too wired, between the competition and screaming at Sofia and the rain and Brendan's rain-soaked shirt and his weird, same-as-always but definitely-not-the-same mood right now.

Brendan crossed to his dresser and pulled out a clean T-shirt. Then he stood there, facing away from me, letting the dry shirt dangle from his fingertips.

"Listen, Brendan, I'm sorry I..."

"Would you just shut up and let me talk for once?"

"I..." My mouth clapped shut.

"Do you know I never really liked her?" He turned and looked me right in the eyes. "I never really trusted her. Whatever was going on...between us... has been over for weeks, really. Since you left. And something stopped me from...I mean, we went out, and we kissed—a lot—but we never..."

"Okay. Now you need to shut up," I said, stepping closer to him. I was on the edge of giddiness. I could feel it starting to creep in. The one thing that could ruin it would be Brendan saying "slept with" and "Sofia" in the same sentence.

He opened his mouth to say something else, but nothing came out. I don't know why, but I was relieved. I wanted to keep him from talking as long as possible. I guess I knew, somehow, that what he said would change everything.

"I've been the biggest idiot on the planet." He took exactly four steps toward me, slow and deliberate. I could see how shallow his breaths were, how tense his shoulders were. He squeezed the hem of his shirt and water dripped from it onto the carpet. I watched each drop explode on impact in slow motion.

He murmured, "I didn't see it. I can't believe I couldn't

see it."

"It was my fault," I said. His eyebrows scrunched in, his expression confused. "I should have told you right away, as soon as I knew they were hacking the system, I wish..."

"Ashley, I swear this is the last time I will ever say this to you. But please. Just. Shut. Up." He came two steps closer, and stopped right in front of me.

He smelled like aftershave and wet T-shirt. It was all I could do not to close my eyes and breathe him in. He looked down, blew out a breath, then looked into my eyes.

"I love you," he said. "I've loved you since the first time you made me climb that damn water tower. That look on your face when you got to the top...like you'd never been so happy. I knew I should be terrified, but all I remember is how beautiful you were. Nothing pissed me off more than seeing you with Vincent, even though I threw Sofia in your face. That's when I really knew. And now, with this whole Mathletes bullshit...you did the right thing, Ash. No one else would have stood up to her. But you did. And I love you for that."

"Brendan, I..."

"You don't have to say anything back." He stepped away, and stared down at the floor again. "I just wanted you to know. And I'm sorry that I didn't tell you sooner. Didn't...realize it sooner." He swallowed so hard I could hear it, then raised his eyes to mine.

Well, an electric fence couldn't have kept me away from

him then. In one smooth motion, I stepped forward, grabbed the front of his shirt with both hands, pulled his body to mine, and kissed him full on the mouth. In a split second, his hands cradled my face, his fingers threading through my hair. His lips moved against mine, desperate, hungry.

The world exploded. My heart thrummed in my chest, or maybe it was his pounding against mine. Nothing mattered but getting closer to him. I wrapped my arms around him and dug my fingers into his back. Suddenly, there was nothing I hated more in the whole world than the thick, soaking-wet fabric that separated my skin from his.

My hands moved under his shirt at the same time my tongue pushed into his mouth. He tasted like cinnamon gum and rain, and nothing was going to stop me from devouring every inch of him. He groaned and pressed in deeper, but then pushed away.

We stood there, foreheads together, gasping, before I managed, "Don't stop."

"What are we doing? What is this, Ash?"

"This is me, telling you I love you too. Always have."

He closed his eyes, and smiled that goofy smile that always melted my heart, no matter how many times I wanted to kill him. He started kissing me again, and after a few seconds I pressed my palms against his chest.

"Let's take care of this wet shirt." I pulled it up over his head and tossed it next to the dry one he'd pulled from the dresser, now long forgotten. He grabbed my waist, pulling me into him again, and when his fingers played under the hem of my shirt, I went for the button at the front of his jeans.

"Whoa, whoa," he said, breathless again. "Are we..."

I bit my lip and looked at him with huge puppy-dog eyes, nodding. My want for him was so intense I thought I would burst. I couldn't imagine ever wanting anything more.

His chest heaved and he walked backwards to his bedside table, pulling me along with him while kissing me again. He reached behind him, rummaging in the drawer of his bedside table and taking out a small square packet. I giggled into his mouth. Of course, Brendan would be prepared for anything. I laughed as he slid his hands down to my legs, picked me up, hitched my thighs around his waist, and carried me to the bed.

And then, the only thing that existed in the entire world was me, and him, and his body, and mine, and this moment.

I didn't think about his strong hands as they clutched and pulled at my waist. I didn't think about his lips and tongue tracing patterns across my collarbones, over my ribs, down my stomach. I didn't analyze the delicious weight of his body pressing down on mine, or the all-consuming heat of skin on skin everywhere, all at the same time. Even in that one incredible instant when we became as close as two people could possibly be, I could only gasp, then sigh, then laugh, and only one thought ran through my mind, over and over·

Brendan. Here. Mine.

Finally.

Ω

After a lot of cuddling and kissing, and a second round, and a little bit of sleeping, Brendan's kisses up and down my jawline woke me up to see the sun beginning to rise.

"Oh, shit. I've gotta go."

"No," he whined in the most adorable way possible, pulling me in to him even closer and tucking the covers around me, trapping me there. "Don't go."

"Well, I'll have to soon," I murmured, pressing my lips to his shoulder. "Before they notice I was gone all night."

He groaned, drawing my lips up to his and kissing me hard. "Yeah, okay. But really. I mean it. Stay with me, Ash," he said into my neck, his breath tickling the wispy hairs at the nape. "Forgive me for being such an asshole, and be...you know...mine."

I smiled and kissed his temple. "On one condition."

"What?" he said as his hand ran up the back of my thigh, stopping at the top, fingers playing at the skin there. "More of this?"

I giggled and squealed, and used my legs to sandwich him and flip myself on top of him. Pulling the sheet to my chest with my right hand, I used my left to push my fingers through his hair, still amazingly, adorably floppy. "Never cut this short."

He grabbed the hand I was using to hold the sheet up, and pulled me down toward him, and kissed me hard. "Is that all I have to do?"he whispered against my lips.

I pressed them into his cheek, then his chin, then the corner of his mouth, until he groaned and opened his lips against mine. I whimpered as his breath rushed into my mouth and his tongue played along my lower lip. At some point, he flipped me back down onto the mattress, and tangled his legs in mine. "And some of that,"I said, breathless.

"You know," he murmured, grazing his lips against my eyebrow, "Dad knows someone who knows someone in CMU housing."

"Of course he does."I rolled my eyes.

Brendan knew all my voices, the sarcastic one especially. "Hey, don't knock it. Do you have any idea what that means? He got me a single room for next year."

My heart fluttered, then dropped into my stomach, which did the same. And then everything burned, low in my belly, and all of a sudden, I had to be close to him again. I pulled the sheet away from my body, and up over our heads. Brendan kissed me hard, his fingers playing along my collarbone and up my neck. And I didn't think I'd ever feel sleepy again.

Brendan...
$$9x - 7i > 3(3x - 7u)$$
$$9x - 7i > 9x - 21u$$
$$-7i > -21u$$
$$7i < 21u$$
$$i < 3u$$

You are so adorable.

THE END

ACKNOWLEDGEMENTS

I wouldn't be able to publish a single word without the help of dozens of people. It never gets easier to write these thank-yous, mostly because there aren't words enough to show appropriate thanks for the selflessness and expertise of every person who helps bring a book to publication. But I'll try anyway.

As always, first and foremost thanks go to my best friend, editor extraordinaire, and partner in publishing insanity, Jamie Grey. I'm so glad you've been by my side for all of this craziness.

And to my publishing mentor and dear friend, Trisha Leigh – I would never have been able to do this publishing thing so confidently, or with nearly as great a sense of humor and perspective, without you. Thank you.

Cait Greer saw this draft from its literal start to its literal finish, and so many steps in between. From brainstorming plot points to reading first drafts to serving as my official math editor to formatting this beauty for digital editions, I literally could not have made this book happen without you. Thank you.

I would be remiss to leave Jane Austen out of the thank-yous, even though she passed away many, many years ago. Thank you for such poignant, heartbreaking, smart, and hilarious original material. There's a reason so many people write reduxes of your work. I hope that this one, published on Mansfield Park's 200th anniversary of publication, is worthy of your approval, wherever you are.

To my earliest readers, Amanda Olivieri, Stephanie Diaz, Valerie Cole, Alexa Hirsch, Cait Greer, Darci Cole, Raven Ashley, and Alex Yuschik, thank you so much for your observations and suggestions that helped shape Solving for Ex into a final product, and for your support and reassurances. I absolutely could not have done this without you.

To Becca Weston, my faithfully awesome copy editor, thank you so much for your time and attention to detail that brought this book to its final polish.

Thanks go out to Hafsah Laziaf, who designed Solving for Ex's cover. It's absolutely perfect.

Book bloggers and early readers are some of the most amazing people on the planet, and some of them have followed me to Young Adult Contemporary from my first two sci-fi books. To the bloggers and my devoted readers who have given so much cheerleading, early reviews, and unsolicited promo to this book, thank you, thank you, thank you.

I wrote this book while on maternity leave after my littlest daughter, Peninah, was born. She won't be able to read this for years, but I want to thank her for being the sweetest little infant, content to eat, be cuddled, sleep, and then sit in her baby seat or under her play mat for hours by my side, watching me type. Everyone thought I was crazy for having a fourth baby, Penny, but you're the only one of my children who has ever let me write in peace - a miracle indeed. I'm glad you're here.

Last but certainly not least, thanks to my husband David for never thinking that writing books and publishing them is anything less than hard, worthy work. Not everyone has as much understanding, let alone support, from their spouses like I do from you, and I don't take it for granted.

ABOUT THE AUTHOR

Raised on comic books and classic novels, Leigh Ann developed an early love of science fiction and literature. As an adult, she rediscovered her love for not only reading, but also writing the types of fiction that enchanted her as a teen. *Solving for Ex* was born of her love for Jane Austen's classics, and how they taught her that love stories could be funny and wickedly smart.

Leigh Ann, her husband, and four children live in Columbus, Ohio. When she's not immersed in the world of fiction, you can find her obsessing over the latest superhero movie or using her kids as an excuse to go out for ice cream (again.)

Turn the page for a sneak peek at another YA romance—the upcoming *Falling from the Sky* by Nikki Godwin.

FALLING FROM THE SKY

by Nikki Godwin

CHAPTER ONE

This is how it always starts. My lungs shut down, and I can't breathe. My eyes glaze over like syrup on pancakes. My eardrums hit their mute button. The world freezes.

At least until the plane is gone.

My crazy grief counselor said I should pray about things. Pray about my dad and the other victims. Pray for the families who lost loved ones. Pray for Mom and Jordan. Pray for myself. I'm not big on prayer, but I did it anyway because I needed to do something to stay sane.

So now I pray for airplanes, like it'll really make a difference, but I don't know what the hell to pray for exactly. A safe flight? No turbulence? A landing on the runway? Lame. How about a pilot who doesn't fuck up and nosedive into a rainforest and burst into flames? If anything, I pray that they don't end up like this—like me.

Maybe I should've prayed for all of that before Flight 722 met its fate. Then maybe they wouldn't have crashed into that rainforest. Maybe they wouldn't have burst into flames and burned to death. Maybe the airlines would've realized the pilot was ultimately going to be responsible for killing the others onboard and replace him. And then, maybe my dad would still be here. I'd still have someone to practice free throws with me, and I'd still have someone to come to my games, and I'd still...

"McCoy!" Terrence shouts. He pushes me toward the sidewalk. "I swear, one of these days there's gonna be a headline that reads 'Ridge McCoy hit by car while praying for airplane.'"

I don't even bother with an apology. Terrence has known me long enough to know that it just happens. I don't mean to freeze in parking lots. I just do.

"You know the guys at camp will think you're a bit off if you do that in front of them," he warns me.

He told me the same thing this morning when I got to Dunson Hills Sports Camp. He met me in the parking lot and climbed into my car before we even signed in. Terrence plays basketball for the school a town over from me back home. I'm just glad to have a familiar face around this summer. He knows about my dad's death and my airplane prayers and my fizzling relationship with Samantha. Fizzling is an understatement. We're as charred as used firewood.

"You know, we're only here because you needed new shoes," Terrence reminds me.

I don't need a reminder, though. These faded Nikes are about to be out of service for good. I've damn near run the soles off of them. I haven't had the heart to ditch them since they were the last ones Dad watched me play in, but they won't make it through the summer.

We push through the double doors and enter the food court. Terrence walks over to the mall map and locates the sporting goods store where his cousin works.

"I'm headed to see Demetrice, so holler if you need me," he says.

I nod. "I think I can handle buying shoes on my own."

Terrence laughs. "You might need some style advice."

He disappears into a crowd of people, leaving me alone with the mall map. I give it a quick once-over. I hate lingering around like I don't know where in the hell I'm going. It can't be that hard to find a shoe store, so I veer off in the opposite direction of Terrence. He may have style, but I don't want any witnesses around in case I have a meltdown over replacing my Nikes.

I find a shoe store wedged in between an airbrush shop and one of those stores that sells eighty-dollar jeans and plays techno music. The limited shoe display has nothing blue or silver on white. I'm not much for these neon colors.

The music isn't much better in here. This stupid pop song bleeds into the techno bass next door, and the only lyric I hear is the one asking me what I would do if I were falling from the sky. This is probably my dad's way of telling me from the other side to run from this store because not only do their shoes suck, but their music screams "plane crash!" in the most effed up way. I push past the Adidas display in the entranceway and escape before the salesman chases me out of the store begging me to give the new yellow-on-black Nikes a second look. Maybe the mall's other hemisphere will have better results.

A faded white marble fountain sits in the center of the mall. Water rushes over the three tiers. Two small kids toss coins in and beg their mom to let them ride the carousel as I approach the fountain. I fish through my wallet for any loose change. I find a penny and weave it between my fingers, trying to think of a wish. I don't really believe in wishing on pennies or shooting stars or 11·11, but right now, I need a wish. Or some good luck. Or just shoes. So that's what I wish for – to find new shoes. I draw my arm back, and in my best jump shot form, toss the penny toward the highest tier.

"Hey Jump Shot! You look lost!" a voice calls out to me.

The guy who works the carousel stares at me with a goofy smile.

"You look bored," I holler back.

Maybe that wasn't the smartest move on my part. He climbs over the side of the booth and walks in my direction. He's shorter than me, probably five-foot-seven, and he's a lot thinner. If he wants a fight, I can take him. I stiffen my shoulders and watch him as he comes closer.

"I am bored, but you're still lost," he says. "Summer camp?"

I nod and relax my shoulders. "How'd you know?"

"No one else would shoot a penny into the fountain like that," he says.

Now I feel like an idiot. Not only am I drawing unnecessary attention to myself by practicing my skills next to spinning horses, but I'm standing here like a lost tourist in front of some Native American guy who needs a haircut worse than I do, still wearing the broken-down Nikes I came to replace.

He pulls a coin from his own pocket—carousel coin maybe?—and stares at it before drawing his arm back and throwing it into the fountain. For a second, I wonder what he wished for.

"Where's the best shoe store around here?" I get straight to my point, hoping he can answer and let me be on my way before his horses stop spinning.

He points behind me. "Down there. Past the candy stand. It's called Finish Line. They always have the best stock," he says.

"Thanks." I turn my back to him and circle the fountain, heading toward Finish Line.

I pull into a parking spot in front of the Dunson Hills Sports Camp sign-in office. Terrence and I go inside to officially sign our souls over for the summer. It's just like any other sports season—signing a form saying you agree to the rules and understand the consequences of your actions followed by peeing in a cup to prove you're not a stoner or meth head. At least I don't have to deal with the lectures about keeping my grades up during summer camp.

"Damn," Terrence says once we're outside. "They take shit for real around here."

Half of the guys on my ball team back home wouldn't pass the preliminaries here. It's a miracle we win any games at all. Terrence's team always beats us, but he knows I got dealt a bad card when it comes to teammates. And my girlfriend. And my dad. Hell, my life is a losing card game.

"See ya back at the room," Terrence calls out from his car.

I glance down at my new Nikes before I get into my own car. Carousel Guy was right. It didn't take long to find blue-on-white with a silver Nike swish. I told the salesman I'd prefer to wear them out, and I avoided eye contact with him as he stuffed my ragged shoes into the box in their place. This is where Dad would talk about how new shoes are a start to a new season and a new chapter in my life, but he's not here to say it, and I'm not as poetic as he was. I glance back at the Finish Line bag in my back floorboard. Letting those shoes go feels like Dad's plane just crashed all over again. Those damn shoes are going in the trunk when I get to the room. I'm not letting them haunt me all summer.

Driving behind Terrence through the campgrounds, I feel like we're in sports prison. The buildings are long, narrow, and white. They remind me more of army barracks than dorms. I expected something a little nicer since they gave us these fancy electronic room keys. We park outside of Building C and roam the hallway until we find room eleven.

Terrence and I lucked up that we knew each other prior to camp so we could request each other as a roommate. If we have a third roommate, I hope he's as laid back as Terrence.

I drop my bags at the end of one of the beds. A single poster of Michael Jordan hangs on the boring white wall. Great - my dad's favorite player. My little brother is named after freaking Michael Jordan. I want to rip him down from the wall. The fluorescent lights make me feel like I'm in an interrogation room. Maybe this summer camp thing is more like a summer prison after all. I send Mom and Samantha the required "I made it here safely" text while Terrence unpacks his things.

I shut the door to room eleven and stretch out on the bed. This mattress sucks, and it's going to be a long, sleepless summer with it. Fortunately for Terrence, he has somewhere else to go. He can crash at his cousin's house all summer and show up for practices. The staff will never know the difference.

"Damn," Terrence mumbles. "This ain't gonna cut it all summer."

"You're reading my mind," I say, tossing on the bed in hopes that I can break this mattress in before the end of camp.

"I hate to say it, McCoy, but I may be bailing on you," he says. "I'm too tall to sleep on this thing, and I'm too young to have a bad back just yet."

I don't even blame him when he repacks his stuff to head to Demetrice's house. He jots down his cousin's cell number in case I need it and says he'll check in with me before practice tomorrow. Then he's gone.

But I'll be here with a stone mattress and a Michael Jordan poster. The words "Don't be afraid to fly" are printed in bold white letters under him. Sorry, MJ, but I'm not flying. Flying results in falling, and I'll be damned if I fall from the sky. This summer, I'm staying planted on solid ground.

Hours later, the mattress still sucks. Guys down the hallway blast rap music, and someone says something about Corona and the river. I don't think they realize I'm even in here. The interrogation room vibe still lingers in the dorm room. I flip over on the bed and bury my face into the pillow to avoid the fluorescent torture. It's only six o'clock. And I'm starving.

I force myself to get up and head to the Dunson Hills cafeteria, but the food is equally as awful as the food in a school's cafeteria back home. I could force feed myself dried out chicken and attempt to blend with the baseball players, but I'm not that desperate. The barbeque place in the food court was calling out to me earlier at the mall. I'll be damned if I'm that guy who sits around camp all summer.

Going to the mall alone isn't much better, though. I find a corner table near the arcade and sit down. I really hate eating alone, especially in public. People stare at me anyway, but I'd rather them stare because I'm doing something out of the norm, like praying for airplanes, than have them think I have to eat alone because I have no friends. At least that's what I think about people when I see them eating alone.

"What's up, Jump Shot?" Carousel Guy sits down across from me.

Does he fucking live here? I didn't want to be the lone loser at camp, but I really don't want to deal with this guy. He must be desperate for friends. I probably look as desperate as he feels.

"That's not my name," I say, tucking my barbeque into the corner of my mouth to speak.

"I figured that much," he says. "You never bothered to tell me your name."

"Ridge. McCoy," I say.

He nods. "I'm Micah. Youngblood."

I was expecting something cooler. Like Blackfeather. Or Wolfcry. Something more Native American than Youngblood.

"Cool," I say. "So what's there to do around here?"

"There's the river, skinny dipping, beer. That's what most of you guys do anyway, right?" he says.

"Most of us." But I'm not most of us. I'd rather slay zombies on Xbox or shoot hoops or drive off a cliff and put myself out of my misery.

He blabs on about how nothing ever happens in Bear Creek, except for the time some rock band's bus broke down in the mall's parking lot, and they had to stay here for a week. Then he says something about a festival that comes every summer and new movie releases.

Basketball doesn't seem like his thing. Sports in general don't seem like his thing. He accepts little silver tokens from excited kids who can't wait for a two-minute ride on a painted horse. Why in the hell is he even talking to me? I don't really care to be alone in my dorm room for two and a half months while my teammates get drunk, but now I can't even hide at the mall because the guy who runs the carousel seems to think we're friends.

He waves his hand in front of me.

"Yes? No?" he asks.

"What?" I wonder if he realizes how spaced out I was.

"I asked if you ever found any shoes," he says.

"Oh. Yeah, I did," I say in between the last bites of my barbeque sandwich. I motion underneath the table. "Thanks for your help."

Fifteen minutes later, I regret my decision to follow him back over to the carousel. If he hadn't been talking about

Xbox games, I wouldn't have. I feel like an idiot for getting sucked into a conversation. Now I can't get away from the guy.

"Uncle Micah!"

The words echo against the high ceiling of the mall. Two little girls run toward us with their arms wide open and big smiles across their faces. One girl is about two or three inches taller than the other, and she gets to the token booth first. They both ram their wrinkled one-dollar bills into the two token slots, like a race to see who can get a coin first.

The clink of a coin against metal sounds twice. Micah laughs at them, watching them scramble against each other trying to get to the gate. Micah's hand purposely covers the lock.

"Sorry, ladies, but I'm closed," he says.

The taller girl folds her arms across her chest and glares at him, but the shorter one looks like she's about to cry.

"I'm kidding, Abby. You know I'll let you guys ride," he says.

He unlocks the gate, and they rush inside, giggling with girly excitement that instantly turns into a screaming argument. They stand on opposite sides of a horse with yellow flowers on it.

"I was here first!" the short girl yells.

"Nuh-huh! I was!" the taller one counters.

Both girls cling to the horse. Micah runs over to play referee. He talks with his hands, pointing to the horse with yellow flowers, to the rest of the carousel, then back to the horse. This is probably my best chance to run like the baller that I am and give these new Nikes a work out. I should run. I should bail right this very second.

But I know that if I do, I'll never be able to show my face in this mall again. The arcade and movie theatre may be the only forms of entertainment I have all summer, so I can't make a scene. Micah would find me anyway. I'd been here a total of three minutes before he found me tonight.

The taller girl stomps away and climbs on top of a horse with pink roses while Micah helps the shorter girl on to the one with yellow flowers. He glances over, makes sure they're both buckled, and starts the ride.

"Sorry about that," he says as he slides back into the token booth. "They're my nieces. Twins, double the disaster."

I nod, having already made that assumption. I could've guessed they were related even if they hadn't called him Uncle Micah. They have his tan skin.

"Abby's the smaller one. And Jade is the other. They're five. They always fight over who rides which one," he explains.

"They're just horses," I say.

If Jordan and I were close in age, I could see him making a scene like that. Hell, he makes a scene over everything, and we're a decade apart in age.

Micah shakes his head. "No, they're so much more than just horses. You see those on the outside? There's ten of them.

They were specially designed just for this carousel."

I don't question his knowledge. The horses spin around, and I take notice of their designs. The yellow flowers. The pink roses. The one with the two fish. The one with the wild mohawk. There's even one with an Indian's head painted on the side of the saddle.

"And they all relate back to my tribe, my life. I'm connected to every one of those ten horses in some way," he says.

He pulls back on the lever, and the carousel slows to a stop. The two girls climb off of their horses and switch places before Micah starts it up again.

"So what do they mean?" I ask.

He leans his head back against the wall of the token booth.

"You really think I can explain all of that to you in a few minutes?" he asks.

I glance at my cell phone. Curfew is in two hours. "I have time," I say.

He laughs and shakes his head. "I need more time than what you have tonight. It'd seriously take all day just to tell you about one horse, much less ten. You know, I could just show you instead," he says.

"What are you suggesting?" I ask.

"Give me ten days this summer," he says.

"I don't know if I can. It's going to be a busy summer," I

say.

Really, I just don't know if I can handle Micah for ten days of the summer. He talks too damn much, and I don't want him latching on to me like I'm his best friend.

He doesn't buy my excuse. "You practice when, Monday through Friday? Do you plan on going home every weekend? Where are you from anyway?"

Yeah. Already getting on my nerves.

"Yes. Maybe. Markham," I answer.

Weekends on campus will get boring. I don't plan on going out with the guys at camp and getting drunk. Terrence won't be around much. And I'm sure as hell not going home on the weekends to deal with Mom's crying, Jordan's complaining, and Samantha's attempt to fake a relationship with me.

But Micah doesn't need to know that.

"I can work my schedule around yours," he offers. He scribbles his phone number down on the back of a mall pamphlet. "Just in case you change your mind or get bored."

He pulls the lever again, and the horses stop spinning. The girls climb down from their mounts and run back over to us. I have to get out of here before they disappear, and he traps me with more Xbox conversation. I glance down at the mall pamphlet in my hand.

"We'll see," I say. "I've gotta head back, so I'll see you around."

I don't give him a chance to persuade me any more than he's already tried to.

Room eleven is still silent when I get back. Terrence won't be back until morning. I don't mind the silence, though. I'd rather be alone. When I'm alone, I don't get fake sympathy and "it'll get better" speeches. I don't get asked stupid questions about how I'm holding up or if I need to talk. It's probably written all over my face that I'm alone and need pity, even here, away from annoying brothers, grieving moms, distant girlfriends, and rainforests that eat planes. That's probably why Micah wants to be my friend this summer. I probably sweat tragedies the way my summer teammates will sweat alcohol.

I empty my pockets and crumple up the mall pamphlet. Micah's phone number falls from the sky and crash-lands in the metal garbage bin by the door. I flip off the light.

I'd rather be alone all summer.

CPSIA information can be obtained at www.ICGtesting.com
Printed in the USA
LVOW03s1802260314

379050LV00021B/1688/P